DYED
AND GONE

An Azalea March Mystery

DYED
AND GONE

An Azalea March Mystery

BETH YARNALL

Entangled Publishing, LLC
2614 South Timberline Road
Suite 109
Fort Collins, CO 80525
Visit our website at www.entangledpublishing.com.

Edited by Stacy Abrams
Cover design by Curtis Shevlak

Print ISBN 978-1-62266-123-7
Ebook ISBN 978-1-62266-124-4

Manufactured in the United States of America

First Edition March 2014

To Lela Aguirre Smith, thanks for all of the adventures in hairdressing.
And to my husband, Mr. Y, for buying into and supporting every single one of my crazy Lucy and Ethel schemes…including the one where I thought I could write a book.

CHAPTER ONE

It was like being drop-kicked into a Lady Gaga video.

Although I'd never actually *seen* a Lady Gaga video, I was pretty sure the k-k-k-ker-ay-zee I was currently witnessing would measure up.

Techno music pulsed from oversize speakers, competing with the fevered, carnival-barker voice hawking the latest, state-of-the-art revolution in hairstyling. A string of models, looking like refugees from the forest scene in the *Wizard of Oz*, shuffled onto the stage, wearing formfitting bark dresses, their hair wired and twisted to resemble bare tree branches. Lights flashed on the main stage, slicing across the gender-neutral forms posed modern-dance style, their hair geometric origami, symbolizing the effect of time and space on society.

Or some such ridiculousness.

I was in Las Vegas with my best friends, Vivian Moreno and Juan Carlos, to attend the North American Salon Trade Expo, or NAST-E, as Juan Carlos called it. As hairstylists, this event was our Cannes Film Festival. If the festival were held at the overblown Las Vegas convention center and the movies were hairstyling presentations so ludicrous it was like New York Fashion Week had thrown up, then rolled around in the notions department of a craft store.

Juan Carlos and Viv had talked me into coming all the way from Southern California to Vegas, practically twisting my arm the whole way here. They'd insisted that the free casino booze, stroke-inducing lights, and *ching-ching-ching* of the slots were the perfect antidote for what ailed me.

I'd been dangling at the end of a string of very poor romantic choices and losing my grip fast when Vivian had burst into my apartment the day before yesterday. She'd yanked the TV cable right out of the wall, ending my three-day, tear-inducing Hallmark channel marathon.

"Please tell me you haven't bid on any more of those horrible flower dresses," she'd said, hands on hips. This wasn't the first time she'd rescued me from floral disaster.

My guilty gaze flew to the laptop on the coffee table in front of me propped up by a stack of bridal magazines, my finger hovering over the return key. "Ah, no?" Not yet, anyway.

"Azalea!" She rushed over to where I sat on the couch and looked at the screen. "Oh, for God's sake. That's the ugliest one yet." She closed the computer, sat down next to me, and pulled my Buy Now hand into hers. "You can't bury your feelings in sappy movies and vintage Laura Ashley dresses. You're getting out of here. Now. Pack a bag."

How did she always seem to know when I was at my lowest? This particular low had been courtesy of a too-hot-to-be-legal cop who'd done the old I'll-call-you thing and then didn't. The jerk.

Juan Carlos had skidded to a stop in the entryway. He'd leaned on the doorjamb, one hand over his heart, huffing and puffing as though he'd run a marathon instead of up my three front steps. "Please tell me we got here in time to stop Laura Ingles Wilder from adding to her Little House on the Depressed Prairie collection."

"Just," Vivian replied. "You're coming with us," she told me. "You've already booked out the time at the salon for the trip, so no rescheduling appointments. Think of this trip as a cleansing."

True. I *had* marked the time off my busy schedule. All three of us had, which was a feat in itself, as our salon was the busiest in the summer. Still, I wasn't sure I could bring my mood up enough to actually enjoy myself.

"Exactly," Juan Carlos chimed in. "Out with the no good, rotten, no-calling-back bastard and in with free drinks, questionable bets, and mile-high buffet plates."

I thought of the dress I'd been seconds away from buying, with its lace collar, flounced skirt, and two-inch-thick shoulder pads, and I knew they were right. I was at the lowest of lows. Plus, I was pretty sure I already owned that dress in blue.

"Fine," I said, confident with the knowledge that the dress was on my watch list, so if this trip didn't work out, it could still be mine.

So there we were, standing at the back of an audience filled with hairstylists from all over North America and parts of Europe, all watching as Dhane, the sexy signature artist for the hip new Scandinavian hair-product company, Hjálmar, prowled the hair show's main stage. He'd become famous enough in our world to garner a single moniker like Prince or Madonna, and seeing him in person, I could understand why.

Gripping Viv's and Juan Carlos's hands, I tried to suppress the excitement rising up the back of my throat. They'd been right. This was exactly what I needed. We had four whole days ahead of us with nothing to do except immerse ourselves in the latest hair-styling trends and products. For the first time in weeks, I was actually looking forward to something.

"So, when I weave my client's hair, the foils represent the spiritual labyrinth of man's quest to fit into the social mores created by society's inability to intellectualize a person's individual creativity, thereby transferring their reality onto me, the artist. Correct?" Juan Carlos asked with a face straighter than a preelection politician promising lower taxes.

"Uh-huh," Vivian answered absently, standing on tiptoes, trying to see over the crowd, her focus fixed on the black-clad man strutting back and forth across the stage.

Decked out in her usual black and white with a red flower pinned in her hair, Vivian looked like a Mexican Betty Boop, all petite curves and what-of-it? attitude. I could never match her attitude, but I had almost as many curves as her. Even though she was a few inches shorter than me and a few shades tanner, we were often mistaken for sisters, which I thought was more due to our closeness than our resemblance. Other than both of us having dark hair, we looked nothing alike. Even though I could only hope for cheekbones like hers, I consoled myself with the fact that my lips were fuller.

"And if I buy their DVD with the bonus, one of a kind, life-altering weaving combs, I'll be taking back my power as an artist. Is that right?" Juan Carlos inquired further.

I clapped a hand over my mouth, trapping the laughter. This was going to be the *best* weekend ever.

"Yes. Yes." Viv waved him quiet. Putting a finger to her deep red lips, she emphasized her point. "Ssh!"

"I see." Juan Carlos stroked his clean-shaven chin as if giving this philosophy great thought. He was trying a new look, very *Mad Men*, with his dark, shiny hair parted and combed to the side and a vintage, man-about-home cardigan sweater with a collared shirt and slim-fit slacks.

The crowd of hairstylists around us watched, enthralled, as more tree people sprang up from the stage like, well, trees, and Dhane, now on bended knee, wound up his pitch to convert every stylist in the room to the Hjálmar, eco-friendly way of doing hair.

"Oh, Mother Earth, forgive us." Lightning cracked on the

screen behind him. The expected thunder shook the floor, making my feet tingle, my exhilaration rising to a new level. "We've killed your trees, your plants, your animals." Images of dead animal carcasses as big as Volkswagens appeared on the screen behind Dhane. "We've desecrated your oceans and streams." Now they showed sea creatures, birds, fish, and other aquatic wildlife, dead or covered in oil. "Please, forgive us." His laser-blue eyes bore down on the crowd from the three Jumbotrons high above the stage, clearly gearing up for the big finale. "We've studied. We've learned. We give you…Hjálmar!"

The stage plunged into darkness, the only light coming from the giant *H* of the Hjálmar logo intertwined with healthy, living plants and wildlife on all four screens. The crowd surged to its feet, the applause, whistles, and shouts loud enough to drop fowl from the air. The house lights came up. I guessed there wouldn't be an encore. Not that he needed one.

An announcement came over the loud speakers, a sexy female voice with a Swedish accent. "Thank you for sharing the Hjálmar vision. Dhane will be presenting the Stylist of the Year Award at the North American Styling Awards sponsored by Hjálmar."

The North American Styling Awards, or NASA, was the most prestigious beauty competition in North America and was considered the hair-styling equivalent of winning an Oscar. As last year's winner, Dhane would naturally present the award to this year's top stylist.

We made our way, herdlike, out onto the main floor of the convention center. Row upon row of manufacturer booths gridded the room, each one promoting the most high-tech, necessary styling tools, products, and equipment a salon or hairstylist would ever want.

Juan Carlos was the first to break our stunned silence. "Holy TV evangelist! I've got the strongest urge to repent. I feel like I've been to church. I'll bet I'm healed. Oh my God! I can't feel my bunions anymore, and my shoes fit better." He examined his hands as we walked. "Ah, darn, I still have that nick on my middle finger from when I was cutting my client Courtney's hair, and she jumped up to chase after her sleazo boyfriend who walked past the salon with another girl." He showed me his cut finger.

"Bummer. Did she catch him?"

"She did." He rubbed the cut. "It was worth it. I got a new client out of it."

"How?"

"The other girl had the nastiest hair, so I took pity on her and booked her the following week."

I gave him a look and shook my head.

"What?"

"I want to check out the Hjálmar booth. Come on." Vivian grabbed my sleeve. I grabbed Juan Carlos's sleeve, creating a chain. Vivian towed us toward the center of the grid, where the big names in hair-care products like Paul Mitchell, Wella, and Sebastian had booths.

The Hjálmar booth was at the center, a choice spot, and was set up like a cosmetics counter in a department store. It was oval in shape and about as long as a double-car garage. The guys and gals behind the counter pranced and posed with the put-out pouts of Abercrombie and Fitch models.

Huge posters hung above the racks of product in the center, featuring more emaciated, disenfranchised youths leaping through meadows, holding various Hjálmar products, their clothing fluttering in the breeze. But these posters were nothing compared to the much larger ones of Hjálmar's star stylist, Dhane. His vivid blue eyes stared down at us from on high as if surveying his kingdom. His gaze was mesmerizing. Looking too long at him made me kind of dizzy.

"Is it me, or do the center of his eyes spin like a pinwheel?" I asked.

"Azalea," Juan Carlos whispered, hitting me in the arm to get my attention, repeatedly, annoyingly.

"What?" I barked, turning to see what he was so wound up about.

Juan Carlos's attention was fixed on the figure headed our way, parting the crowd like Moses.

Dhane strode purposefully as a captain would to the helm of his ship. He was flanked by suits who I assumed were Hjálmar executives, his pale shoulder-length hair rippling behind him. Seeing him up close was nothing like seeing him onstage or in a picture. I'd thought he was attractive. I was wrong.

He was stunning. Beautiful. But it was the careful, fragile beauty of a delicate orchid, easily marred or crushed.

Juan Carlos made a sound like a balloon losing air. I knew the feeling. If I'd been capable of more than staring gawk-eyed and gape-mouthed, I might've thrown myself at Dhane's feet.

Dhane spotted us and made a slight change of direction, heading our way. Juan Carlos hit my arm again, like I hadn't been watching every move Dhane made. Vivian shifted her stance, putting out a hip, and patted her hair. What in the what? I glanced back and forth between Vivian and Dhane, my brows bunching tighter together with every step he took. Did they know each other?

Dhane reached us and my first thought was that he was taller than I'd imagined he'd be. My next thought was thoroughly naughty and completely unrepeatable.

He grasped Vivian's hands, kissing both in turn. "My Vivian." His accent was much more pronounced in person, sounding vaguely European and kind of forced, as though he'd practiced to get it just right. "I'd know you anywhere."

"It's been a long time." Vivian smiled, batting her eyelashes at him.

My brows bounced up and I stared in openmouthed

astonishment. Vivian *did* know Dhane. From where? When? How? And why in the hell didn't I know about this?

"And yet you look the same. How is this possible?"

Vivian giggled. Giggled! Viv didn't do smitten teenager. Not even when she had been a teenager. Um, hello! *Somebody* was forgetting all about her boyfriend of three years back home.

Juan Carlos nudged me out of the way, hinting at an introduction. But it was as if Dhane and Vivian were alone in the room, their gazes so entwined not even Juan Carlos's throat clearing and posturing could break their bond. It took a sharp nudge in the shoulder from Juan Carlos for Viv to return to us.

"Oh, sorry. Dhane, I'd like you to meet my friends. This is Juan Carlos. He's a stylist at my salon and a dear friend."

Dhane kept ahold of Vivian's hand while extending his other to shake Juan Carlos's. "Pleasure to meet you."

"Mine, too," Juan Carlos purred.

"And this is Azalea, my best friend and business partner."

Dhane turned his brilliant blues on me. Were it not for the hand he'd clasped, I'd have swooned like a lovesick boy-band fan. "Azalea, so nice to meet you at last."

At last? I looked a question at Vivian. Boy did my best friend have a lot of explaining to do.

"How long are you in town?" Vivian recaptured Dhane's attention, leaving Juan Carlos and me to exchange looks of confusion and conjecture.

"I am to stay for the awards and then return to Europe for another event." They were in the vortex again, just the two of them. "Will you meet me later?"

"Of course."

Dhane smiled, and I could have sworn a choir of angels sang. "We have much to discuss, no?"

One of the executives tugged Dhane's sleeve. "She's waiting. We have to go."

Dhane cast him an annoyed look mixed with something else—fear, maybe?

"A moment," he told them, then turned back to Vivian. "I am looking forward to spending time with you." They exchanged cell phone numbers and a lingering good-bye.

Vivian, Juan Carlos, and I stood shoulder to shoulder, watching Dhane leave. The crowd that had gathered made room for his departure, surreptitiously casting furtive glances at him in that way you do with celebrities when you recognize them but don't want to pester them. A few gave Vivian curious looks, no doubt wondering if she was someone they should recognize. A few others didn't bother to hide their jealousy before they turned their backs and followed Dhane.

I shoved Vivian's shoulder. "Why did I not know that you knew Dhane?"

Juan Carlos joined in. "I cannot believe it! I should shun you. This is unforgivable...but I might consider forgiveness if you tell all. And I do mean *all*."

Vivian spun away, leaving us to scramble after her.

"Come on, Viv. How'd you meet him? How long have you known him?" I would have continued peppering her with questions, but she stopped me with a, "Ssh" and a, "Not here."

Juan Carlos and I followed her out into a hallway and down a corridor to a small, out of the way windowed alcove with a view of the famous Las Vegas strip.

"Okay, you can't repeat what I'm about to tell you, got it?" She seemed nervous, casting furtive glances around as though she were about to give up state secrets or something.

Juan Carlos and I bobbed our heads. In that moment, we would have traded our finely honed, ridiculously expensive hair-cutting shears to hear what she had to say.

"All right." She cast a wary eye around us, making sure she wouldn't be overheard. "I met Dhane when I was sixteen during the summer I went to stay with my aunt Tita in Wichita."

So just before Vivian and I had met in beauty school. I felt a little pang of jealousy at the thought that Dhane had known her longer than I did.

"She'd just had twins and my mom sent me to help her, since all of our family is in California." Vivian paused. "I really shouldn't be telling you this. I promised."

"We won't tell. We swear." I glanced at Juan Carlos to get his agreement.

"Absolutely," Juan Carlos agreed. "Even if you dipped me in hot oil and pulled my fingernails out one by one. Or did that water-torture thing with the drips on the forehead, my lips would stay sealed. Cross my heart, hope to die—"

Vivian stopped him with a hand. "Got it. You won't tell." She took a deep breath and another look around. "Aunt Tita had put the babies down for a nap, so I had some free time. I decided to go for a walk."

She stopped again and looked out the window, but her gaze was unfocused, as if she were looking more within than without. I got the impression that she'd buried this part of her past so deep for so long that it took a great deal of effort for her to pry it loose.

After a moment, she continued, "I was walking, not really paying much attention to what I was doing. I was just so glad to be out of the house. It was hot, really hot. I put a hand up to wipe the sweat off my forehead and that's when I got grabbed from behind and pulled into a space between two apartment buildings."

She turned and paced a couple of steps away, then back again. "I was scared out of my mind. I thought he'd kill me. He told me to give him my watch and the pearl earrings I got from my grandma for my fourteenth birthday. He was big, huge. Like I said, I was really afraid. But my grandma had given me those earrings right before she died. I couldn't just hand them over."

She crossed her arms tightly over her chest, hugging herself.

"He hit me. I went down and stayed down. I figured if he thought I was dead, he'd leave me alone." She rubbed her arms. "But he didn't. He bent down over me. I held my breath and tried to be as still as possible. And then he was on top of me. I panicked and screamed, kicking and hitting at him, but he was just too heavy."

"Oh, Viv." I took a step toward her, but she waved me off.

"I'm fine. I was fine because of Dhane. Only his name wasn't Dhane then."

Juan Carlos's eyes bugged out of his head. "What…what happened? Go back. What happened with the guy?"

"He was heavy because he'd been hit in the head with a brick. Dhane hit him. He saved me." I could tell her emotions were right there at the surface, reflecting in her dark brown eyes.

"Then what?" I asked, knowing there had to be more, a lot more.

"Dhane was skinny then, you know, in that young kid, gangly kind of way. But he was really cute even then." She cracked a hint of that secretive smile I was already beginning to associate with Dhane. "He helped me up and then he handed me my watch back, but not before he'd kicked the guy in the gut." She laughed. "I think I fell for him right then."

"You and Dhane?" Juan Carlos asked with more than a hint of awe and an obvious twinge of envy.

"Well, no. I was a good Catholic girl. But we did fool around a bit." She looked off, that grin playing around her mouth again. "I sneaked out as often as I could to see him. And then the summer was over and I had to go back home."

"Did you see him again?" I asked.

"Yes, a few more times. Another summer and then he came out to see me. By then I was in beauty school and we were just friends. I showed him a little of what I was learning. He picked it up quickly. He had a natural talent for working with hair."

"You said that his name wasn't Dhane then," Juan Carlos

reminded her.

She looked confused. "I did?"

We nodded.

"Oh, well, I guess he wanted a new identity, a new name. His home life wasn't the greatest and he wanted to distance himself from it. He came up with the name Dhane and I thought it fit."

"Wow, you helped create Dhane." Juan Carlos said this as if Vivian had invented a flying car or something.

"No, Dhane created Dhane. He worked really hard and he deserves his success.""What was his real name?" I asked.

She shook her head, scanning the small alcove as if she'd already said too much. "That's for Dhane to tell."

"If he's from Kansas, then how'd he get the accent?" Juan Carlos asked.

"It was part of reinventing himself." She bit her lip, and her voice took on a pleading, desperate tone. "Look, please don't say anything to anybody. This is important. Please promise me you'll keep what I'm telling you to yourself."

She'd told us everything she was going to, and I got the impression she regretted even that small amount. I examined Vivian's face in that way we did when we wanted to know what the other is thinking. She avoided meeting my eyes.

I knew Vivian better than I knew myself. There was something else going on here. And as soon as I could get her alone, I was going to find out just what that was. The one thing I knew for sure was that Vivian seemed very protective of Dhane, and keeping his secret was extremely important to her. Being the keeper of more than a few of my secrets, I knew Viv would never spill Dhane's.

I also knew without a doubt that the story she'd told us was at best incomplete and at worst a total and complete lie.

Giving her my word of honor to keep what she'd told us to myself, I couldn't help but wonder what she'd left out…and why.

CHAPTER TWO

Vivian, Juan Carlos, and I went our separate ways, each of us heading to the workshop or class we wanted to see. I made my way to my friend Lisa's class, where she would be demonstrating a new deep-conditioning treatment from Spain that promised one formula to flatten hair with too much volume and another to volumize hair that was too flat.

A miracle if there ever was one.

As I sat and watched Lisa run a brush through her model's hair, the special conditioning vapor billowing from it nearly obscuring her, I replayed Vivian's story in my mind. It didn't add up. True, she had an aunt Tita who lived in Wichita and had five kids including a set of twins, but as far as I knew, Vivian had never been to Kansas. Or if she had, she'd never mentioned it before today.

And why the secrecy surrounding Dhane's real name? I mean, who cared? A lot of celebrities change their names to make them more exotic…or less exotic. It wasn't like Juan Carlos and I worked for the IRS or something. We're trustworthy. Well, I was, anyway.

What hurt the most was not what she'd told us, but what she hadn't told us. The thought of Vivian holding back left me feeling a little lost. I went on a long, mental trip around Speculation Island, trying out one far-fetched theory after another. The stakes had to be pretty high for Vivian to have kept this from me for so long. We knew everything about each other right down to our bra sizes and tampon preferences. So what was the deal?

I was so absorbed in my thoughts, I didn't notice the person sitting down next to me until he tapped me on the shoulder.

"Excuse me."

I turned to see a guy of indeterminate age and nationality staring at me with exaggerated anime cartoon eyes. He wore large, dark, round contacts that obscured a good portion of the whites of his eyes, giving them a Kewpie doll-like look. He'd used white eyeliner on the inside of his lower lids and mascara to spike his lashes, which intermingled with the spikes of black hair hanging in his eyes.

At least I thought he was a guy. His facial features could have gone either way, but what threw him over to the masculine side, besides the lack of feminine curves, was his outfit. He wore a long, nearly to his knees, black vest riddled with zippered pockets and topped with a mandarin collar. Slim black pants and boots completed the look. He wore no shirt and his arms were thin yet toned, like that of a young man.

"Yes?" I answered after a too-long stunned silence.

He smiled and handed me an envelope. "I was told to give you this."

I eyed it as if it were a subpoena. "What is it?"

"An invitation." He nudged it in my direction. "Take it."

The plain white envelope seemed innocent enough, so I accepted it. "Who's it from?"

"You'll see."

He turned to leave, but I stopped him with a hand on his arm. "Do I know you?"

"No, but I know you…now."

"What's your name?"

"I call myself Jun." He said this with expectation, as if I should've been impressed. "It means obedient."

There was something about this boy I kind of liked. Maybe it was his full-out commitment to Japanese animation and the adolescent confidence it took to parade around in public dressed like a comic-book-convention reject. Or it could have been the optimism and anticipation that radiated from his young face. I'd lost the shiny expectation that the world would be kind to me, that life was simple and fair. I missed it. Whatever drew me to him, I had the feeling Jun and I were destined to be friends.

"And are you?" I asked, a bit tongue in cheek.

He grinned with teeth so white I had to resist the urge to cover my eyes.

"Sometimes." He tapped the envelope in my hand. "Come," he cajoled.

"Maybe," I hedged, knowing I wouldn't be able to resist. My curiosity was already shoving aside any other plans I might have had.

My answer seemed to satisfy him, and his face settled into a comfortable just-us-buds smile. "Until then."

Twisting in my chair, I watched Jun leave until the heavy conference room door closed behind him with a quiet *click*.

I turned back around and stared at the envelope he'd given me. It suddenly hit me how freaky it was that Jun had found me in a convention full of thousands, and goose bumps scattered over me. I tightened every muscle in my body, suppressing the urge to shudder.

I mentally debated whether or not I should read it. Turning the envelope in my hand, I felt a bit like Pandora about to open a box and unleash who knew what. Once done, knowing what it contained could not be undone. I might be better off if I dropped it in the nearest trash can and forgot about it.

Oh, who was I kidding? There was a reason I'd become a

hairstylist—and it wasn't for the long hours standing on my feet. The cutting cape was like Wonder Woman's lasso. Once on, clients would spill their deepest darkest secrets, like coins from a winning slot machine. My rampant curiosity fed on a consistent diet of hush-hush info and hidden agendas. There was no way I could stop myself from peeking inside.

I opened the envelope and unfolded the plain white paper, smoothing out the creases on my jeans. Taking a breath for courage, I read the three simple lines:

10:00 P.M. RAINE TOWER, SUITE 3848
I LOOK FORWARD TO SEEING YOU.
DHANE

Dhane? Of all the people I'd expected the note to be from, Dhane would have been at the bottom of the list, along with the president of the United States and Buffy the Vampire Slayer. What did Dhane want with me?

I looked around the room, expecting someone to jump out and tell me this was all a joke. Lisa was inviting the audience to come up and feel her model's before-and-after hair. The crowd moved toward the stage, but I stayed where I was, alternating baffled glances at Dhane's invitation and the door Jun had disappeared through. I debated going after him, but that shiver I'd suppressed earlier shook me and I had a feeling Jun had vanished as abruptly as he'd appeared.

I refolded the paper and stuffed it into my oversize hobo bag, the one with so many pockets Vivian called it my Mary Poppins purse. Then I texted Juan Carlos: *What are you doing?* I was testing the waters, unsure if I should mention Dhane's note or not. For all

I knew, I was overreacting and Dhane had invited all three of us to his suite…late at night…clandestinely.

"Hey, Azalea." I glanced up to see Lisa standing over me. We were the only ones left in the room.

I popped up and gave her a hug. She'd put on a few pounds since the last time I'd seen her. But then who was I to judge, what with glass houses being vulnerable to stones and all. I'd packed on a few post-breakup pounds myself. And Lisa looked good. The extra weight softened the sharp angles of her face, giving her a kind, almost benevolent look. She'd clipped her hair short and it shot out from her head in a profusion of tightly coiled black curls.

"How did you like my presentation?" she asked.

I shuffled my feet, not wanting to confess that I'd missed a good portion of it. "You did great." That wasn't a lie. I'd noticed the audience had been very involved in what she had to say.

"You didn't feel the before and after."

"I was waiting for the crowd to die down."

"Sheila!" she exclaimed. "Sheila, come over here and let my friend Azalea feel your hair."

A young blonde with a milquetoast face plodded over to us and offered me two hunks of hair to touch, with all the lackluster enthusiasm of a diner waitress reciting the daily special.

I obediently ran my hands through Sheila's hair. "Wow." I turned my attention to the "after" side. "There really is a difference."

"Do you think you'd be interested in adding this treatment to your salon service menu?" Lisa asked.

"Possibly. But I'd need to run it by Vivian first."

"Of course." Lisa turned to her model. "Thank you, Sheila. Come back in an hour for the next presentation."

"Okay." Sheila started to turn, then bent down and picked something up. "Is this yours?" She held out a plastic hotel key card.

I felt my face go hot and quickly tucked the card into my front pocket. "Yes, thank you."

We watched Sheila traipse away, and then Lisa turned to me. "What are you doing later?"

"There are a couple of classes I want to see. Why?"

"I'm one of the judges for the student competition. I have to watch them prep their doll heads this afternoon to make sure no one cheats. Want to hang out and observe with me?"

As a salon owner, I knew this was a great opportunity. We were always on the lookout for new talent. "Sure."

She gave me the particulars and we parted ways. I wandered out onto the main exhibition floor, not really paying attention to the booths I passed, my thoughts swirling around Dhane's invitation. A part of me couldn't help but feel flattered. Dhane was seriously hot. Of course my ego liked the idea that he might be interested in me. And it wasn't as though I currently had a love life. Well, I guess I sort of did, if you counted made-for-TV-boyfriends and pints of Ben & Jerry's a love life.

Even so, I refused to entertain the notion that I was so very desperate as to risk my relationship with Viv for whatever Dhane might have in mind.

My phone vibrated in my pocket. Juan Carlos had texted: *Watching Dick Stain make an ass of himself. Wanna watch with me?*

Richard Stain had been an employee at our salon until a few months back. To say he and Juan Carlos hadn't gotten along would be like saying Democrats and Republicans had a few minor disagreements on occasion. Those two fought worse than two stags in season. And the trick of it was that no one could figure out why.

I stopped near a booth with racks and racks of colorful, clip-in hair wefts and made a mental note to pick up a few pink ones for my niece, even though I knew it would irritate every single woman's liberation cell in my mother's body. Mom's idea of childhood dress-up had included a briefcase and a judge's gavel.

She'd hate me giving her granddaughter something so frivolous. Must compete with men, even at playtime!

I returned Juan Carlos's text: *Stop calling him that! Where are you?*

He responded: *The Torrid Toolz booth.*

I pulled out my convention map, found it, and made my way over.

Torrid Toolz had a booth large enough for a small platform stage to be wedged into it. I found Juan Carlos watching Richard smooth out his model's hair with TT's new ceramic flatiron.

Juan Carlos immediately began scrutinizing Richard's performance as if he were an *American Idol* judge. "Dick should have taken larger sections of hair. I could make those micro mini sections smooth with just the heat from my bare hands and a dab of relaxing liquid. For cripes sake, his model looks like she's part Asian. Why would an Asian person need her hair straightened when she already has the straightest hair on the planet? It's a fix, I tell you. The Dickster couldn't style his way out of an underwater beauty pageant."

I put my hand on his arm to stop the tirade before Richard's mike picked it up and broadcasted it to the crowd. "Jealous?"

He gave me a look that was the ocular equivalent of the middle finger.

I turned my attention back to Richard winding up his spiel onstage. He was good—convincing yet trustworthy. A respectable combination in a sales person.

"He's done. Let's get out of here."

Juan Carlos made to leave, but I grabbed his sleeve and jumped with my hand in the air. "Richard!"

"Shut up! What are you doing?"

Waving higher, I moved forward with Juan Carlos twisting to free himself from my grip. "Richard!"

He saw me and beamed with recognition. Then his dark eyes

moved past me to Juan Carlos and his smile slid into a slit-eyed scowl. At the edge of the stage, Richard helped me up and gave me a big hug. He was a bear of a man. Built out of blocks, he was all squared-off angles and thick slabs of beef. He reminded me of a Rock 'Em Sock 'Em Robot. Hugging him was like embracing a Buick.

"I'm so glad to see *you*, Azalea." The mutual love/hate society was now in session.

"I didn't know you'd be here. How have you been?"

Juan Carlos joined us onstage, a stone statue of obstinacy.

"Good. Good. I just started working for Torrid Toolz a few months ago, and they asked me to be one of their demonstrators for the show."

"You look great. Doesn't he look great, Juan Carlos?" Maybe it wasn't well done of me to provoke him, but it sure was fun.

"Like a Mack truck," Juan Carlos deadpanned.

"Love the new look, Juan Carlos," Richard returned. "But isn't it a little early for Halloween?" He tapped his chin. "Let me guess, Ward Cleaver?"

Juan Carlos came back with, "Aren't you a little west of the Jersey Shore? Snooki and The Situation must be missing you big time."

Richard took a step forward, nearly knocking me off the stage. "Your grandpa called from 1963. He wants his wardrobe back."

"Easy, Roid Rage wouldn't want you to get angry and turn all green or anything."

Richard really got in Juan Carlos's face then. "Are you insinuating that I take drugs?"

"Either that or your mama did."

Uh-oh. The two things I knew about Richard were that you don't mess with his styling tools and you do not insult his mother.

Richard grabbed the front of Juan Carlos's shirt and lifted him off his feet. "Take that back." He shook Juan Carlos, making his hands and feet jerk like a marionette. "No one disses my ma and walks away whole."

"Guys. Guys. Come on. Everyone's staring. Someone's going to call security and then you'll get hauled off to jail," I pleaded.

"First he apologizes."

I smacked Juan Carlos's arm. "Say you're sorry."

Juan Carlos turned to me. "But I'm not—"

"Oh, yes you are. Do it now, or you're fired." There was no heat in this statement—I was totally bluffing.

Juan Carlos threw me another dirty look, then mumbled his apology.

Richard planted Juan Carlos back on his feet but didn't release him. "No, say it to my ma." Richard punched in a number, then handed Juan Carlos his cell phone.

"Is this jock itch for real?" Juan Carlos asked me, earning him another hard jerk that dislodged a hunk of his perfectly coiffed hair.

"Just do it!" I ordered, ready to get off the stage and disappear back into the crowd.

"Hello, Ma? Yeah, yeah, I know. I will later. Listen, this guy Juan Carlos said some disparaging things about you and he wants to apologize." Richard handed the phone to Juan Carlos. "Make it sincere."

Juan Carlos took the phone. "Hello, Mrs. Stain. Yes, that's me." Juan Carlos's eyes bugged out of his head and he turned crimson. "Uh-huh."

"Tell her you're sorry," Richard prompted with another jolt.

"I'm, uh, real sorry for what I said about you, Mrs. Stain. Uh-huh. Okay. Thank you." Juan Carlos handed the phone back to Richard.

"Ma? *What*?" Richard released Juan Carlos and turned away, sputtering Greek with a lot of short, choppy hand gestures.

Juan Carlos smoothed the front of his shirt. "Can we go now?"

Giving him a sideways glance, I caught Juan Carlos watching Richard with a look on his face that I'd never seen before. And then it hit me. Juan Carlos *liked* Richard.

Whoa.

Suddenly the months and months of squabbling, nitpicking, and hostility in the salon made perfect sense. I couldn't wait to tell Vivian. This was the tastiest bit of gossip to come my way since I'd found out how the lady who owned the card shop next to our salon paid her rent. My hand twitched toward my cell phone.

"What did Mrs. Stain say to you?" I asked Juan Carlos.

"Nothing. Let's go."

"Wait," I implored. "I have to say good-bye to Richard." But Juan Carlos was already off the stage and heading toward the exit. I debated going after him for a moment and then decided against it. I knew Juan Carlos well enough to realize that I'd get nothing out of him while he was in the mood he was in. So I let him walk away. Whatever Mrs. Stain had said, it rattled him to the point of panic. If I had a hope of finding out what had happened, it would be from Richard.

On the other side of the stage, Richard was packing up his equipment, tossing things into his bag as fast as he could get ahold of them. He was in such a rush, he didn't notice me until I walked up and tapped him on the shoulder.

He yelped and spun around, clutching his heart. "Oh, Azalea, you scared half a year off my life." He searched the faces around me. Seeming calmed by what—or I should say *whom*—he didn't find, Richard relaxed into his usual mellow self. "Did you like my presentation?"

"Very much." I paused, thinking how best to go about getting the information I was after. "Sorry for the things Juan Carlos said. He gets a little carried away sometimes. I hope you and your mom weren't too offended."

"No. No. It's fine." His words were meant to be nonchalant,

but he sounded more panicked than indifferent. He loaded the last of his items into his bag and turned toward me.

Rocking back on my heels, I gave him my best you-can-confide-in-me smile. "Juan Carlos seemed kind of, um, upset when he spoke to your mom. I wonder what that was all about."

"Sometimes my mom says things she shouldn't." He hitched his messenger bag higher on his shoulder.

"Is there something going on between you and Juan Carlos?"

"No." He huffed out a frustrated breath. "There could've been... There almost was, but he's just so damn stubborn, I..." He shook his head. "Never mind. It was good seeing you, Azalea." He gave me a quick hug. "I'm sure I'll see you around. Give me a call when you get back home and we'll do lunch or something." He sketched a wave and then he, too, disappeared into the throng.

The convention floor pulsed to the beat of a nearby speaker, snippets of conversations drifted around me, and every now and then someone jostled me with a muttered apology. I stood there a moment in that vastness of humanity, feeling rather abandoned. I hated being alone in a crowd.

It felt a lot like that time when I was six and kinda, sorta wandered off from my mom at the mall to check out all the lighty, blinky toys at another store and got lost. By the time I was finally discovered, I was hysterical, and my mother had threatened to sue the owner of the mall and every single employee in it. I hated the mall and crowds after that. Thank goodness for online shopping. And therapy.

So far this trip hadn't been the life-cleansing, forget-my-troubles-and-all-the-lousy-men-I've-dated weekend getaway that I'd expected it would be.

Contemplating what to do with myself, I shoved my hands in my pockets and froze. I cast a look around, then scampered to an out-of-the-way corner. Pulling the hotel key card from my pocket, I felt nervous to the point of nausea. The card Lisa's model had picked up off the floor and given me wasn't mine—Dhane had included the key to his hotel room with his invitation. Examining the Raine Hotel logo, a feeling of foreboding swept over me, creeping up my spine and settling into a headache at my forehead.

Whatever Dhane's motives were for inviting me to his suite, they weren't good. Certainly they wouldn't be good for my relationship with Vivian.

I considered dropping the key and invitation in the nearest trash can. A part of me resented Dhane for putting me in this position. Was I supposed to be flattered? *Hi, I'm a long-lost boyfriend of your best friend. Wanna come to my hotel suite late at night under the cover of secrecy? Wanna jeopardize your friendship for a clandestine meeting with a hot, rich, famous hairstylist?* Who does that to a person?

And yet the other part of me had to know. Why me? What did he want? Another thought struck—what if the note and key hadn't been meant for me? It wasn't addressed to anyone. What if it had been meant for Vivian? People got us mixed up all the time.

I flipped the key card over, hoping to find a clue to this mystery. The words "Please come" were written in thick black ink, reminding me of Jun's persuading.

Jun.

Jun had seemed pretty confident that I was the intended recipient. And how smart of Dhane to send him. Sweet, innocuous Jun. Who could resist? Maybe that was the point. Sending Jun was like sending a singing telegram. Dhane must have counted on Jun's charms to strike up enough curiosity in me to ensure my attendance. I didn't appreciate the manipulation. And yet, it had worked. Knowing I shouldn't, I wanted to go. I told myself it was because he was interested in me as Vivian's friend, not in me romantically.

Maybe this was an invitation to a party and Vivian and Juan Carlos had also been invited. That scenario made more sense than any of the other crazy ones I'd come up with. A party. That was it.

Making my decision, I tucked the key into the front pocket of my jeans and lost myself in the crowd.

CHAPTER THREE

That afternoon, I met up with Lisa in a stark, stuffy room where twenty-five fledgling hairstylists sweated over doll heads attached to rickety tables, each one trying to distinguish him or herself from the others. You could almost smell the ambition pumping off them in hot waves.

Lisa and the two other supervisors kept a sharp eye on the contestants as they cut, curled, coaxed, and coiffed their mannequin's hair into competition perfection. The blank-eyed stares of the doll heads should have long since lost their creepiness for me, and yet they hadn't. There was something inherently unnatural about severed heads being shoved onto rotating posts, then attached to tabletops just so stylists could play with their hair. It didn't help that the mannequins came with names like Annie, Rachel, or Derek, as though they were real people who had bequeathed their heads to the science of hairstyling.

Representing each sex and every nationality, loose doll heads lay topsy-turvy in bins along one wall, waiting to be chosen and transformed. Curly, straight, dark, light, long, short, anything and everything a stylist could want or want to make over.

They gave me the willies.

A student along the sidewall caught my attention. He painstakingly smoothed each strand of his doll's hair into the shape of a tulip. But what drew me to him was the color technique he'd used to create a deep red at the base that gradually lightened to pale pink "petal" tips. I stepped closer to get a better look. The shading was near perfect, no blotches or steps, just a slow transition from dark to light.

I pulled a business card from my bag and laid it on the table where he was working, taking a chance he'd be interested in a job in California. Startled, he glanced up, then nodded at my encouraging smile. I hoped he'd call. Naturally talented hair colorists weren't thick on the ground.

Moving on, I watched another student tease a large section of her doll's hair. After packing the hair thick with her comb, she then flipped the section toward her and smoothed one side with a plastic bristled brush. She gently turned the hair under, forming it into a Liberty Roll made popular in wartime 1940s, and then secured it with bobby pins. Although nice, there was nothing special about the style—until I caught a glimpse of the drawing sitting on the table in front of her. The finished product would have American flags and…were those sparklers?

I suddenly had the urge to make note of the fire sprinklers and emergency exits. Hairspray and fire didn't mix. Continuing down the row, I studied each student's creation. Two of them had very similar designs. I was speculating on who had copied whom when a voice whispered in my ear.

"Holy catfight, that's going to get ugly." Juan Carlos seemed to have recovered from his run-in with Richard and was back to his usual sarcastically observant self.

"How'd you get in here?"

"*Please*. I'm more connected than a mob boss's barber's bookie. I should be asking how *you* got in here, but I won't because I'm just so happy I found you. Guess who I ran into?"

"Who?"

"Guess."

He knew I hated this game. "Just tell me."

"Don't be such a Crankerella Crankenstein. You take the fun out of everything. Fine," he huffed. "I'll tell you. But I want it on record that I tried to surprise you." He paused, then with great dramatic flair announced, "Bobby Brickhouse!"

I groaned. Bobby Brickhouse was not a time in my life I wanted to revisit. Neither was the memory of finding him with his hand up my assistant's shirt.

Juan Carlos looked genuinely disappointed. "I thought you *liked* him liked him. What's the deal? How could you not like him? He's built, stacked."

"Yes, I know. Like a brick house. Ha-ha. That joke's not too old." At his glare I explained, "I did like him. But Bobby Brickhouse is a two-timing, empty-headed jerk." Why couldn't I ever find a guy who just wanted me? Not me *and* my assistant.

"Whoa, whoa, whoa. How did I not know you and Bobby Brickhouse hooked up? First Viv and now you with a secret. What is this world coming to? Doesn't anybody tell anybody *anything* anymore?"

The sting of Vivian's dishonesty hit me anew and my cheeks went hot with shame for not having told Juan Carlos about Bobby Brickhouse. "You're right. I'm sorry. I should have told you. I was just so embarrassed that I—"

"What is *he* doing here?"

I turned to see who had nabbed Juan Carlos's attention. Richard Stain's dark head was bent toward Lisa's and they appeared to be in deep discussion.

Juan Carlos shifted as if the ground beneath him had suddenly turned into molten lava. "I gotta go." He glanced around, looking for another way out, but the only exit was directly behind Richard. "I gotta go," he repeated, the panic in his voice rising.

I reached for his hand, not knowing what else to do. "Do you want me to distract him so you can leave?" I offered.

He seemed to take some comfort from our contact. Visibly

summoning his strength, Juan Carlos gripped my hand in both of his and took a deep breath. "No. I'm fine." Then he shook himself loose and straightened his sweater. "I'm fine. It's fine. Whatever. I don't care. He can be here. I can be here. It's fine." He turned his back on Richard and directed his attention to one of the students instead. "That's gorgeous! Look at that."

The style the student had created *was* amazing. We inched closer for a better look.

"Wow."

"Do you think she'd show me how she did that?" Juan Carlos asked.

"Probably, if you asked her."

"I'm going to grab a doll head just in case." Juan Carlos scooted around the tables, bound for the doll head bins on the other side of the room.

"Ten minutes!" Lisa announced, galvanizing the students into a panicked frenzy of hairspray clouds and last-minute checks on the competition.

"Oh. My. God! You are such a cheater!" shouted a young man—one of the two students who had really similar designs.

"What?" At the accusation, the other student, a redheaded girl, stared back and forth between the two hairstyles, obviously surprised by what she was being accused of. Then her indignation kicked in. "I didn't cheat! You're the cheater. I'm telling." She jumped up with her hand in the air. "Judge!"

"I'm telling," the boy mimicked. "Go ahead. Confess your cheating ass off. Tell them how you stole my idea then ruined it." He flicked a finger at a curl on the redhead's doll, causing it to fall. "See. Crap. A total knockoff."

The redhead clenched her fists at her sides and screamed, "You ruined it!" Then she launched herself at the boy, knocking her doll head off its stand and onto the floor.

The poor loose head rolled across the floor, tripping up Lisa and one of the judges who was coming to the girl's aid. Realizing what she'd done, the redhead made a grab for the boy's doll head. Grappling with her, the boy juggled the head in the air like a football receiver trying to clutch a just-in-reach pass. The girl slammed her body into his, causing him to knock into the table and lose his battle to save the head. It flew out of his hands and collided with the tulip-shaped doll head.

After that it was every man for himself. Those who had stations near the brawl ripped their doll heads off the stands, trying to protect them. As the fight rippled out, involving more and more students, craniums became the projectile weapons of choice.

I ducked, narrowly missing a blow to my own noggin and crawled under a nearby table. A second later I was joined by Richard Stain, his large body nearly crowding me out and into the clash.

"This is like being in the court of Henry the Eighth. Because of all the severed heads, I mean," he explained with a shy grin.

I cracked a smile and nodded. "I got it."

"Holy Anne Boleyn." Juan Carlos wedged himself in behind me. "I feel like I should be singing the chorus for that Henry the Eighth song." He nudged me to scoot over for him, pushing me into Richard. "Give a guy some room."

I could hear Lisa and the other judges trying to calm everybody down.

"There is no more room. I'm not the only one under here," I complained.

Juan Carlos caught sight of Richard and glowered. "Figures. Quit hogging all the cover, Gigantor."

"That's it!" Richard reared up, taking the table and our hiding place with him. As he stood, the table flew off his back and crashed to the floor behind him, narrowly missing a student. He pointed a meaty finger at Juan Carlos. "You're going to stop insulting me. Right now!"

The sudden violence seemed to have a startling effect on the students. They stopped pelting each other with doll heads and turned as one to watch the new fight.

Juan Carlos slowly unwound from the floor and puffed up to his full five-foot-ten-inch height. He pointed a finger back at Richard, right up in his face. "I'm sick of you telling me what to do!" He jabbed his finger to punctuate his point. The doll head he had clutched in his fist swung back and forth by the hair, hitting Richard in the chest.

Everyone froze, and the room went eerily quiet.

Something wasn't right.

A scream, sharp and staccato, slashed the air. The sound created panic. Chaos rose up all around as if the three of us, Richard, Juan Carlos, and I, were in the center of a tornado. People whirled and twirled, generating a cyclone of pandemonium and noise.

So much noise.

That piercing, penetrating scream never stopped. I clapped my hands over my ears, trying to shut it out.

Juan Carlos reached for me, but I shrank away from him. His gesture brought with it the realization that it was me who was crying out.

Richard made a move to come to my aid, then froze. Horror etched his face, curling back his features, the skin pulled tight as his attention fixed on the head dangling from Juan Carlos's fist.

Juan Carlos followed our gazes, his eyes moving slowly from his fist clutching the long, snowflake-white hair, to the dulled ice-blue stare, over the fragile, ashen beauty, finally resting on the jagged edge where the head should have met the body.

Juan Carlos opened his mouth to scream, but unlike me, no sound came out. He began to shake, quaking so hard the head bobbed back and forth. The head's movements seemed to snap something inside of him. In his panic, he flung the head away from him, scattering the remaining people in a flurry of yelps and shrieks.

As the head came to rest, the crowd stopped and stood there, gaping. Then as a group, they inched closer, sealing away from me the sight of Dhane's face lying broken and wrong on the dirty, industrial-grade carpeting.

Chapter Four

My nose stinging from unshed tears, I stared at the scarred linoleum floor of the well-used hallway where I sat with Lisa, Richard, and a handful of students waiting to be questioned by the police. Memories of Dhane kept flashing over and over in my mind's eye like a flickering, old movie. Snippets of scenes: Dhane, unbelievably handsome, gazing back at me from his TV commercials, dynamic and compelling as he prowled the Hjálmar stage, and then the overwhelming physical sensation of meeting him in person.

He'd been so vibrant, so young, and now he was just gone.

I couldn't believe it. Who would do something so awful to Dhane? And why?

It was the first time I'd seen death. There was no way to prepare myself for the tragic strangeness of it. Or the overwhelming sadness. None of it seemed real, and yet sitting here in this hallway, I had to face the fact that it was very real. Dhane was dead. Someone had murdered him and left his head to be found in that bin of doll heads.

I thought about Juan Carlos and the expression on his face

when the police had whisked him away. If it hadn't been for Richard holding Juan Carlos and calming him down before they'd gotten there, the police might have carted him off to the mental hospital. I'd never seen him so distraught, panic distorting his features, making his handsome face so pale, he'd looked close to passing out.

Looking down the long line of chairs, I thought about Vivian and worried about how she'd take the news of Dhane's death. I sniffed back threatening tears, wishing more than anything that I could talk to her, but the policeman guarding us had forbidden conversation, which included cell phones.

A door finally opened down the hall and a very short man with very nice hair, wearing a very nice suit, appeared. The clipboard he consulted would have looked awkward and too large in his small hands if he weren't clutching it with so much authority. Again the word *very* came to mind. Everything about him was excessive, from his expensive haircut to the way he scanned the line of witnesses, as if reading our minds.

He zeroed in on Richard. "Richard Stain, you're next."

I exchanged a curious look with Lisa, and her dark brown eyes held the same question I was asking myself. *How'd he know who was who?*

"Azalea March, you're with me." I turned from Lisa to find the man staring directly at me.

For a moment I sat frozen, pinned in place by his stare. Then Richard brushed past him through the doorway, breaking our eye contact. Compared to Richard, the man looked like a child playing dress up. That thought made the corner of my mouth want to kick up.

As I passed him, the man asked, "Something funny?" Saying it in such a way so that I *knew* he knew what I was thinking.

I ducked through the doorway, feeling guilty in the way you do when your parents have caught you doing something you shouldn't, something they'd told you not to do a thousand and one times. But being a kid, you did it anyway and there you were, caught red-handed and ashamed. That was me. A lot.

The small man closed the door behind me and marched over to a set of chairs identical to the one Richard sat in with another police officer across the room.

"Have a seat." He motioned to the chair facing the wall, then sat in the opposite one with the best view of the room. "I'm Detective Weller." He set aside his clipboard and pulled out a small notebook. "I need to ask you a few questions." He paused pen over paper to nail me with his scrutinizing stare. "Are you comfortable?"

"What?" Was I comfortable? Like it would make this experience or my memories easier to deal with if I had a comfy chair and a cold beverage? "I guess."

"I was being polite. I'll get on with it, then. What were you doing in the competition room? I understand only judges and contestants were supposed to be there."

"My friend Lisa is a judge. She invited me to watch the competition. I own a salon…" I started babbling, spilling my guts like I was turning state's evidence or something. I was on the verge of confessing about the frosty-pink eye shadow I'd stolen from a drugstore on a dare when I was fifteen when he stopped me with a hand.

"Thank you. You've given me a great deal of information. Now if you could narrow it down and tell me about what brought you here today, that would be great."

"Sorry."

"Happens all the time. I'm pretty sure the statute of limitations has run out on most of those crimes you've confessed to, so you're okay." He broke out an understanding smile that was just this side of patronizing. "What happened when you walked into the competition room? Keep it short. If I need more information, I'll ask. Okay?"

I nodded like the idiot I apparently was. "Okay."

"Okay." He waited, pen hovering, that smile permanently affixed.

I started in again, concentrating hard on keeping my story as concise as possible. When I'd gone through it once, he wanted me to go over some of it again, asking me about a few details that seemed totally unimportant to me.

"Thank you, that was very helpful," he said. I was about to stand, assuming we were finished, when he hit me with the zinger. "You knew Dhane. Tell me how you met."

I gripped the hard plastic seat of my chair. If I told him about how I'd met Dhane, then I'd have to tell him about who had introduced me to him. And then I'd have to tell him about what Vivian had told Juan Carlos and me after she'd introduced us to Dhane. I wasn't entirely sure on the friendship code of ethics here. Does a sworn-to-secrecy friendship oath supersede my obligation as a witness of a crime or vice versa?

He must have guessed at the predicament I was in because he warmed up his smile and dropped his voice, turning all confidential and friendly on me. "I know you want to help. You've helped me solve the case of the missing hundred-dollar bill in front of Rally Burger back in 1997." That corner of his mouth kicked up, again just short of condescending. This guy was good, better than me by far. I didn't have a chance of keeping anything from him.

"I didn't know Dhane. I'd just met him briefly this morning." There. That was the truth.

"I have a feeling there's more to the story."

"No. Not really." *Yes. Totally.*

I folded my arms over my chest and clamped my mouth shut, sure I'd get lockjaw from the effort. Nothing was going to get past my lips. He could glare at me with that penetrating stare, quirk his lips in that trust-me smile, and use his authority over me all day long. I owed Vivian more than I could ever repay. She'd been there for me more times than I could count. Now it was my turn to stand by her.

"Don't you want to help me find the person who did this to your friend?" Once more he made with the just-buds, you-can-tell-me, you-know-you-want-to grin.

I had the strongest urge to kick him in the nuts.

Instead I tightened my arms harder against my chest, pressed my lips into a thin line, and gave him my coldest stare. I tried to imagine an invisible shield going up between us, preventing him from reading any more of my thoughts. Maybe to keep myself from kicking him in the nuts, too. I was pretty sure I'd be in more trouble for doing that than for not answering any more of his questions.

He flipped his notebook closed and pulled out a card. After he wrote something on it, he handed it to me. "Here's my card with the case number on it. If something should come to your notice or events should occur that require you to confide in me, call me. My cell number's the one at the bottom."

"The one marked 'cell'?"

"That would be the one." He sat back and searched my face. "Before you go, there's something I want you to remember." He paused, making sure I was listening, and then he recited something about dancing in rings and secrets knowing stuff. "That's from a Robert Frost poem," he finished.

"Uh-huh." If that poem was supposed to be some kind of ominous statement, it hit its mark. "Can I leave now?"

He waved me off. "Go. But don't forget what I said."

As if I could. As if I wouldn't be up half the night trying to figure out what the heck he was warning me about and worrying that I'd be carted off to jail for trying to protect Vivian. "Secrets know. Right." I managed to not roll my eyes. "Words to live by." I headed for the door with the hairs at the nape of my neck standing on end.

Lisa was still sitting in one of the chairs in the hall. I gave her a small wave and a thumbs-up that had no truth in it. I felt more miserable leaving than I had going in. I hustled out of the convention center and into the taxi line out front, needing as much distance between Detective Weller and me as possible,

Good gracious, Vegas was hot in July. Dry heat, my Aunt Fanny's fanny. I swiped at the sweat puddling on my forehead, knowing it wasn't all from the weather. I was second in line, so I was out of the heat and into an arctic taxi faster than a Vegas drive-thru wedding.

As I sat in the back of the taxi on my way to my hotel, I thought about Dhane and Vivian. Where was she? I pulled my cell phone from my pocket, bringing out the hotel card key Dhane had given me along with it. Looking at them in each of my hands, I had the oddest feeling. My thoughts bounced back and forth between the two items, trying to sort out what exactly had me so on edge.

Making my decision, I punched Viv's speed-dial number and gave the driver a new destination. "Can you take me to the Raine Tower Suites instead?"

The taxi driver lifted a hand off the wheel. "Sure. No problem. I go where you say." Then he flipped a U-turn, sending me flying across the backseat just as Viv's voice mail kicked in.

"Viv, call me as soon as you get this message. I mean it. Call me!" For emphasis, I texted her, too.

Then I texted Juan Carlos, hoping he was all right after being questioned by the police. I wasn't sure how he'd deal with finding Dhane's head in that bin of doll heads. Thinking about him made my stomach churn with worry, not that the cabbie's driving helped. Holding on to the seat back and door handle, I braced myself for another turn.

This was supposed to have been a friends' weekend, a little fun in Lost Wages to help me move past my past. The worst I'd

expected to happen was Juan Carlos throwing his panties at a
Celine Dion impersonator or Vivian forcing us to sit through a
cheesy Michael Jackson tribute. Murder certainly hadn't been on
the agenda.

Where are Vivian and Juan Carlos?

I got my first look at the famous Raine Hotel as the cab pulled
up to the front drive. A gleaming, curving tower with the famous
Raine signature at the top, I couldn't help but gape at the grandeur.

I wasn't entirely sure why I was here. You know that feeling,
that niggling voice in the back of your head that sometimes
whispers at you to go in a particular direction or avoid a certain
situation? It was yelling at me now, so I followed it, blindly letting
it lead me to the Raine Hotel. The voice had been wrong before
and maybe it was wrong now, but I had to go with it. When it was
right, it was really, really right. And the sense that it would be right
this time rode me hard.

Oh, who was I kidding? I was dying of curiosity, practically
vibrating with it.

I stumbled out of the cab and paid the fare, happy to see the
car disappear back into Vegas traffic. The heat touched me briefly
before I was sucked into the climate-controlled interior of the
hotel. I was immediately struck by the understated elegance, the
restrained wealth. This was a place where the truly affluent played.
Trying not to gawk like a slack-jawed hick, I found the elevators.
Slipping the hotel key card in the slot, I punched the button for
Dhane's floor.

This was such a bad idea and yet I couldn't help myself. My
avid curiosity was as much a part of me as my hazel eyes, big boobs,
or the birthmark on the small of my back in the shape of Mickey
Mouse. I was the kid who unwrapped and then rewrapped all of my
Christmas presents to avoid any disappointing surprises and then
unwrapped my sister's, too, just to make sure hers weren't better
than mine. One time hers *were* better so I switched them. That was

the last time my parents put out presents before Christmas Day.

The elevator doors slid open without a sound, delivering me into a sparsely furnished space. I paused before going down the eerily quiet hall, not entirely sure why I'd come here. I checked my phone—still no calls or texts.

Maybe I should turn back.

I mentally shrugged. In for a penny, in for a pound, I supposed. Taking a deep breath, I braced myself and headed down the hall.

The plush carpet muffled my footfalls, amplifying the sound of my heart beating so hard, I was surprised it didn't echo off the walls. I felt like the too-stupid-to-live girl in a horror movie, sure there was an audience somewhere shouting at me to not go down the hall. Stopping to wipe my sweaty hands on my jeans before making another turn, I knew I was stalling. The same something that had propelled me to be here was now telling me to hang back. I leaned against the wall and peeked around the corner and down the hall. Empty.

This was silly. What was I doing here? *Stupid curiosity.*

I'd just made up my mind to turn around and leave when I heard a noise. I peered around the corner again. A door was open down the hall and two men stood in the corridor, looking back into the room.

"But the guests," the taller man pleaded. At closer inspection, I could see he wore a blazer embroidered with the Raine logo.

"I understand." The shorter man adjusted his belt over his stomach. "We'll try to be as discreet as possible, but this is a crime scene. In about ten minutes this place is going to be crawling with techs and supervisors." Pulling his jacket back, he hooked his thumbs in his waistband, exposing his substantial belly. "I'll do what I can to accommodate your guests."

The tall man twisted his hands. "You'll use the stairs and go out the back way?"

The other man waved this off. "Sure, sure. It's not like this is our first murder. Somebody's always getting offed in this town. Or offing themselves. We know the back ways in and out of every hotel and motel on or off Strip."

The Raine man made a noise like a small, furry creature being stepped on.

"Hey, Barnes!" the other man, obviously a police officer, shouted into the room. "Are we taking her in, or are we supposed to wait for Kennedy?"

Barnes muffled a response from inside the room.

"Figures. Our day wouldn't be complete without King Kennedy gracing us with his presence." The officer turned to the taller man from Raine. "We'll let you know if we need your help."

The Raine man started to say something with a finger pointed at the officer, but he got interrupted.

"Yeah, yeah. I know. Discreet. We'll call you if we need you." With that, the officer went back into the room, shutting the Raine man out.

The Raine man looked at the door like he wanted to cry, then turned and headed in my direction. I had a decision to make—go back down in the elevator or hide. Hitching my purse higher on my arm, I marched around the corner like I belonged there. The man gave me a startled look, then glanced over his shoulder back down the hall. To his credit, he gave me a pleasant smile and how-do-you-do, the very picture of discretion. Mr. Raine would have been proud.

I walked far enough down the hall to be sure the Raine man had turned the corner, then stopped at a door and pretended to try to open it. A quick peek told me the Raine man was gone, so I retraced my steps and stopped in front of the door the policeman had gone into. Suite 3848. Dhane's room. As quietly as I could, I bent and put my ear to the door. Nothing.

A commotion at the other end of the hall caught my attention. People were getting off the elevator, headed this way. The suite doorknob clicked.

Uh-oh.

I jumped, suppressing a yelp. Glancing up and down the hallway, I quickly assessed my options. The door started to open. I gripped my bag and just as I had before, I acted as though I belonged, walking decisively back toward the elevators.

A group of people rounded the corner led by the now very flustered Raine man. "The back way. Detective Platt assured me you'd use the back way."

"I'll remember that for next time," replied an auburn-haired man at the front of the pack.

"Next time?" the Raine man squeaked. Even in his agitated state, he still gave me a nod and how-do-you-do as I came even with the group.

"Hold up." The red-haired man put a hand on the Raine man's arm. He held up his other hand to stop me. "Can I see some ID?"

"What?" My surprise wasn't faked.

"She's a valued guest," the Raine man defended.

I held up my key card. "Is there a problem?" I had this acting like I belonged thing down pat.

"No, no problem. Thank you for staying at the Raine. If there's anything we can do to make your stay more enjoyable, please give me a call." The Raine man handed me his business card. It read Dave Strickland, Supervisor.

The red-haired man studied me like a wanted poster. "She's registered on this floor?" he asked Dave.

"Detective Kennedy, please," Dave pleaded.

"Detective? A police detective?" I turned to Dave. "Has there been a crime?" I put the proper shock and fear in my voice. "Am I safe?"

"Yes, yes. We take great care with our guests' safety here at the Raine. There's no problem. No problem at all." Dave handed me another card. "Please accept a complimentary brunch at Mangé,

Raine's beautiful Zagat-rated restaurant overlooking the pool."

"What's your name?" Detective Kennedy asked me.

"My name?"

"Detective." Dave sounded like he was on the verge of a stroke.

Detective Kennedy shifted his weight, leaning toward me, nearly nose to nose. "Your name."

"Azalea." Oh, crap. Why'd I give him my real name?

"Azalea what?"

"Detective, please," Dave whined, wringing his hands like a wet dishrag.

"Azalea Smith." Way to go stealth girl.

Detective Kennedy looked like he either wanted to roll his eyes or arrest me. "What room are you staying in, *Ms. Smith*?" He coated "Smith" with so much sarcasm it had multiple syllables.

I bumped out a hip and propped a hand on it, trying to match his attitude. I figured the more I acted like an aggrieved guest, the more likely they'd believe it. "I'm in 3853. You want to come in for a drink?"

Right away, I could tell my attempt fell short.

"Kennedy," the potbellied Detective Platt called from the open doorway of suite 3848. "She's requesting a lawyer."

"Shit," Kennedy muttered. With one last hard look at me, he marched off down the hall, his ragtag band of techs and officers following in his wake.

Dave monitored their departure until the suite door closed behind them, and then he turned to me with a grin so huge it looked like it hurt. "Are you enjoying your stay with us here at the Raine?"

"I was. What happened? Why are the police in that suite?"

He blinked, then blinked again. Ratcheting his smile up another couple of notches, he recited, "The Raine is considered to be one of the finest hotels in the world, having earned the coveted

AAA five diamond, the Mobil five-star, the Forbes five-star, and the Michelin five-star ratings. The Raine also made Forbes Award history by earning five-star ratings in every category—hotel, restaurant, and spa two years in a row." He jabbed another card at me. "Please accept this card for a complimentary spa service of your choice."

"Thank you, but—"

"It would be my pleasure to escort you to the elevator." He gripped my elbow and steered me toward the elevator bank.

I glanced over my shoulder back down the empty hallway. "There were so many police officers. I hope it's nothing—"

"The Raine Hotel boasts one of the largest casinos in Las Vegas at over one hundred square feet. Please accept this fifty-dollar casino credit with our compliments."

We waited for the elevator in silence. I was afraid if I opened my mouth again he'd make me a partner in the hotel. But it was eating me up not knowing what happened in suite 3848. As soon as the doors whooshed closed on us, beginning our descent, I started in on him again.

"I think some of those people might have been crime-scene techs, you know, like on *CSI*? You can be honest with me. I won't tell anyone."

His robotic smile still in place, Dave turned to me. In the close proximity of the space, I could see that the strain of holding it together had carved hollows under his bloodshot eyes and his mechanical grin showed signs of slippage. "Do you golf? The Raine Golf Course is the only one on the Las Vegas strip and was codesigned personally by Mr. Steve Raine." He produced another card. "Please"— he put so much emphasis on the word, it became more of a prayer than a request— "accept this card for a complimentary round of golf."

I took the card he offered and gave up trying to get any more information about what had happened from poor Dave. As the silence settled over us, I thought about all I'd seen and heard in that hallway.

In the suite, the police were holding a woman who had asked for a lawyer. I got that much. But who? And why? Could that woman be Dhane's killer? What would they do with her? Bring her to the police station, most likely. If she'd asked for an attorney, then she was probably considered a suspect.

The elevator doors slid open. Dave bolted, leaving a fading, "Have a pleasant stay at the Raine Las Vegas!" in his wake. I looked around for something to do with myself. If the police were going to take that woman into custody, I figured they would most likely escort her out the front. Detective Platt seemed to enjoy irritating poor Dave, and Kennedy didn't strike me as someone who cared what people thought.

I spotted a small grouping of chairs with a good view of the elevators and front door. This was where I'd wait. I knew it was silly, but having met Dhane just that one time, I felt connected to him. Plus, I felt a sort of responsibility for having been there when his head had been, ah…found.

Then there was his relationship with Vivian. I also felt tied to Dhane through her. Plus, if I were honest, I'd have to admit my rampant curiosity was burning holes through me.

I checked my phone, but still nothing from Vivian or Juan Carlos. Lowering myself into the plush leather chair, I sighed. *Where are they?*

I thought about calling our hotel, but I didn't have the number or a fancy phone to look it up on. Instead, I texted them both again, with lots of exclamation points.

Watching people come and go, I mentally played Does the Carpet Match the Drapes? It's a game Juan Carlos made up where you try to figure out who colors their hair and what their natural color really is. But after half an hour, I got bored. It seemed like no one in Las Vegas had natural hair and most of them had bad do-it-yourself drugstore dye jobs. The worst were the men with their shoe polish black, she's-into-me-for-my-youthful-looks-not-my-buckets-of-money, painted-on hair. Yeesh. You'd think with all that money, they could afford to spring for a colorist to do it right.

I was busy admiring a gorgeous brunette's walnut-and-caramel-highlighted locks when Detective Kennedy's fiery mane caught the corner of my eye. He'd just gotten off the elevator and had turned to look back at a blond woman escorting another woman from the elevator.

The air backed up in my lungs, constricting my chest. Before I knew it, I was standing, then walking toward them, my arm outstretched. "Vivian!"

Viv twisted toward me. She gave her head a small shake, stopping me midstride. Then her gaze darted away and it felt like the door she'd closed on me earlier had just been bolted shut. Shocked, my feet sticking to the floor, I stood there like a stranger, watching Detective Kennedy haul my best friend and business partner out of the hotel, her hands cuffed behind her back, and into a waiting police car.

CHAPTER FIVE

Three things happened at once. Detective Kennedy spotted me through the glass doors. Juan Carlos called me back—I could tell by his ringtone. And I sat down hard, right there on the exquisite Italian marble floor. Just plopped down on my behind while people continued to mill about, walking around me as if guests threw themselves to the ground in the middle of plush hotel lobbies every day. If they gave me an askance look, I was too overwhelmed to notice.

Vivian arrested!

Her story about knowing Dhane trickled back to me, the holes in it even more glaring than before. What had she been doing in Dhane's hotel room? Why would they arrest her? What had she done? They couldn't think she had anything to do with his death. Unless…

Several Raine employees rushed me, hovering over me like nervous mothers. One of them asked the group if they should call Dave.

"Please, don't do that," Detective Kennedy said from above me. "*Ms. Smith* will be just fine. Won't you?" Gripping me by the upper arms, he hauled me up. "Atta girl. Why don't we sit down, have a nice chat?" He steered me to the chair I'd been sitting in. "Have a seat."

One of the Raine employees, a chubby-cheeked girl with an explosion of freckles, leaned over me and shook her head with a frown. "She looks kinda pale. You aren't going to be sick, are you?"

Her question flung the rest of the group into twitching panic.

Kennedy threw up a hand. "She's fine." He made a shooing motion, his attention never wavering from me. "Go."

The freckled girl looked for a moment like she wanted to argue, then thought better of it and faded away with her coworkers.

Kennedy sat down opposite me. He didn't have that creepy, searching gaze Detective Weller had. His was more direct, like a laser beam or a bullet. "Well?" he asked.

I stared at him. He stared back. We went on like that for several long moments. All the while, thoughts ping-ponged around in my head. I was concentrating so hard on keeping it together that I didn't realize my nails had pierced the leather on the arm of my chair until Kennedy tried to pry them loose.

"Easy. You'll hurt yourself." He folded my hands into my lap, sat back, and asked the question that made me want to vomit on his shoes. "You want to tell me how you know my suspect?"

"Suspect?" Oh, cripes. Hearing myself say it aloud was almost more than I could take. I propped an elbow on the arm of the chair and rubbed at my throbbing forehead, willing my stomach to be still.

"You want to tell me who you really are? Or do you want me to haul you in and find out my own way? I can guarantee it won't be pleasant. We have this new officer—her specialty is cavity searches. Hagatha just loves a good strip search—"

"Azalea," I answered.

"Yeah, I gathered that much upstairs. What's your full name?"

"Azalea March."

He nodded, his suspicions about me confirmed. "And how do you know Ms. Moreno?"

I swallowed back the rising bile in my throat and swiped the sweat off my upper lip. "Vivian?"

He dipped his head.

"We're friends."

"Okay. Are you really staying in suite 3853?"

"No."

He inclined his head again. It was an annoying, arrogant gesture and I was beginning to see why they called him King Kennedy. "What were you doing upstairs?"

I bit the inside of my lip.

Relaxing back, he rested his arms on the chair, giving the impression that he had all day to wait. My dad used to use this technique and I hated it, mostly because it worked so well on me. And he'd had to use it so often. I'd been a rather precocious child.

But what to say? I had been snooping around, trying to figure out why a dead man sent me a note for a clandestine meeting? *Right*. Vivian's having been found in that suite combined with my skulking around the hallway outside of it did not look good. For either of us.

I suddenly viewed Detective Kennedy's questions with new trepidation. At best, I was in the wrong place at the wrong time. At worst, I was an accomplice to whatever it was he thought Vivian had done.

I didn't trust myself to speak. Anything I said would only make me look guilty and confirm his suspicions about Viv. So I did the impossible. I said nothing.

"Hagatha especially likes brunettes," he provoked.

Thinking of Viv, I bit my lip harder. The coppery taste of blood filled my mouth, but I held my ground.

"That usually works."

I blinked. He was kidding around with me.

"Oh, good, you got my joke. I find humor helps to put people at ease." His smile creased the corners of his eyes, making him look almost reptilian. Initially I'd thought he was kind of handsome, but now he repulsed me. Some of what I was thinking must have shown on my face because he backpedaled. "The sooner you tell me, the sooner you can leave and I can help your friend."

"Help? Now there's a joke."

He bowed his head. "From your point of view, I can see how that might be difficult to believe—"

"Difficult? No, not really. I'm sure *Your Highness* helps all kinds of innocent people."

His brows shot up his forehead. "I see you've done more than be in the wrong place at the wrong time."

Crap. He'd nailed me for the eavesdropper I was. I crossed my arms over my chest and put on my best defiant face.

"You can be as pissed as you want, but you will answer my questions. Either here, or after you've sat in a jail cell for a few hours. Your choice."

He wasn't going to give up. If I went to jail, I couldn't help Viv, who was the real person in trouble here. My mind raced to find a plausible explanation for my being in that hallway. The most believable lies always held a measure of truth. So that's what I decided to go with—the truth...sort of.

"Dhane asked me to meet him at his suite. He gave me his card key." I pulled the key out of my purse and handed it over as proof.

"Why were you meeting him?"

I arched a brow, hoping he'd draw his own conclusions and I wouldn't have to answer his question.

He bobbed his head. "I see." He pulled out a notepad and pen. "And how long had the two of you been together?"

"We'd just met."

He looked up sharply. I'd surprised him. Good. I'd rather he thought I was a slut than a criminal.

"When did you meet?"

"After his Hjálmar presentation."

"Today?"

"Yes."

Detective Kennedy bent his head, hiding his expression in his notebook. "Do you always visit the hotel rooms of men you've just met?"

"No." My answers came easier, but like watching a rattlesnake shaking its tail, I didn't trust Detective Kennedy for a minute.

"Where were you between the time you met Dhane and your visit to his hotel room?"

"At the convention center."

"Can anyone verify that?"

I thought about Juan Carlos and his finding Dhane's head in a doll bin. I thought of Lisa and Richard, who had also been there. I worked out the best person to use as an alibi. "My friends Lisa and Richard."

"I'll need their contact information."

In the middle of handing over their info, my phone rang again. Juan Carlos. I ignored it.

"Where are you staying?" Kennedy asked.

"The Luxor. Room 617."

He closed his notebook. "I'll want to talk with you again. Stay available." He got up.

That was it? I couldn't let him leave without finding out about Viv. "Wait. What did you arrest Vivian for?"

"Murder." He dropped that little bomb, watching me for a reaction.

"*Murder*? No, that can't be right. You have the wrong person. Vivian would never—"

"She was found with the body."

"*No.*" It was too much. I dropped back into my chair from the weight of it.

Detective Kennedy seemed to soften from my reaction. "You're scaring the Raine employees." He motioned toward Freckle Face and her cohorts, hovering at the edge of the reception desk. "Go back to your hotel. I'll take good care of your friend." Then he turned and walked away without a backward glance.

I pulled out my cell phone and called Juan Carlos back. "Where are you?" I shouted loud enough to earn a few stares.

"Oh my God! Where are *you*? Where's Vivian? What is going *on* in this crazy world?"

"Juan Carlos. Focus here. Tell me where you are."

"My hotel room."

"I'll be right there. Don't move!"

I snapped my phone shut and leaped up. I was in a taxi, rolling down Las Vegas Boulevard, faster than you could say "hot in Vegas." The rich didn't seem to have to wait long for anything, that's for sure. I could get used to this.

Juan Carlos whipped open the door as soon as my knuckles hit the wood. He grabbed my wrist and pulled me into the room. "Where have you been? Where's Viv? Do you have any idea what they did...? What I had to...?" He shook me harder with each question.

"Have you been drinking?" He reeked worse than a bar-room floor. "There better be some for me." A large hand handed me a glass of amber liquid and I took a gulp without hesitation. "Argh, it burns. In a really, really good way. Thank you." I took another hit, sure I was seeing things. "Richard?" I turned to Juan Carlos. "What's he doing here? I thought you two hated each other."

Richard held up his flask.

"Oh, who can hold a grudge when I pulled a...and his head was...and I was...and then it...and then you...and then they..."

Richard splashed more whiskey into Juan Carlos's glass. "He's calmed down quite a bit, actually. You should have seen him after the cops got through with him."

Juan Carlos took a big gulp and threw himself on the bed, wrapping an arm over his face for added drama. "They broke me…beat me till they got what they wanted. Which was nothing. How would I know how it got…that I would…that he was…"

"He's almost forming sentences again." Richard tipped the flask into Juan Carlos's mouth. "That's a good boy." Richard held Juan Carlos's hand. "Do you want me to sing for you again?"

Juan Carlos nodded without dislodging his arm from his eyes.

As Richard sang Juan Carlos a song that sounded like some kind of Greek lullaby, I dropped into a nearby chair and set aside my glass of firewater. How was I going to tell Juan Carlos that Vivian had been arrested? What was I going to do about it? I ground my fists into my eyes, pushing back the tears that wouldn't help Vivian and would only upset Juan Carlos more.

Richard's song ended and the only sound was Juan Carlos's soft snores. I looked up to find Richard considering me with a sympathetic smile. He placed Juan Carlos's glass on the nightstand and came over to sit with me. For a while we both watched Juan Carlos sleep.

"What happened?" he whispered.

My gaze stayed on Juan Carlos. "They arrested Vivian for Dhane's murder."

He muttered something in Greek I was sure his ma wouldn't have approved of.

"Yeah, that pretty much sums it up." I recovered my glass of whiskey and took a sip.

"How did you find out?"

I relayed everything that had happened since Detective Weller had called us into the interrogation room. When I finished, he issued another Greek expletive.

"What should we do?" he asked.

"I don't know." A knot of sickness lay heavily in my stomach, turning the whiskey sour. "I've been asking myself that question since I saw her handcuffed and perp-walked out of the Raine Tower Suites." I set my glass back down. "I guess we have to try to help her. What else can we do?"

"Okay. What's our first move?"

Richard looked at me with so much expectation, it nearly tore me open. I dropped my gaze to the ostentatious hotel carpeting, trying to summon a droplet of the courage he expected from me.

"The Hjálmar booth. And then we'll see if we can't spring Viv from the Big House."

Richard and I shot Juan Carlos a startled glance. Either he'd been faking sleep or our conversation had woken him up. He looked focused and ready for action, not at all like the wreck he'd been earlier.

"What did you hear?" I asked him.

"Almost all of it. Vivian needs our help and we're going to give it to her." Juan Carlos swung his legs over the side of the bed and sat up. He weaved a little and grabbed his head.

"Easy." Richard rushed to his side. "Here, have some water. And we should probably get some food in you." He looked to me.

"Right. Okay. We'll grab some food, then head down to the convention center. But first we need to call James." The thought of calling Vivian's boyfriend gave me some measure of courage and purpose.

"Oh, I forgot all about James. That's a good idea. He has that hot friend who's a cop. Call him—he'll know what to do."

I shot back the rest of my whiskey, my cheeks burning as badly as my stomach lining.

The hot cop Juan Carlos was talking about was Alex Craig. We'd met at Vivian and James's New Year's party. He'd asked me out. We went on a couple of dates and had hit it off...or so I'd thought. He said he'd call and then had somehow lost all knowledge of how to use a phone. He was the reason I'd sworn off men and had been binge-buying Laura Ashley dresses.

As much as I hated to admit it, he was probably Vivian's best chance. Still, the idea of my having to deal with this *particular* police officer was right up there with having a root canal or a gynecological exam by a doctor with unusually large hands.

CHAPTER SIX

Twenty minutes later, we were cruising toward the convention center in the back of a taxi. Juan Carlos was shoving fries in his mouth like a competitive eater in the final seconds of competition as I wrapped up my phone call with James. It had not gone well. I'd delivered the news badly and he'd taken it even worse. I was pretty sure the worry cracking his voice would haunt me in the wee small hours of the morning.

"When does James arrive?" Juan Carlos asked around a mouthful of fries.

"He should be here sometime after midnight depending on the flights coming out of Orange County. He said he'd call when he landed."

"That's good."

Juan Carlos tipped the fry cup into his mouth, gulping down the last of them as we pulled up in front of the convention center. Richard paid the fare and we all traipsed into the chaotic entry hall.

"That was fast." Richard pointed to a larger-than-life poster of Dhane draped with an RIP banner.

"How would you...where would you...how could they...?"

Juan Carlos expressed our puzzlement perfectly.

"Come on." I gripped his sleeve and pulled him toward the main convention floor before he stuttered himself into the ground.

The Hjálmar booth was packed with gawkers and groupies all trying to be a part of the tragedy. A life-size Dhane cutout had been turned into a makeshift memorial layered with flowers, stuffed animals, and notes. I overheard a woman offering a rather large sum of money for one of the display posters of Dhane. I didn't want to think about what she was going to do with it.

"Now what?" Richard asked.

"Follow me." Juan Carlos plunged into the crowd.

I tagged along behind Richard who, because of his size, made a handy crowd-parter.

Juan Carlos had snagged a spot at the counter and was waving down a very overwhelmed-looking young Hjálmar employee when we caught up to him. "Mateo!"

The boy spotted him and came over. "Dude." They exchanged a series of complicated hand bumps ending in a half hug and hearty back slaps across the counter.

"Can you take a break?" Juan Carlos asked Mateo.

Mateo took a quick look over both of his shoulders, then nodded. "Yeah. I gotta get out of here. Meet me at the bar in five." They executed another set of hand gestures and then Juan Carlos led us out of the throng.

"Holy hangers-on. Those people are crazy-pants. If ever I get so knocked over by a celebrity that I start acting that way, feel free to slap me," Juan Carlos said.

Richard slung an arm over Juan Carlos's shoulders. "You won't. But I will." Then he hugged Juan Carlos to him.

I nearly tripped over my own feet. This shift in their relationship was weirder than weird. Ever since we'd come to Vegas, nothing was the same. Vivian had suddenly become secretive and distant, Juan Carlos and Richard were getting along, and then there was

Dhane. His invitation to meet him, his death, Vivian's arrest... none of it seemed real, and yet knowing it was, going through it, didn't make it any easier to absorb.

I got so caught up in my thoughts I nearly missed it. A flap of dark fabric, the sharp spikes of hair, and those odd, unnerving eyes.

Jun.

I told the guys I'd catch up with them, then veered off. Getting a glimpse of Jun as he rounded a corner, I picked up my pace, scuttling after him. I turned where he'd turned only to come to a screeching halt. The corridor was packed with people wearing head-to-toe anime. Everywhere I looked there were rainbow-hued spikes, pigtails, and puffs from florescent to pastel. How was I ever going to find him?

I excused my way through the swarm, searching for the odd boy whose appearance in my life had begun this tsunami of strange events.

"Azalea?"

I turned to find Jun standing before me with his glaring smile and Kewpie doll eyes.

"Are you attending the anime and manga hairstyling workshop, too?" His gaze roamed over my ordinary outfit, making me feel like the only one who hadn't dressed up for the Halloween party.

"No. I was looking for you."

"Me?" His grin widened in surprise and I was struck anew by his childlike charm, making me want to reach out and touch the side of his sweet face. He reminded me of my nephew who also liked to play dress up. Only my nephew preferred to dress like a soldier or firefighter and not an extra from *The Matrix*.

I mentally shook some sense into myself. I was not here to befriend this boy but to grill him for information. "I need to talk to you."

"Okay. Sure." He continued to smile at me like a puppy

waiting for a treat.

A set of doors off to one side opened and the caricatures began filing through it. Jun didn't appear to notice, staring down at me like I was about to give him a present.

"Is there somewhere more private we can speak?"

He bounced his head. "I know a place. C'mon."

He turned back the way we'd come. I trailed after him, mentally rehearsing the questions I wanted to ask. He veered off down another hallway and ducked into an empty classroom. The door closed behind us with a quiet *snick*.

The room was so still and cold that I had to cross my arms over my chest and try to rub some warmth into them. Jun turned to me, his face full of expectation. I couldn't fail Viv. If I was going to help her, I needed to know everything Jun knew.

Eyeing Jun, I looked for something sinister inside him, wondering if he might know the person or persons who killed Dhane. With his honest, eager face, the kid was about as evil as a basket of kittens under a rainbow. I took a deep breath and dived in. "How did you find me to give me that note?"

"Easy. I followed you."

I opened my mouth, then closed it. He'd followed me? I didn't remember seeing him before he'd sat down next to me in that workshop room. "Why did you give me the note?"

He tipped his head to the side like a dog searching for the source of a sound. "It was for you."

I could tell I was going about this all wrong, so I tried another tack. "How do you know Dhane?"

"Hjálmar Dhane?"

"Yes. Hjálmar Dhane."

"I don't."

I huffed out an exasperated breath. This guy was as clever and stealth as a kindergartener. "Who gave you the note to give to me?"

"Sora."

"Who's Sora?"

He did that tilty-head thing again. "The one who gave me the invitation to give to you."

I would have screamed if I didn't think it might scare him. "Okay. Let's try this another way. Tell me exactly where you were when Sora gave you the note for me."

"We were with Trinity and Ace."

"Yes, but *where* were you?"

"Oh, right. Sorry. We were standing with Tenchi on the main floor near the Hjálmar booth."

"Thank you."

He grinned, obviously happy to have pleased me. "You're welcome."

"What did Sora say when she gave you the note to give to me?"

"Nothing."

"What do you mean nothing?"

"She didn't say anything. She just handed it to me."

"Then how did you know to give it to me?"

"Tenchi told me to give it to you, then he handed it to Sora and she handed it to me."

We were finally getting somewhere.

"Who is Tenchi? And what did he say when he gave you the note?"

Jun's smile dimmed and a quizzical line appeared between his brows. "Why are you asking me these questions? Is something wrong?"

He obviously hadn't heard about Dhane. My stomach sank. I felt like the mean big sister telling her kid brother there was no Santa Claus. "Dhane's dead."

"Hjálmar Dhane?"

"Yes."

"Oh, no." Jun blinked back tears. "Why? What does this have to do with me?"

"That's what I'm trying to find out. The invitation you gave me was supposedly from Dhane. I need to know who it came from and why."

"I didn't know it was from Dhane. Promise."

"I believe you."

"Wow, Dhane's dead. That sucks. His poor sister."

My ears perked up. "His sister? What sister?"

"Trinity." Jun snapped his fingers. "I get it."

"What?"

"Trinity."

"What about her?"

"It was her. She was with Tenchi when Sora, Ace, and I met up with them at the Hjálmar counter."

"Uh-huh." My head started to hurt. I needed a translator and a scorecard to help me keep track of what Jun was trying to tell me.

"Don't you see?" he asked.

"See what?"

"Trinity."

"Jun, I really need you to focus here. What are you trying to tell me about Trinity? And where can I find Dhane's sister?"

"Trinity."

"Jun," I warned. "Stop saying Trinity and answer my questions."

"That's what I'm doing."

My exasperation got the better of me. "Stop talking in circles!"

His face bunched up like he was about to cry.

Aww, jeez. "I'm sorry. I shouldn't have yelled at you."

"That's okay I guess." He plopped down into a chair and stared at the floor.

I sat next to him and rubbed my temples with jerky hands. "Let's back up a little. Who is Trinity?"

"I told you. Trinity is Dhane's sister. She's the one who wanted to meet you."

CHAPTER SEVEN

I dragged Jun with me to the bar to meet up with Juan Carlos and Richard. I had a strong feeling he was going to be important and I would need him and his circular logic to help Vivian. I also needed him to find Dhane's sister, Trinity, whom I was certain had information that would help me figure out what had happened to Dhane.

Juan Carlos's Hjálmar friend, Mateo, was already sitting in a booth with Richard and Juan Carlos when Jun and I got there.

"Azalea, where have you been?" Juan Carlos's irritated glare moved from me to Jun standing over my left shoulder. "Holy Comic-Con!" He waggled a finger at Jun. "Who's your little friend, Zee?"

I made introductions all around, taking special note of Richard's irritation at Juan Carlos's interest in Jun.

Juan Carlos scooted over and patted the booth seat next to him. "Come sit next to me, Jun."

"Thank you." Like the eager-to-please puppy he was, Jun plopped down next to Juan Carlos, oblivious of Richard's glowering.

I slid in next to Jun just as the waitress strolled up and asked for our drink order. Everyone ordered a cocktail except Jun.

"Cherry Coke, please."

"Cherry Coke? No, no, no. He'll have a Singapore Sling," Juan Carlos informed her.

The waitress propped her tray on her hip and asked Jun, "Can I see some ID?"

Jun blushed and ducked his head. "I just want a Cherry Coke, please."

The waitress looked to Juan Carlos.

Juan Carlos shrugged. "Cherry Coke."

The waitress pivoted and headed off to place our drink order at the bar.

Juan Carlos turned to Jun. "No fake ID?"

Jun shook his head.

"That's cool. Love your hair. Who cuts it?"

"I'm sure Mateo has better things to do than watch you strike out with an underage cartoon character," Richard interrupted.

Juan Carlos turned on Richard, but I cut him off before they could have an all-out brawl. "Mateo, what have you been hearing about Dhane's death?"

"That's all everybody's talking about. I've heard lots of stories." He tossed his head, flipping his long black hair over one shoulder. "There's the one where he gets jumped in the elevator of his hotel. There's one about it being a mob hit. And then there's my favorite one. Hookers and blow." Mateo bobbed his thick black brows, his too-pretty-to-be-a-boy's mouth curving into a naughty smile. "You know, like an erotic-asphyxiation thing."

Ewww.

"Then how do you explain his…and its being…?" Juan Carlos stammered.

Richard stepped in before Juan Carlos hurt himself. "He's asking how any of that could be true, since he was decapitated."

The image of Dhane's head lying on the carpet, his beautiful hair fanning out around it, popped into my head. I shivered uncontrollably. Then I thought about Vivian being accused of doing that to him and I just couldn't imagine it. Not my Vivian.

"Yeah, they didn't really talk about that part. I mean they did, but just not the details of it. You know?" Mateo said.

We all nodded.

Mateo's statement got me thinking. How would a person go about decapitating someone? What kind of person would do such a thing?

"What...what did it look like?"

We all turned toward Jun, surprised by his question. Then Juan Carlos, Richard, and I exchanged glances. Having firsthand knowledge of the experience put us in a club no one would willingly join. I didn't have the words to describe it for him and even if I did, I wouldn't want to be the one to put such an image in his innocent little head.

"Bad," Richard answered. "I won't ever forget it," he finished quietly.

The silence hung heavily over us, weighing down all our moods. Someone sighed.

"Vodka Collins?" the waitress asked, disrupting our thoughts.

Mateo put up his hand. The last to get his drink was Jun.

"And a Cherry Coke for the young master." She sat down a tall glass with a purple straw and three maraschino cherries in front of Jun.

His face lit up like a child's on Christmas morning.

"How *would* a person do that?" I asked, unable to rein in the thought.

"Do what?" Juan Carlos asked.

"Decapitate someone."

We looked around the table at one another. It was one thing to speculate on what might have happened. It was another to break it down and piece it back together.

"You'd have to be strong, I would think," Mateo said. "I mean, it can't be easy. You'd need a chainsaw or an ax or something. And it would be messy. Blood everywhere."

Jun audibly gulped.

"There's no way Vivian could have done it," I defended.

"Yeah, she's a miniature little thing," Juan Carlos added.

"Not just that," I said. "She just doesn't have it in her. I've known her forever. Sure, she gets an unholy glint in her eye when she kills a spider, but that's an insect, not a person."

"Who's Vivian?" Jun asked.

Mateo sat up in his seat. "Is she the one they arrested? I heard about that. I heard she was covered in blood, soaked in it. She a friend of yours or something?" He cast a scandalized glance at Juan Carlos and me.

"Yes. And none of that's true," I argued. "She didn't have a drop on her." And then it hit me. How Detective Kennedy hadn't seemed confident in Vivian's arrest. The blood—or lack of it— would make it difficult for charges to stick. So why arrest her? Just because she was found with the body?

I needed to talk to Vivian and soon.

"Who's Vivian?" Jun asked again.

Mateo asked, "How do you know she didn't have any blood on her?"

His question had me frowning over how much information I should share and whom I should share it with. At this point I didn't know whom to trust outside of Juan Carlos and Richard. To protect Viv, I let Mateo's question slide.

"If she didn't have any blood on her, then why did they arrest her?" Juan Carlos thankfully slipped in.

I turned to Mateo. "What do you know about how Hjálmar is run? Was Dhane more than the face behind it? Have you heard anything unusual either before or since Dhane's death?"

"As co-owner, Dhane was very involved in product development. His partner ran the business side. There was a rumor about the company maybe being for sale, but I don't know if it had sold or not."

"Has anything out of the ordinary happened lately?"

"Like what?"

"Like someone hanging around who hadn't before or a change in the company's policies or procedures, something like that," I said.

"No, not really." Mateo stared off for a moment, his dark eyes fixed on a spot in the distance. "Wait." His attention returned to us. "There was one thing that was kind of strange."

"What?" Juan Carlos asked.

"This lady came to the counter early this morning while we were finishing setting up, you know, before the show floor opened."

"Yeah?" The thrill of a possible clue vibrated inside of me.

"She was asking for Dhane. Got kind of mad when she found out he wasn't around. Like she was expecting him to be there or something. Like they had a meeting scheduled."

"Who was she?" I asked.

Mateo's shoulders hitched up. "Don't know."

"Could you find out?"

"Maybe."

Juan Carlos joined the questioning. "What did she look like?"

Mateo's glance veered off again. "Kind of small. Dark hair. Hispanic. Smokin' body." He flashed a wicked grin. "All T and A, just the way I like them."

His description sounded kind of familiar. "How was she dressed?" I held my breath for his answer.

"Black dress, tight. I liked that. Her hair was up. I liked that, too. Oh, and she had a big red flower in her hair. She kinda reminded me of Salma Hayek."

My heart slid into my stomach. He'd described Vivian perfectly. Juan Carlos was staring hard at me. The same shock and disbelief I felt was being reflected right back at me.

I twitched a shoulder, trying to shake loose the bad feeling I was getting. "If you can think of anything else or if you hear something, please give me a call." I slid my business card across the table to Mateo. "Even if it doesn't seem important, okay?"

"Sure. Will do." Mateo tucked my card in his jeans pocket and stood. "I'd better get back to the counter. See you, Juan Carlos. Say hi to George for me." They exchanged hand pumps and fist bumps with each other. Juan Carlos's part in it was lackluster at best.

"Later," Mateo called to the rest of us as he left.

Richard slid over in the booth so we all could spread out. "So what's with Cartoon Junior here?" he asked me, gesturing toward Jun.

"My name is Jun."

I sipped my drink, needing a moment to sort out my scattered thoughts. "He's helping me." I briefly explained about the note and the gist of the conversation I'd had with Jun earlier.

"Where can we find this Trinity?" Richard asked Jun.

Jun hitched a shoulder. "Tenchi would know."

"Would he put me in touch with her?" I asked.

"Probably." Jun sucked up the last of his drink. "But you can't talk to her."

I exchanged a long look with Juan Carlos. "What do you mean?"

"She doesn't talk to people," Jun replied.

"Then how did she tell Tenchi to give you the note to give to me?"

"She didn't."

I slapped a hand to my forehead. "But you just told me she did!"

Jun sucked an ice cube into his mouth and talked around it. "I didn't mean her."

"Okay, wait." Juan Carlos held up a hand. "I'm lost. If this Trinity chick didn't tell this Tenchi dude, and I'm assuming it's a dude, to give Azalea the note, then how did he know to give it to her?"

"Through Curio," Jun answered, digging out another ice cube, totally oblivious to our frustration with him.

I dropped my head on the table.

"Who's Curio?" Juan Carlos asked.

"Well, he's really a what not a who." Jun lassoed a cube on his straw and spun it around until it flung off and hit Richard. "Sorry," Jun told him.

Richard took the straw from him. "It's fine. *What* is Curio then?"

"A skunk."

That brought my head up. "A real live skunk? In here?"

"Well of course not live." Jun smiled as if we were all in on the joke.

"A *dead* skunk?" Juan Carlos shouted.

"Oh! No." Jun squinted at me. "Did I say Curio was dead?"

Finally catching on to Jun's path of logic, I asked, "Is Curio a stuffed animal?"

Jun tipped his head to the side, his wide eyes blinking slowly. "Of course."

"Of course," we all chimed.

"Where did you find this guy?" Richard mumbled to me out of the side of his mouth.

I waved him away and started in on Jun again. "So Trinity told Curio, the stuffed skunk, to tell Tenchi, a real guy, to tell you to give me the note?"

"Yes!" Jun beamed.

I lifted my glass. "Huzzah!" Then gulped down the last of my drink.

Juan Carlos's eyebrows bunched up. "Why does she talk through a stuffed skunk? What is she, a child?"

Jun's mouth flattened into a frown. "You're being mean."

"He's not trying to be." I laid a hand on Jun's arm. "We're just struggling to understand what happened so we can help our friend."

"That's okay, I guess," Jun said. "Trinity is…different."

"Look who's talking," Richard mumbled.

I shot Richard a dirty look, then turned back to Jun. "How is Trinity different?"

"She's not like you and me." Jun stabbed at the ice in his glass with his purple straw.

"What do you mean?"

"Well, I don't know for sure so I probably shouldn't say."

"We won't tell anyone, promise." I had to get him to talk. He knew more about the people in Dhane's life than anyone I'd met.

Jun looked around the table, checking our expressions for the truth. He bit his bottom lip. "I asked Tenchi about her. He said something happened to her a long time ago. Curio helps her." He jabbed at the ice again. "That's all I know."

He wasn't looking us in the eyes anymore and I got the feeling he hadn't told us all he knew. I was really getting tired of people doing that. "Jun. We're friends, right?"

He bounced in his seat a little, his expression wide open again. "The best."

"Uh-huh. And friends help friends, right?"

"Always."

"I need your help."

Jun bobbed his head. "Okay."

"I need you to tell me what Tenchi told you about Trinity."

Jun looked at Richard and Juan Carlos.

"Hey, guys. Why don't you get Jun another Cherry Coke from the bar?" I suggested, loading it with tons of amscray and I'll-tell-ya-later facial expressions.

As soon as Richard and Juan Carlos were out of earshot, I started in on Jun again. "What did Tenchi tell you about Trinity?"

"He told me not to tell. I keep my promises."

I took his hand and gentled my voice. "Jun, my friend Vivian is in really bad trouble. She needs our help. What Tenchi told you might help me find a way to help her. Don't you want to help?"

He nodded, but he didn't look convinced.

"Tenchi would understand you telling me just this once, don't you think?"

He twirled his straw around the inside of his empty glass. "I guess so."

I sat back and waited. I could see the struggle all over his face. He wanted to help, but he didn't want to betray his friend. I knew exactly how he felt. I was in the same predicament. I wanted to help Vivian, but I had to do it without betraying her trust.

After a moment he took a breath and gave up on the straw with one final stab. "Tenchi said that when Trinity was little, like maybe five or six, Dhane killed their father. Right in front of her."

Of all the things I'd imagined he'd say, that was nowhere on the list. It wasn't even in the same stratosphere as the list. I rubbed at my forehead, searching the far recesses of my mind for a follow up question, but Jun beat me to it.

"I guess Dhane's father married Trinity's mother after Dhane's mother died. Then one day the dad just snapped, attacked Trinity. Dhane killed him to protect her, but he didn't have to go to jail. Because of what happened, Trinity doesn't deal well with people. She needs Curio. That's all I know." Jun turned away from me and stared down at his empty glass.

I found my voice after a few moments of stunned silence. "Thank you, Jun."

Jun didn't answer. I wanted to reach out to him, let him know how much I appreciated his help. I had the strongest urge to hug him hard and tell him he did a good thing, but I couldn't quite find the words.

We sat in silence for a few moments with me trying to summon the courage to ask him to go one step further. I thought about

Dhane. Then I thought about Vivian.

"Do you think I could meet Trinity?" I asked him.

"I guess I could call Tenchi and find out." He stood up just as Juan Carlos and Richard returned to the table. "I'll be right back."

Juan Carlos waited a beat. "Okay, he's gone. Spill."

I knew it was a terrible betrayal, but I trusted Richard and Juan Carlos. So I filled them in on the most pertinent parts of what Jun had told me, glossing over or not relaying the bits that I didn't think were important in determining who had killed Dhane. I really needed their help in sorting through all of this. The sooner we figured out what had happened, the sooner Viv would be released.

"So," Richard said. "What do you think Dhane's sister will know that might help Vivian?"

He posed a good question.

"I don't know," I answered. "But at least we'll know what we're dealing with when we talk to Trinity. Jun is arranging that now." I turned to Juan Carlos. "I've been wanting to talk to you about the story Vivian told us of how she met Dhane. A couple of the things she said have been bothering me."

"Me, too."

"It just didn't make sense. And it didn't match some of the things she'd told me before. I can't stop thinking about it."

Juan Carlos got excited. "I know! There were more holes in her story than a punk-rocker's head. I thought it was just me. Why would she tell us a story that isn't complete? What's she hiding?"

"I don't know." That was the million-dollar question. What was she hiding and why? I was especially curious to know if and how it would tie in to Dhane's murder.

Jun returned, looking a little concerned. "Tenchi said that Trinity will see you. But it has to be now and you have to go in alone."

CHAPTER EIGHT

Standing outside of Trinity's suite, directly across the hall from Dhane's, gave me the heebie-jeebies. The hallway was eerily quiet and so still that I could clearly hear over the hammering of my heart the voice in my head screaming to *get out*. I thought about my dad. Not because I was scared and wanted my daddy, but because if he were here he'd tell me to suck it up and do what needed to be done. So I sucked it up as best I could.

Just as I lifted my hand to knock, Dhane's door opened behind me, scaring a startled yelp out of me.

"Well if it isn't *Ms. Smith*. Fancy meeting you in this hallway twice in the same day."

Clutching my hands over my chest to prevent my heart from leaping out and running off down the hall for safety, I turned to find Detective Kennedy leaning against the doorjamb, arms crossed like he'd been expecting me. He regarded me with glimmering verdant eyes, a smug smile playing around his mouth.

God I hated him.

I dropped my hands and rolled my eyes. "Don't you have a crime to solve and an innocent person to release, or is it case closed? Time for coffee and donuts for you."

I seemed to have amused him even more because his eyes bunched up at the outside corners. "You're very good at the best-defense-is-a-good-offense strategy. Sure you're not a lawyer?"

I stared hard at him, trying not to huff and roll my eyes. All I'd be missing then would be a firm stomp and a whine like a teenager who'd just been put on restriction. Why did this jerk bring out the worst in me?

"I hope you're better at being a cop than a stand-up comedian," I countered. Good. That was good. I sounded the right amount of annoyed and indifferent. "Shouldn't you be out setting up surveillance or checking in with the crime lab or something?"

"Jesus. Everybody who's ever watched an episode of *CSI* is suddenly an expert on police procedure."

I balled my hands, hating the way he pushed my buttons. "You're a tremendous ass, you know that?"

He put his hands up, palms out. "Easy, *Ms. Smith*. Wouldn't want to have to take you in for police brutality."

I narrowed my eyes at him, vibrating with anger. "Go away."

"Sure thang, sweetheart. Just one pesky little question. What are you doing here…again?"

I folded my arms over my chest and shook my head.

"You always go about everything the hard way?" he asked.

A voice called to him from within Dhane's suite, drawing his attention away from me. He told them just a minute, then returned his attention to me, running a hand through his hair. "I really don't have time for this. As much as I'd like to stand here and exchange barbs with you all day, I do have a murder case to solve. So just tell me what you're doing here so I can get on with it."

I studied him closely, noticing for the first time the strain around his mouth. His tie had been pulled loose and hung off center, and his auburn hair wasn't carelessly rumpled but disheveled from hands raking repeatedly through it. His eyes appeared a brighter green because of the tired redness around them. I imagined those eyes had seen more than their share of horrors and human depravity.

Inwardly, I sighed. Really, why was I arguing with him? I hitched a thumb over my shoulder. "I'm here to see Dhane's sister."

Kennedy's brows climbed. "Really?"

"Yes, really."

"And why would the, ah…recent acquaintance of her deceased brother be paying her a visit?"

Oh, crap. Yeah, why would she do that? I went with my earlier measure of truth tactic. "She asked me to."

I'd surprised him even more. Good. I supposed it was wrong of me to enjoy it, but this day had held so much suckiness, it felt good to get something over on Old King Kennedy.

"Really?"

"Wow, you're a real tough interrogator. If you'll excuse me, I have an appointment." I started to turn away from him, but his voice brought me back around.

"Tell me why she asked to see you." He shifted his stance, letting the door close behind him. "This ought to be good." He folded his arms over his chest.

"Well…" *Make something up. Make something up. Make something up quick!* "She's a friend of a friend of mine." I licked my lips, trying not to look up to the left…or was it the right that gives away a lie? Jeez, I really did watch too much *CSI.*

"Uh-huh." He did that regal head nod thing, inviting me to continue digging my hole.

"That's it, really."

He frowned. "I'm disappointed in you."

"Look, what do you want from me? You've locked up my best friend for no good reason and now you're wasting time chatting with me instead of looking for the real killer."

"I'd say a full confession is a pretty good reason to lock up a suspect."

"A what?" There was a sudden clanging in my head from a dozen warning bells. Tiny dots filled my vision and I swayed a little, blurring the dots. "What...what did you say?"

"Ah, Jesus. You're not a fainter, are you? Here, sit down." He made a move to grab ahold of my arm, but I jerked away from him.

"You're wrong. You must be wrong. Vivian would never...she couldn't...you must have misunderstood."

"This is a real shock for you."

He reached for me again, but I batted his hand away. "I want to see her. You're wrong. This is all wrong." I turned my back on him and headed for the elevators. "I'll talk to her. She always tells me the truth."

But she hadn't told me the truth about her and Dhane. I pulled up short. A sickness clenched my gut and I fisted a hand over it, pressing back against it. Confessed. No. No, no, no, no, no. That was not right.

"I need to see her." I started forward again, but Kennedy's words stopped me.

"You can't. She's in custody. The only person who can see her is her attorney. So unless you studied torts and crimes along with cuts and perms, you won't get in to see her."

That did it. I turned on him. "Look, you arrogant son of a bitch—"

"Ah, your color's back. Thank Jesus. For a minute there I thought I'd have to deal with old Dave again. Sorry for the insult. But I don't have time to deal with a fainter and you looked like you were going to keel over at any moment."

"You're crazy. You know that? You drop that bomb on me, then insult me. What's wrong with you?" I wanted so badly to shed myself of him, I felt like I was suffocating. I brushed past him, purposefully knocking him back a step. I banged my fist on Trinity's door. I could feel Kennedy's eyes boring holes into the back of me.

The door swung open enough to reveal an Asian man who I assumed was Tenchi, but I really didn't care. I walked in, seized the door from him, and took supreme pleasure in slamming it in Kennedy's arrogant face. Then I brushed off my hands and turned to find a small group of people gawking at me.

As if they had a right to stare, garbed like rejects from a Clowns-R-Us catalog. Really, where did these people get their clothes?

"You must be Azalea," the one who'd answered the door said.

"Yup. Ah, sorry. That guy is kind of a pain."

"We know." A tall, scarlet-haired woman uncoiled from the sofa. "I'm Sora." She held out a hand and when I shook it, the phrase "wet noodle" popped into my head. I resisted the urge to wipe my hand on my jeans, but only narrowly.

"I am Tenchi." The doorman's handshake was much better, but I still wanted to rub his creepy cooties off.

"Ace."

I turned to find a young man with the striking high cheekbones and long raven hair of a Native American warrior. After our handclasp, I closed my fist, sealing in the contact our hands had made. Not creepy. Not creepy *at all*.

"We'll excuse ourselves." Sora motioned to Ace and he followed her out of the room like a hound scenting his dinner.

Then I was alone with Tenchi. His weird eyes and weirder blond pageboy haircut made me wish I were back in the hallway exchanging insults with Kennedy again.

"First the rules." He signaled for me to take a seat. When we were settled he continued, "Talk directly to Trinity, not to Curio. He merely serves as an interpreter, if you will."

"Interpreter. Like for a foreign person?"

"Correct."

"Okay." I'd never been good at rules and hoped there weren't very many more.

"Don't look Trinity in the eye. Don't say the words 'three,' 'fortune,' or 'skunk.' She especially hates the word 'skunk.'"

"Skunk. Got it."

"You can't chew gum, but breath mints are permissible. You can cross your right leg over your left, but not your left leg over your right."

"You're making this up."

He tried to pull a brow up into his bangs but his Botox-frozen face wouldn't oblige him. "Do you want to speak with her or not?"

"Yes. Sorry. Carry on. Right leg yes, left leg no. Got it."

"You're not an Aquarius, are you?"

"No, a Cancer." Jeez. Was this guy for real?

He nodded approval. "There's just one more thing."

Thank goodness.

"You can't mention Dhane's name. This is important. Just his name sets her off and we've finally gotten her calm again after the police left." He shook his head in pity, but oddly his hair stayed still. Nothing on this guy moved. "Do you agree to the terms?"

I anxiously bobbed my head, but how in the world was I going to pull this off? Right leg and breath mints yes. Gum no. Don't say three, fortune, skunk or Dhane's name. Don't look at Curio and don't look Trinity in the eye. Oh, and that thing about Aquarians. I supposed it was a bad time to mention that my rising sign was Aquarius.

"This way." He stood and walked to a closed door. "Just one more thing. I need to hold your cell phone. She hates cell phones, especially since they started making them with cameras."

I pulled my phone from my bag and stared at it for a moment. This was my last link to the sane world, and I really didn't want to be without it, but I handed it over to him anyway. I was deep in the crazy den, about to meet the queen of the crazies. It would have been nice to be able to call for help, should they try to eat my brain or something.

"Remember, talk to her, not Curio." Then he opened the door and shoved me through it, quickly shutting it behind me.

It took a moment for my eyes to adjust to the dimness in the room. The faint mocking scent of bubble gum hung in the air, competing with the smoke from a recently extinguished candle. I shuffled my feet and rubbed my arms. It was much colder in here than the rest of the suite. Unease crawled up the back of my neck. I fought to control it, clamping down on my fight-or-flight reflexes.

A match ignited, illuminating the hand that held it. The smell of sulfur tinged the air as three candles were lit. Three. The irony was almost a relief. But the thing that really struck me was the face revealed by the match before it was blown out.

Pale as the moon and framed by hair darker than night, Trinity's face was eerily perfect, freakish in its symmetry, as if it had been made by a machine. I supposed some would have called her beautiful, with features exactly the size and shape as they should be. But there was something wrong, something altogether ugly and unstable about the way they came together.

In the meager candlelight, I could just make out her shape on the bed piled in pillows. Afraid to blink, I froze in place with the door at my back and the unknown before me.

And then she spoke with the voice of a child, high and tinkling, edged with unrestrained irritation. "She's wrong. Wrong, wrong, wrong. Why is she here? Here and not there? Tell her to go away!"

"I asked to see you. I wanted to know why you sent me a note from Dh…ah…y-your brother."

"No note. No notes for her. For her but not *her*. It's all wrong. Wrong, wrong, wrong."

"The note wasn't for me?"

"Why is she here? No notes for her. Notes for her not *her*. Tell her to go away and bring me the one. It's wrong. Wrong, wrong, wrong."

"What one?" This whole speaking to me like she was reading from a Dr. Seuss book was frustrating.

"I want the little one, the one who made all the red. Tell her to bring me the one who made the red."

What the hell was she talking about? I squinted in the darkness, trying to get a better feel for what I was up against here.

"Red, red, red. Red flowers, red lips, red hands. Hands dipped in red, dripping red, all red. Red, red, red."

Oh, no. Somehow I understood what she was trying to tell me. Dread washed over me, pinning me in place. The room seemed to narrow. I took a step forward, then another. I'd been here before. Disappointment warring with hurt, and over it all a desperate need to believe that this was not happening.

CHAPTER NINE

"Do you mean Vivian?" I asked, fearing the answer.

"Why is she still here?" Trinity stormed. "I want the one with the red. Red, red, red."

"You sent the note for Vivian?"

"Notes for red, red notes. Red hands read red notes. I want the one who made the red. Tell her to bring me the one who made the red!"

"I can't."

"Can't, won't."

"You don't understand." I moved a few paces closer.

I could see her now. She stroked a matted and worn stuffed skunk on her right shoulder, her face tilted toward it. I focused my gaze on the unusual star pendant hanging from her neck. It had the same awful symmetry as her face.

"Vivian is in jail," I explained. "I'm trying to help her. I was hoping you could tell me why you sent her the note. Was it from you or Dh…your brother?"

"All the red mixed with red makes more red. The red makes dead. Dead makes red and they all know it. They know it. Dead wanted red so dead is red. But she's not red." Trinity pointed a finger at me, then resumed her vigorous petting.

In a strange way, I began to understand what she was trying to tell me. "Your brother wanted Vivian, am I right? So he sent the note?"

She turned to me so sharply it took all my focus to keep my eyes from her face.

"Red should be with dead. Red, dead. Dead, red. Yeah." She turned back to Curio with a smile. "Dead red. That's good, isn't it? Am I right? Time to go," she chirped, popping from her bed and quickly blowing out the candles. "It's time. Time to go. Time to take. Time to let go and be let go. She's not the one. Not the red and not the dead. She's gone. Gone, gone, gone." I felt more than saw Trinity coming toward me in the darkness. "Tell her to tell the one to tell them all that red is dead and dead is red."

She grabbed my hand and held it to her face. I stood stock-still, afraid to breathe and accidentally inhale some of her crazy.

"Pretty is pretty. She's not the one, but I like her. Tell her to come back and be pretty again."

"I'll come back," I said. In that moment I would have agreed to stick my hand in a meat grinder. If lunacy was catching, I was sure to come down with it now.

"I'm happy! Are you happy?" she asked Curio. "Happy is as happy was. Every day and all day. Happy, happy, happy." She spun away from me, twirling in the darkened room like a deranged ballerina. "Happy day today. Happy, happy, happy. Happy day."

I backed toward the door, afraid to take my eyes off her. Feeling for the knob, I couldn't help but wonder what would happen to Trinity now that her brother was dead. She clearly needed to be taken care of. Would Tenchi and the others watch out for her, or was there some other relative who would step in?

As the door closed on Trinity's dance, I breathed a sigh of relief to finally be away from her. My visit with Trinity had yielded at least one tidy tidbit — Trinity had sent the note with Dhane's key card to Vivian, not me. Somehow Jun had gotten it wrong.

"Well?" Tenchi startled me with his abruptness. He stood hands on hips, waiting for a report.

"She's fine. I didn't upset her. She was happy when I left, honest."

"Happy? What do you mean happy?" He strode past me to the door and put his ear against it. Then he stood up straight and gave me an odd look. "What did you say to her?"

"Nothing really. She did most of the talking."

"You'd better go." He slapped my cell phone into my hand and disappeared into Trinity's room.

I half expected to find Kennedy still lurking in the hall, but thankfully my getaway was quick and uninterrupted. It was full dark when I got outside and still hotter than a backstage dressing room. Vegas at nightfall was something to behold. The lights from casinos and hotels illuminated the night, giving off a feeling of endless celebration, as though it were perpetually five minutes to midnight and Las Vegas was the world's largest New Year's Eve party. I could almost hear the artificial clinking of coins hitting the trays of a million slot machines and smell the stench of cigarette smoke and cheap booze mixed with the hopeful anticipation of the gamblers.

God, I loved Vegas.

Sitting in the back of a cab, I mulled over what I'd intentionally and unintentionally learned. I could not get over Kennedy's words. Vivian had confessed. But why? Setting aside what I knew about her as a person, there was still no way she could have done it. Yes, she was found with the body, but she didn't have a drop of blood on her. At least none that I could see.

And what would be her motive? She had been looking for Dhane earlier in the day, so she was obviously anxious to see him. And when she finally did, she'd seemed really happy and he did, too. Why would she kill someone she hadn't seen or talked about in years? As far as I could tell, there was no motive.

That left opportunity. The truth was I had no idea where Vivian had been while I walked the convention and sat in Lisa's class. I imagined there had to be some level of security in the hallways of the Raine Hotel, most likely cameras. The police would likely be looking at the comings and goings of suite 3848 very closely. I would have given anything to get a look at those tapes, even if it meant playing nice with Kennedy, but that was highly *unlikely* to happen.

I should have caught up with Juan Carlos and Richard after my visit to loony town, but Kennedy's words haunted me, almost daring me to verify them. As the cab pulled up in front of the police station, I scrounged the depths of my brain to come up with a way to get in to see Vivian. I had to see her. I just had to.

The cab pulled up in front of a building built block on top of block with little or no imagination. I paid the fare, then stood staring up at the forbidding facade. Vivian was in there, encased in a building that looked more like a crypt than a police station. What must she be thinking? Feeling? The image of someone as bright and colorful as Vivian entombed in this concrete block was sadder than I had words for.

I hitched my bag higher on my shoulder and marched into the large foyer, where spare ultramodern met incarceration chic. An officer stood behind a wall of glass as thick as a mattress, helping someone who talked to her over a telephone attached to the wall. I got in line behind a woman with two children huddled to her like limpets and began a mental list of questions to ask Vivian.

I was debating whether or not I should bite off a hangnail and ruin my manicure when a door to the left of the glass wall opened. Two suits walked out, deep in whispered conversation. I recognized them as the guys Dhane had been walking with when I'd met him at the convention. I'd have given anything right then for bionic hearing, but the best I could do was to try to read their body language.

In an amazing flash of brilliance, I nicknamed the shorter one Shorty. The other one I called Jerk because he had the pinched mouth, uptight attitude, and beady eyes of a real asshole.

Shorty looked panicked—not the ordinary kind of anxiety that comes from losing your keys or something, but the bone-deep fear his world was about to come to an end. He punctuated his speech with short, choppy hand movements and swipes across his sweaty forehead.

Jerk seemed to get more and more annoyed with Shorty, until he finally grabbed him by the back of the neck and propelled him toward the exit as fast as Shorty's little legs could go. I tried not to show any interest as they passed me, Jerk digging his fingers into Shorty's neck. Shorty let out a protest—something about not telling—but Jerk didn't let go until they were through the front doors.

Even though I was now second in line, I abandoned my post to follow them. Pressing my face to the glass door, I tried to see where they'd gone, but they'd disappeared into the darkened parking lot. I glanced back at the line, then back at the door.

Really, there was no question. I knew I would follow them from the first moment they appeared. They'd been close to Dhane, close enough to know who had access to him and who might have wanted him dead. The police must have thought they had knowledge about the case.

I pushed out into the night, the warmth radiating up from the earth wrapped around me like a heating blanket. I immediately slipped into the shadows, away from the lights of the building so my eyes could adjust to the darkness. I spied the suited pair standing next to a nondescript rental car, their argument now in full swing.

"They check these things out, man. They're gonna know." Shorty seemed even more agitated now, pacing back and forth like a caged animal.

"Don't be an idiot. We didn't tell them anything. Calm the fuck down," Jerk replied, puffing out cigarette smoke.

"Calm down. Calm down? You're not the one with his ass hanging out. I knew it. I knew I shouldn't have listened to you."

Jerk grabbed Shorty by the neck, jabbing his cigarette fingers in his face. "When the fuck did you listen to me? When you were boning that crazy bitch? No. When you bragged to her and set fire to this whole shit pile instead of keeping your god damned mouth shut? No." He pushed Shorty away with a disgusted grunt. "I knew I shouldn't've brought you in. You're a total fuckup."

"I didn't say anything, man. I keep telling you that. Not a word. Not one single word."

"And you keep saying *that*." Jerk drew hard on his cigarette, then flicked it away. "If you didn't talk, how'd she know? Huh? Bitch have superpsychic powers or something?" Jerk shook his head. "Fuckup."

"I'm not a fuckup!"

"Just get in the goddamned car. They probably got this parking lot bugged."

Shorty moved to the passenger side of the car. "I'm just saying, I didn't say anything. I didn't screw up. I don't know how she found out, but it wasn't me, man. You gotta tell Mac it wasn't me."

"I ain't gotta tell Mac shit. Your ass hanging out is your problem, not mine. Would you get in the fucking car already?"

Shorty looked like he wanted to protest, but he got in the car without another word, slamming the door harder than was necessary.

"Total fuckup," Jerk muttered, then he, too, got in the car.

I flattened myself against the building as their car passed. What were they talking about? The only crazy bitch I knew in this whole mess was Trinity. But I didn't see how and why she would have hooked up with Shorty. Who were those guys and how were they involved? And who was Mac? What would Shorty have told Trinity that would have gotten Dhane killed?

I turned to go back into the building, my head spinning from what I'd heard, and bumped into a wall of hardened chest. "Ooph."

Large hands wrapped around my arms, pushing me back a step. "Just the person I was hoping to see."

CHAPTER TEN

My past slammed into me like a rake handle to the face, all six-foot-some-odd inches of what-ifs, recriminations, and abs so tight you could bounce a quarter off them.

"'Cause this day hasn't sucked enough," I muttered, peeling his fingers off my arms.

"Join the club," Alex replied. "This day hasn't exactly been beer and nachos for me either."

Detective Alex Craig and I had had a very intense, but way too brief, attempt at a relationship. At least I'd thought it was intense. I'd been harboring a little crush on him since I'd first met him a few years ago, but it wasn't until James's party when Alex had *finally* noticed me. We'd gone out fairly steadily until a few weeks ago when all of a sudden he started canceling and postponing dates or running out in the middle of them when he actually did show up.

On our last doomed date, I'd answered the door to his retreating back and a quickly dashed off, "Sorry, gotta go, I'll call you!" as he jogged back to his car. I'd considered it a sign. A power greater than us was clearly at work here, and we obviously weren't meant to be.

I just wished he wasn't so darned cute. Or such a good kisser.

"What are *you* doing here?" *Don't do it. Don't look up into those pale baby blues. Don't...ah, damn.*

"I'm here for Vivian." He crossed his arms over his chest, which made his shoulders double in width. "Why were you lurking in the shadows?"

"I wasn't *lurking.*"

"Then what were you doing?"

I held up a finger. "Wait for it…"

He looked at me like I'd sniffed too much perm solution and was still riding the high.

"Huh. That's so strange," I said after a few moments of his phone not ringing and calling him away.

"I'd say the only thing strange here is you."

"You know I didn't even recognize you arriving. I'm so used to you leaving."

He tipped his head back in realization. "So that's why you haven't returned any of my calls. You're mad."

"Not mad. Just over it."

"It wasn't my—"

"Fault. I know. It was obviously fate intervening."

"Not fate. Just a murder case that wrapped up today. I was gonna call you tomorrow."

I'd been deceived too many times by was gonnas from men. I was gonna call…I was gonna pay you back…I was gonna tell you about her…

"I almost bought another Laura Ashley dress because of you!"

"What?"

"Just forget it."

Alex pulled his cell phone out of his pocket, jabbed at it with his thumb, and put it up to his ear, turning his back to me. The jerk.

My phone warbled from the bottom of my purse. I pulled it out and looked at the display with a frown. Against my better judgment, I answered it, moving away from Alex.

"Hello."

"I really am sorry I got called away," Alex's voice rumbled in my ear and from somewhere behind me. "I'd much rather have dinner with you than interview a meth addict with info on the lowlife who killed a grandmother for a forty-dollar fix."

And just like that I wasn't mad at him anymore. How could I be with the image of my own sweet gram now at the front of my brain?

"I'm sorry, too."

"Maybe we could try again?"

"I don't know. Maybe."

"What would it take to turn that maybe into a yes?"

I was just about to answer when James, Vivian's boyfriend, poked his head out the door.

"There you are," he said to Alex. "There's some paperwork you have to sign." Then James spotted me. "Hey, Azalea."

I forgot all about the too-cute-to-resist cop working his way under my resolve. "Did you get in to see Viv?" I hung up on Alex as James stepped outside with us.

"Thanks to Alex she can have one visitor, supervised, for five minutes."

"Okay, where do I go? Do I have to sign something?" I asked.

"Not you. James," Alex replied. I could tell he wasn't happy about having to disappoint me. Again.

I turned on him. "I really need to talk to her. You don't understand." I spun back to James. "Please, let me go in. I really, *really* need to ask her some questions."

James adjusted his glasses. "We came all this way and I really want to see her, too."

"James asked me to set this up for him," Alex said with a what-can-I-do? shrug.

"I'll go out with you again if you let me be the one to see Vivian," I offered Alex. "Please."

Alex dipped his hands into his pockets and rocked back on his heels. "This isn't exactly the way I'd planned it."

"Pretty please?"

"Any night I want?"

"Hey, wait a minute," James said. "I'm the one who brought Alex here, so I'm the one who gets in to see Vivian."

"I'll give her a message from you," I told James, then to Alex, "Any night you want. Totally your pick."

"But—" James tried to protest, but Alex interrupted him.

"You'll change your schedule for me?"

Jeez, this guy. *"Yes."*

"And if something should happen that's out of my control, you'll reschedule with the same stipulations?"

James made another attempt. "Hey! What about me?"

"Yes. Yes. Yes," I answered, ignoring poor James.

"She's in," Alex told James. "Sorry, man."

• • •

I was ushered into a small room with a large mirror, a metal table, and three chairs. Alex stayed with me. If I hadn't already known how serious a situation this was, his demeanor would have tipped me off. Gone was the carefree charmer. In his place sat a sharp, stern-eyed cop with the stiff shoulders and puffed-up chest of a man in charge. I'd never seen him like this, and frankly he would have scared me if he weren't on my side.

The door opened and in walked a handcuffed Vivian followed by Detective Kennedy.

"Jesus, you're like a bad penny," he said to me.

But I didn't even give him a glance. I couldn't tear my gaze away from Vivian's face. It felt like forever since I'd seen her. We both looked like we'd walked a thousand miles since then, especially her. They'd taken away her flower and the pins in her hair. All that was left of her lipstick was a slight stain. Her eyes were red and puffy, but her chin was high, her gaze even with mine.

"Five minutes," Kennedy reminded us, then propped himself against the wall, arms and ankles crossed, standing guard.

Vivian kicked the chair away from the table and sat down. When she placed her cuffed hands on the table, her stare was strong and steady.

I nodded toward Kennedy. "He says you confessed."

"Yes," Vivian replied.

I eyed her closely, looking for that connection we had, the one where we could almost hear what the other was thinking.

"Did you do it?" I could hardly get the words out. The thought of Vivian committing murder was so wrong, so totally opposite of everything I knew about her, just asking the question felt like the ultimate betrayal.

Alex interjected, "I suggest you don't answer."

"We could end this now," Kennedy threatened.

Alex sent me a warning glance. It was pretty clear that Kennedy was looking for any reason to pull the plug on this whole thing. There was no way I'd give him that satisfaction. I was getting my full five minutes with Vivian.

I looked at Vivian, and what I saw both comforted me and increased my concern. She didn't kill Dhane, but she was willing to go to jail for it. Why? Who was she protecting? This was not the conversation I'd been expecting to have with her.

I licked my lips and tried another tack. "I met Trinity today."

Something flashed across her face for a moment. I quickly looked at the men in the room to find out if they'd seen it. Kennedy gave a good impression of being bored, while Alex looked interested but uninvolved. Academy Award winners had nothing on those two.

"That's nice. How is she?" Vivian asked.

"Happy," I answered.

"Really?" Vivian's response sounded normal, but I could tell she was surprised. Very surprised. Something was really off here. Vivian gave me a look like she wanted something from me, but I wasn't sure what.

"I'm worried about her," I said.

"I'm sure over time she'll be fine," she said with so much insistence that it raised a huge red flag for me. Trinity was never going to be fine, especially now that her brother was gone.

"How's Juan Carlos?" she asked.

The abrupt change of subject threw me off for a moment, but since she was the one in handcuffs, I didn't feel like I should argue with her. For the moment. "I think there might be something going on between him and Richard."

"I knew it!" There was a glimpse of my Vivian. She even smiled a little. "I always suspected those two would get together if they ever got over loathing each other."

I hated to do it, to change the look on her face, but I had to know. "Vivian, *why*?" My voice cracked and I felt a little piece of my heart give way. This was not how this weekend should have gone. I should not have been sitting across from my handcuffed best friend in this cement tomb while two cops jockeyed with her future. And she stood accused of murder.

Alex cleared his throat, and I could almost hear Kennedy straining to listen in.

Vivian stared hard into my eyes like she was trying to send me her thoughts. "You'll know why and I hope you'll understand." She reached for my hand, but Kennedy glared and shook his head so she pulled back. "Take care of the salon. Take care of yourself." She stared down at the table, hiding tears. "I'm sorry."

"Vivian—"

"Time's up." Kennedy peeled himself off the wall and gripped Vivian's arm, hauling her to her feet.

"Wait!"

Vivian turned back to me. "I'm fine," she said, then disappeared through the door with Kennedy.

But I knew she wasn't fine, nothing was fine. Everything was upside down and backward.

Alex slipped an awkward arm across my shoulders. "She'll be okay."

I tossed his arm off and stood up, knocking my chair back against the wall. "She's not fine. I wish everyone would stop saying that. None of this is fine. It's crazy and messy and doesn't make any kind of sense. Vivian didn't kill Dhane. Can't you all see that?"

"Of course we can."

"Then do something!"

"I'm doing the best I can. I got us a meeting with her, which was not easy, and I've arranged for her attorney. They haven't arraigned her yet, which could be a good sign. All we can do now is wait."

"Wait," I repeated. I wasn't good at waiting under normal circumstances, and this was anything but normal.

"I don't like that look on your face. What are you planning?"

"I plan on waiting."

"Uh-huh." Alex looked like he wanted to say more, but Kennedy interrupted.

"My lieutenant wants a word with you," he said to Alex.

Alex gave me a measured look. "Stay here until I get back," he told me, then walked out with Kennedy.

Like a good girl, I dropped into a chair. A few moments later, Kennedy reappeared, alone.

He sat across from me, arms folded. "Your boyfriend has good connections," he said conversationally, but I knew there was something more behind it.

"He's not my boyfriend."

Kennedy inclined his head. "Okay."

"What do you want?"

He waved a hand. "Well, if I were to make a wish, it would be for you to tell me why you keep showing up in the middle of my case. Every time I turn around, there you are." He leaned toward me, his eyes bright green lasers. "Why is that?"

"I don't know what you're talking about."

"Right." He sat back and studied me, tapping the tips of his fingers on the table. I tried not to squirm.

"I half expect you to be waiting on my doorstep when I get home tonight," he said.

"You really should think about a career in comedy. You're quite hilarious."

"So I've been told." He sat up, all seriousness. "You were there when the victim's head was found." At my surprised expression he said, "Yeah, instead of getting doughnuts, I read the reports on this case. Your name popped right out at me. Funny that, don't you think?"

When I didn't answer, he continued, "Then you show up outside the suite where the body was found…twice. Now you're here pulling strings and asking my main suspect questions." Placing an elbow on the table, he propped his head in his hand and smiled. "If I weren't so racked by your beauty, I might begin to wonder if you were perhaps an accomplice in this case."

He'd wrapped his sarcastic compliment in a threat meant to scare me. It worked. I opened my mouth to speak but was stopped by Alex's return.

"Let's go," he said with a hard warning glare for Kennedy.

As I passed by him, Kennedy got in one last shot. "I'm sure our paths will cross again, *Ms. Smith*." He bowed slightly. "Until then."

CHAPTER ELEVEN

Sitting in the back of a cab with Alex while James rode in the front seat, I replayed the bits of my conversation with Viv over and over in my head.

Cryptic.

That was the word I'd use to describe my conversation with Vivian. Now that the emotional impact of seeing her and the frustration of not being able to carry on a real conversation with her had worn away, what I was left with was a strong sense of urgency. She'd been trying to tell me something. But what?

I wished I'd paid better attention. I wished I had the kind of memory that recorded everything like a video camera. Most of all I wished I could hit the rewind button on this whole trip.

Alex took the hand that had been fidgeting with the cheap pleather piping on the taxicab seat and squeezed. "Easy. We're almost there."

I didn't answer. Instead, as we slogged our way up the strip through the traffic to my hotel, I propped my elbow on the windowsill and looked out at the lights. Their cheerful brightness mocked me. This was supposed to have been a fun trip, a crazy, stay-up-all-night, drink-till-you-puke weekend. Instead I was sitting in the backseat of a cab worrying about how I was going to prevent my best friend from being prosecuted for a murder she didn't commit and feeling guilty for enjoying all of the attention Alex gave me because of it.

Alex.

I wasn't being entirely truthful with myself about my feelings for him. I liked him way more than I should, way more than I wanted to. The truth was I would have given him another chance at a date even if he hadn't let me in to see Vivian instead of James.

I slid my eyes sideways to sneak a peek at him. Dang it! Why couldn't I fall for a handsome, *available* man? Why did I always pick the ones who put me second after their favorite sports team or their buddies or the woman they were banging on the side? It wasn't like I was ugly or desperate.

Oh my God, that was it. I *was* desperate. Pathetic and desperate. I was going to end up hoarding cats or making a world-record-breaking giant foil ball or something.

Out of habit I started to reach for my cell phone, thinking to call Viv for one of her famous talk me down from the ledge speeches. And it hit me all over again. Vivian had confessed to murder. What had started as a fissure seeing Vivian in handcuffs for the first time was now a yawning, gaping wound. What would I do without her?

She'd been the only one to stand by me when my life had come crashing down around my ears. When I'd lost my job, my credibility, and a big chunk of my friends. Viv had been the only one who'd stuck when all the others had scurried away like rats. She'd helped me find a new job. She'd been the one to loan me the money to pay back our old boss so I wouldn't be prosecuted for theft. Money I hadn't stolen. Not only had Vivian believed in my innocence, she'd even tried to help me prove it by trying to get the real culprit, my ex-boyfriend, to confess to taking the money. She'd done her best, but the selfish jerk just wouldn't 'fess up, leaving me with the reputation of being a thief.

Over the next few years, I'd scrimped and saved and paid Vivian back. She'd never mentioned it again. Not even the couple of times when I was late paying her. When I was back on my feet financially, she was the one to suggest we open a salon together.

And now it was my turn to try and prove *her* innocence. I didn't know if I could do it. I was probably stupid to even try, but I had to help Vivian. I had to. Swallowing the lump in my throat, I summoned all the courage I could scrape together and thought about what to do next.

I'd formulated a fairly competent plan by the time the taxi pulled up in front of our hotel. Okay, maybe competent wasn't the right word, since I was fairly certain it rode hard the line between this just might work and a crazy-Lucy-and-Ethel scheme. But it was the best plan I could come up with.

I left Alex and James at the front desk to book themselves a room and headed up to Juan Carlos's. I needed him to tap into his vast network of friends for someone who could give me information on Dhane's company. I also wanted to know more about Dhane's past, most specifically the murder of his father. That was a task I was saving for myself.

Outside Juan Carlos's door I could hear music playing. I knocked, hoping he could hear me over Frank Sinatra. *Sinatra?*

There was some shuffling and then Juan Carlos opened the door enough for his head to pop out at me. He looked a little rumpled.

"Oh, I'm sorry. Did I wake you?"

"No." He looked a little guilty. Or was it embarrassed? "I'm up. Whatcha want?"

"Aren't you going to let me in?"

"Ah, yeah, sure, hang on a sec." He slipped his head back in and closed the door.

"Juan Carlos, open this door. It's not like I care what you look like." I rolled my eyes at the closed door. Really, what was the matter with him? "Come on, open up." I knocked again.

A moment later he opened the door, smoothing his hair back into style. "Sorry. Come in."

"What are you—" I stopped short at the sight of an equally rumpled-looking Richard. I swung my head from one to the other, my dropped jaw swaying. "Were you…? Are you…? Oh, gosh, I'm so…" *Wait a minute.* I swatted Juan Carlos on the arm. "What is the matter with you? Vivian's in trouble and you two are in here going at it like a couple of teenagers?"

"I should head out." Richard scooped his phone off the nightstand and started for the door, head down, avoiding me.

I blocked his path. "Where's Jun?"

"Jun?" Richard stopped and looked to Juan Carlos to field my question.

"You know, Jun? The comic-strip kid? You guys were supposed to keep an eye on him."

"Yeah, about that," Juan Carlos began.

"Oh, no. Don't tell me you lost him. I don't have any way to get in contact with him."

"What was I supposed to do? He's an adult—"

"Sort of," Richard interrupted.

"He said there were some things he had to do. I did get his cell number for you," Juan Carlos offered as consolation.

"That's all right, I guess." I eyed the two of them. I should have been more annoyed than I was, but in reality I was glad to see them together. "So, you guys…?" I made a back-and-forth motion with my hand.

"No!" At Juan Carlos's cross-armed glower, Richard corrected himself. "I mean, we were just, you know…" Richard broke out in a bright pink blush.

"You're such a prude," Juan Carlos admonished him. "We *were* just about to have wild, crazy monkey sex, but then you showed up and ruined it. Thanks a lot." Juan Carlos held up his finger and thumb. "I was this close to finding out just how well-proportioned the big guy really is."

Richard looked like he wanted to melt into the horribly patterned carpet.

I cast a dubious eye at the perfectly made bed, then back at them. Really it was none of my business what went on between them, and besides, seeing the two of them get together was the best thing to happen all crappy day.

"I hate it when that happens," I teased Juan Carlos.

"I know!" He pointed a finger at me. "You owe me."

I cracked a smile, feeling the most normal I'd felt all day.

"I, ah…'bye." Richard made for the exit so fast he nearly spun me around.

"You embarrassed him. He's never going to let you find out now," I joked.

Juan Carlos looked at the closed door like it held everything he ever might have wanted.

"Oh my God," I whispered.

Juan Carlos turned to me, his face full of the hopeful joy and near-painful rush of falling hard. What I'd seen a hint of earlier was now broken open, naked and free, filling the space between us. He didn't just like Richard. He was falling in love with him.

I'd felt that once. With my ex-fiancé. And he'd handed it back to me, broken and rejected.

"He'll be back," I offered, not knowing what else to say.

"You know what his ma said to me on the phone?"

I shook my head.

"She asked me what was wrong with me. Why I'd throw away a perfectly good man like her son." He looked at me with eyes filled with disbelief. "I thought he hated me."

"I always thought you hated each other."

"I did hate him."

"Do you want me to leave?"

"No." He shook his head, throwing off his mood and returning to himself. "You can stay if you tell me what happened with skunk girl. And don't leave anything out."

"Jeez, it feels like forever ago." I relayed every detail I could remember. By the time I got to the part where Trinity danced around the room, Juan Carlos was in stitches, gripping his stomach, bent nearly in half. I couldn't help but laugh right along with him.

"Holy Dancing with the Crazies. You have got to be making some of this up." He swiped a tear off his cheek. "Please tell me you got it on video."

"No cameras allowed."

He dropped into a chair. "Oh, man. That's the best story I've heard in a long time."

"And I saw Vivian."

"What?"

"Yeah."

"You should have started with that! What is the matter with you?" He rushed me, pulling me down onto the bed next to him. "What happened? What did she say? How'd you get in to see her?" He shook my arms. "Start talking, *chica,* before I pass out from lack of information to my brain."

I filled him in on my visit with Vivian, from my spying on Jerk and Shorty to Kennedy's parting words.

"Holy whodunit! This mystery is more twisted than my aunt Sandy's morals. And they don't call her Randy Sandy for nothin', you know." He stood up to pace, tapping a finger to his chin. "Something's way off here...more than just Trinity's rocker. I don't like those guys, what did you call them? Jerk and Shady?"

"Shorty."

"Right, Shorty. So, Shorty bopped a bimbo and spilled some super hush-hush secret that may or may not get back to Big Mac, whoever that is. And Vivian is covering up for someone. Someone worth protecting enough that she's willing to become Big Bertha's prison bitch." He threw up his hands. "I don't get it. What are we missing here?"

"I think it might have to do with Trinity and Hjálmar. Remember how Mateo said he'd heard a rumor that the company was for sale?"

"Yeah."

"We need to find out if that's true or not. I also think we need to find out how the company was structured and who takes over now that Dhane's gone, especially since Trinity isn't exactly in a position to step in. You wouldn't happen to know someone who knows someone who could look into that for us, do you?"

Juan Carlos cracked a smile so wide it made the Cheshire cat look like he was frowning. "You know I do."

"Get on it. I want to do some digging into Dhane's father's murder. I have a feeling that was the big something Vivian left out of the story she told us about how she and Dhane met."

"Oh my God, you're right! That witch."

"Vivian trying to gloss over accidentally spilling the fact that Dhane had changed his name made me really suspicious. I knew she was hiding something. The thing I don't get is why? Why would you and I care twenty-some-odd years later about a murder he was never charged for?"

"Use my laptop." He ushered me over to the desk. "Go, go. I got some phone calls to make." Then he began furiously tapping commands into his phone.

I twitched the mouse to bring the screen to life. *Where to start?* I had a feeling if Dhane had changed his name, then so had Trinity. I did some quick math to guesstimate the year Vivian had gone to Wichita and met Dhane. I typed in Wichita, murder, and the year. All I got was a bunch of hits for Wichita Falls murders so I narrowed my search by adding Kansas.

An hour later my eyelids were drooping so low I had to prop

one open while I clicked the mouse with the other hand.

"Don't do that, you'll give yourself wrinkles. And if you get eyes like a Shar-Pei, I'm not gonna want to hang out with you anymore." Juan Carlos came over and closed the laptop. "It's late. I need my beauty sleep and you need your…sleep."

"Ha-ha. Suddenly everyone's a comedian. Must be Vegas." I yawned so deep I almost blacked out. "I can't do it. I can't go to sleep in a nice plush bed knowing Vivian's sleeping on a wafer-thin, lice-ridden cot in a jail cell. It doesn't seem right."

He brought me in for a hug. "I know how you feel, but there's nothing we can do about it right now. We need our sleep if we're going to help her." He rubbed my back and I nearly dropped off standing up. "I'll tell you what, the minute she gets out we'll delouse her and take her to a nice spa. How does that sound?"

"All right, I guess."

He turned me around and pushed me toward the door, grabbing up my purse on the way. "Here." He handed me my bag. "Get some rest. We'll begin again bright and early." He kissed my forehead and pushed me through the doorway.

"Will you set your alarm and call me?" I was terrible at waking up early.

"Absolutely. Go." He shooed me away.

I dragged my bag down the hallway after me. I was too tuckered to hoist its heft onto my shoulder. At my door, I had to search its depths for my key card, reminding me of the one I'd gotten to Dhane's suite. What if I'd been the one to find his body? I shuddered at the thought. The door slid closed before I could find the light switch, but I was too tired to care. I padded my way across the room, feeling for the end of the bed.

Big hands grabbed me, pulling me onto the bed. My scream got cut off by one of the hands clamping over my mouth. I tried to struggle, but I was held too tight. Panic gripped me and blanked out everything but my desperate need to escape.

CHAPTER TWELVE

"Easy, Azalea. It's just me."

"Alex?" I mumbled into his hand, my heart banging around like a bat in a cage.

"If I let you go, promise not to scream?"

I let out a breath, blowing air over the hand on my mouth.

"Is that a yes?"

I nodded, narrowly resisting the urge to bite his fingers off.

He released me and I immediately came out swinging, hitting him anywhere I could land a strike.

"I'm sorry. Stop it! Don't… Ow!" He captured my wrists so I used my feet and knees. "Azalea…ow…watch it…oof—" He let me go and curled up like shrimp, covering his crotch half a second too late.

I swatted him in the shoulder. "What the hell is the matter with you? What are you doing here?" I punctuated each question with another whack. "Don't you ever do that to me again." I pushed off the bed and switched on the bedside lamp. It was quite satisfying to see the damage I'd done.

But I was still mad, so I picked up a pillow and hit him again. "Why are you in my room?"

He held up a hand, gasping, his face mottled red.

"You deserve it, you rotten jerk. Never, ever sneak up on a woman in her darkened hotel room." I threw the pillow against the headboard. "You scared me half to death. My heart's still racing. Jeez." I turned away and paced the foot of the bed, trying to calm myself down.

"Sorry," he wheezed out.

I stopped and glared at him. "You should be." Pity got the better of me—he just looked so pathetic. "Are you all right?"

"Do you have a permit for that knee?"

Crossing my arms, I cracked a smile. If he was making jokes, he was feeling better. "I'd apologize, but it's your own fault. Why are you in my room skulking about?"

He leaned up on his elbows to look at me. "I wasn't skulking. I was sleeping."

"Why?"

"It's nighttime?"

"Alex," I warned.

"There are no more rooms, so I flashed my badge and got James into Vivian's room."

"That doesn't explain why you're in *my* room."

"I'm not sleeping in a king-size bed with James."

"Well, you're not sleeping in a king-sized bed with me either."

He sat up, and the bedsheet slipped down his chest and right on down his chiseled abs, landing so it barely covered his, ah, broken bits and pieces. "I have nowhere else to sleep."

"Are you *naked*?"

He pulled the sheet up under his arms. "Just shirtless. Please. I promise to keep my hands to myself." He showed me his palms, turning them forward and back, perfectly innocent.

"What is the matter with you?"

"Other than some bruised parts—" He lifted the sheet to have a look at himself.

I fixed my stare to the ceiling.

"—thank God," he whispered to himself. "My ego included, nothing's the matter with me."

"You can't sleep in my bed." I pointed to the couch, which was really more of a love seat. "You can sleep there."

"Half of me could. What should I do with the other half?"

I honestly didn't know what to say. I was afraid to look at him for fear I'd launch myself at him, so I scurried off to the bathroom, leaving a "You'd better be dressed and out of my bed by the time I get back!" in my wake.

I closed the door behind me and sank down against it. The tile floor was cool beneath me, helping to ground me and stanch my rampaging emotions. I wanted to stretch out, letting the hard coldness of it seep into me. Instead I got up and switched on the shower, setting it for colder than I usually took it.

By the time I came out of the bathroom, Alex was sitting up in bed, watching some sports channel.

"You were supposed to be dressed and out of there by the time I finished."

"I am dressed, see?" He flicked the sheet back to reveal board shorts.

Aw, jeez. I didn't look away in time, and so I got hit with the full effect of a very toned, very male, mostly nude, super-way-hot Alex from about the knees up. I clapped a hand over my eyes, but the image was already there, burned into my memory bank.

"I can put a shirt on if it bothers you that much."

A challenge. I didn't do well with challenges. I'd yet to meet one I wouldn't take, which always ended with me in all sorts of hot water. I had a feeling spending the night in the same bed as Alex would be a losing bet. He might be able to control himself, but I wasn't all that sure I could.

He switched off the TV. "Come to bed. I promise to keep my hands to myself." He patted the mattress beside him.

Climbing into bed, I gave him my most stern look. "You'd better keep that promise. My other knee is just as lethal."

He pulled the covers back and tucked me in. "I'm sure it is."

• • •

The trill of the phone startled me awake. Without opening my eyes, I reached a hand out, feeling for the receiver. "Hello?"

"Good morning, sunshine!" Juan Carlos chirped.

"Uhnn." I flipped my hair off my forehead and found myself staring into Alex's baby blues. Somehow during the night I'd draped myself across him, leaving a pool of drool on his chest. "Oh, God."

I tried to get up, but Alex wrapped an arm around me, pinning me in place. He put his other hand behind his head and looked down at me with the kind of grin that got girls like me in big trouble.

"Rise and shine! I've been a busy, busy boy this morning," Juan Carlos blabbed on. "I have so, so, sooo much to tell you. Are you awake? Hello?"

"I'm awake." I gave Alex a hard shove in the chest and he released me. I scampered off him onto my own side of the bed.

"Good. Meet me in the café downstairs in half an hour."

"Half an hour? That's not enough—" *Click*. "Damn."

I handed Alex the phone to hang up for me.

"Something wrong?" he asked, using the bedsheet to wipe down his chest.

I rolled my eyes and sighed, frustrated with him, this whole situation, and if I was honest…myself. "Yes. No."

He looked me over slowly, searching for what, I didn't know. When he spoke, his voice was gentle, soothing. "I want you to know that I'll only take what's freely given."

His words made me tingle in places that hadn't so much as twitched in months.

He reached over and took my hand. "Okay?"

Damn! Did he have to be hot *and* sweet? Not to mention half-dressed, interested, and so freakin' close? As much as I wanted to, and Lordy did I want to, I couldn't. Not with Vivian in trouble.

"Okay," I answered, getting up to look at myself in the mirror over the dresser. I looked like I felt: out of control and messy. "Yikes."

"I like it. You have that morning-after look." Alex dropped his feet to the floor and stretched.

I nearly fell face-first into the mirror. The thin light streaming through the crack in the curtains lit up his torso, deepening the shadows and highlighting the oh-so-delicious rises.

"Do you have to do that?"

He turned to me. "What?"

"Nothing. Just get dressed. We're meeting Juan Carlos in half an hour."

"Mind if I take a quick shower?"

Oh, the images...

While Alex showered, I changed into a vintage Western-style button-up shirt with tiny pink-and-white flowers on it and my darkest jeans. Dark circles rimmed my eyes, so I applied shimmery, peachy-pink and taupe eye shadows and lots of mascara. To keep the focus off my eyes, I patted my cheeks with a rose-colored cream blush and followed with a dark fuchsia lipstick. I looked like a cowgirl pinup.

Grabbing a brush, I began hacking away at my mass of hair, trying to get it all to go in the same direction. It wasn't working, so I pulled out my box of bobby pins and MacGyvered myself a pretty cute updo. I found a small pink flower and tucked it in over my right ear. The flower reminded me of Vivian.

Alex came out of the bathroom, smelling of fresh aftershave and clean man. This roommate situation was *not* going to work. "Why are you always naked? Don't you own any clothes?"

Alex looked down at himself, all innocence. "I'm wearing pants."

"Just hurry up." I bent to grab my snakeskin peep-toed pumps and spied his computer case. I never did find out what had happened when Dhane's dad died. "Can I use your computer?"

"Sure. Cord's in the bag." He grabbed a shirt from his suitcase and finally covered up. Not that I watched his every move or anything.

I booted up the computer and began a new search. It took less than five minutes to find the information I had searched two hours for the night before. Apparently I searched better with a few hours sleep under my belt. "Bingo."

My cell phone rang.

"It's been thirty-*five* minutes. Where are you?" Juan Carlos wanted to know.

"I'll be right down. And you won't believe what I found out."

"And you won't believe what *I* found out. Hurry!"

In my rush, I snapped the computer shut, grabbed my bag, and was halfway down the hall before I remembered I'd left Alex in the room. I spun around and plowed right into his chest. "Oomph."

"You really should watch where you're going," Alex said.

"Every time I turn around, you're there!" Buoyed by the excitement of what could be a real clue in all this mess, I shook off my irritation and grabbed him by the hand. "Just come on."

I fidgeted the whole way down in the elevator. When the doors finally opened, I sprang free, bolting toward the café.

Juan Carlos and I began talking at once.

"You'll never believe what I found—"

"Guess what I dug up—"

"You first," we said in unison

"No, you," we said again.

"Azalea goes first so she doesn't explode," Alex said, taking a seat next to Richard and introducing himself.

"Well, hello there." Juan Carlos held out his hand for Alex. "It's so nice to see you again." Then he threw me a dirty look. "Azalea didn't mention you'd come with James." He turned and whispered to me behind his hand. "You should have told me Detective Delish was here. I would have spent more time getting ready." He smoothed the hair over one ear with the palm of his hand. "How do I look?"

"You look fine. Same as always," Richard said, not looking up from his menu.

"Good to see you, too," Alex said. "New look?"

"Yes. Do you like it?" At Alex's nod, Juan Carlos simpered, turning side to side.

"If you're done barking up the wrong tree, Azalea has something she wants to tell us," Richard interrupted, earning a sniff and head toss from Juan Carlos.

"I swear, Alex, if you weren't straight I'd be all over you like Bob Mackie on Cher," Juan Carlos said.

Alex laughed. "And if I were gay, I'd let you."

"Hello?" I slapped a hand on the table. "Anyone remember Vivian? You know, our friend who's in jail?"

"Please, let me go first," Juan Carlos said, bouncing in his chair. "I promise, this is big. Huge."

"All right, go." I waved him on. "But hurry, mine's big, too."

"It's like being in the men's room at the Leather Mustache," Richard deadpanned.

Alex and I smothered our laughs while Juan Carlos ignored him, pressing on.

"Okay, so you know how you wanted me to find out about the company?" At my nod, Juan Carlos continued, "I know who Big Mac is."

"Who?" I asked.

"MacKenzie Todd, better known as Mac, was Dhane's partner in Hjálmar, but she was more like a silent partner. You know, she did the behind-the-scenes kind of stuff like product development. And apparently she was developing a really top-secret product that was going to launch Hjálmar into the outer stratosphere."

"What kind of product?" I asked.

"Some kind of revolutionary new hair color formula that doesn't fade even on really porous hair."

"That's not revolutionary," Richard said.

"That's not the revolutionary part, no. But get this." Juan Carlos paused for dramatic effect. "What makes this color so innovative is that it can be changed with only one shampoo."

"Like a rinse or toner?" I asked.

"Yes, but it won't be sheer like a rinse or toner. This new color formula will give coverage like a permanent color, but will wash out completely when you use the special shampoo," Juan Carlos explained. "In essence, a client could change her hair color for as long or short of a time as she wants."

I could practically see the piles of money stacking up. My heart leaped in excitement. "That would be incredible. I could give my client a different hair color every day if she wanted."

"Yes!" Juan Carlos enthused. "Think about it. A blonde could be a redhead for a weekend or a brunette for a month."

"Yeah, but it wouldn't work in reverse without lift," Richard pointed out.

Alex looked puzzled. "What's lift?"

"To put it simply, lift is how hair gets lightened. The greater the lift hair color has, the lighter the hair gets," I explained. "I see what you mean, Richard, a brunette couldn't be a blonde or a true redhead for a weekend. You could maybe get auburn, but with all that brown occurring naturally in the hair, you wouldn't get a bright red."

Juan Carlos jumped in. "Ah, here's the thing though. Big Mac was supposedly testing just such a product."

"Are you kidding? That's not possible." I shook my head in

disbelief. "Can't be done."

"But what if it could?" Richard asked, looking for the first time like he was really interested in our conversation. "How much would a product like that be worth to a company? Millions? Billions?"

"Exactly," Juan Carlos said. "And how pissed would you be if you developed such a product and your partner sold the company and your new product right out from under you?"

"He sold the company?" Richard blurted out.

"It was for sale. And from what I understand, there was a buyer, but no, Dhane died before the sale could go through," Juan Carlos said.

"You'd think they'd have a partnership agreement to prevent that kind of thing, though," I said. "Vivian and I have one. There's no way either of us could sell our portion of the salon, let alone the whole business, without the other's approval."

"The LLC only lists Dhane. There's no mention of Big Mac in any of the paperwork."

"Oh my God," I gasped, my mind spinning with new scenarios. "But why would Dhane do that when they were on the verge of something so huge?"

"That I don't know," Juan Carlos said.

I looked over at Alex. He was scribbling in a small notebook.

"I'm taking notes," he explained.

That was a good idea. I wished I'd thought to do that. But then he did this sort of thing for a living. I dug around in my bag and came up with the sparkly silver notepad I carried to write down color formulas, and one of those fat pens with four different kinds of ink. Not exactly police issued, but it would do.

Just as I bent my head to write in it, I caught Alex's approving half grin.

"Now you," Juan Carlos said to me.

I set aside my notebook. "I think I might have found out what happened when Dhane's dad died."

"How? When? You had nothing when you left my room last night."

"I used Alex's computer."

"How…but…oh! You are such a Two-faced Tilly." Juan Carlos eyed me like I was his teenage daughter coming home past curfew. "What'd you do, hook up in the hall? And after you gave me such a hard time about me getting in some hard time with Rambo here." He jerked his head toward Richard, who slumped down in his seat.

"I did not! He was already in my room when I got there."

Juan Carlos sucked in air. "You had him on hold, pretending to be all tired so you could cut out early and do the mommy-daddy dance with Officer Awesome here."

"I didn't even know he was there!"

"She's telling the truth," Alex interjected on my behalf. "There weren't any more rooms. Azalea was kind enough to let me share hers."

Juan Carlos looked back and forth between Alex and me. "Right. And you're telling me nothing happened."

"She was all over me, but I managed to resist," Alex said, a teasing smile playing around his mouth.

"Can I tell you what I found out now?" I asked. Juan Carlos gave a reluctant nod, so I continued, "Last night I must have looked at a thousand news articles and I'm sure I'd already read this one particular piece, but this morning something popped out at me. The article was dated ten years ago, so Trinity would have been about fourteen. Older than Jun's story led us to believe, which is why I probably overlooked it the first time.

"What caught my eye was a small, grainy photo just below the byline. It was a yearbook photo of a young man named Daniel Ware of Newton, Kansas. The article was about how he'd come home to find there'd been a house fire and the only survivor was his younger sister. Arson was suspected then confirmed. In the rubble, two bodies were found."

"Two? I don't think you found the right article," Juan Carlos said.

"Just wait," I said. "The two bodies were determined to be the parents. They'd died from smoke inhalation. Because he hadn't been home at the time, Daniel wasn't charged."

"What makes you think that article is linked to Dhane?" Alex asked.

"The photo," I answered. "He was younger and had a really bad mullet, but I'm positive it was Dhane. There's no mistaking those eyes."

"That's for sure," Juan Carlos agreed. "But I'm confused. Jun said Dhane had killed their father and that's why Trinity's ten pounds of crazy in a five-pound sack."

"Right. But here's the thing. Dhane didn't kill anyone," I replied. "He had an alibi."

"Then who killed the parents?" Richard asked.

"According to the newspaper report, there was only one suspect." I looked around at everyone at the table, anticipating their reactions. "The little sister."

CHAPTER THIRTEEN

"Holy Twisted Sister!" Juan Carlos exclaimed. "We all knew Trinity was one twist short of a slinky, but that level of crazy's in the blood. Poor Dhane."

Alex remained quiet, his head bent over his notebook, scribbling furiously.

"What are you writing?" I asked him.

"I'm making a note to contact someone in the Newton, Kansas, PD to find out if any charges were ever filed in that case. It's doubtful I'll get much, since Trinity was a minor and those records are usually sealed. But I may get lucky enough to get the detective's impressions and maybe some insider info on the case."

I don't know why Alex's willingness to help surprised me. He *had* come all this way to help Vivian. I guessed I expected him to be more like Kennedy, obstinate and closed-mouthed.

"Do you know anything about Dhane's personal life?" Alex asked.

Jeez. I hadn't thought about that. "No. Why?"

"Just covering all the bases," Alex replied.

"I have a question," Richard said.

We all looked at him.

"If Trinity killed her parents, it's likely she may have also killed Dhane. And if so, why would Vivian take the fall for a known murderer?"

• • •

Richard's words ricocheted around in my head all through breakfast and during our cab ride to the convention center. Why, if Vivian knew Trinity had killed once, would she take the rap for her? Why wasn't Trinity locked up in a psychiatric ward, bouncing off padded walls instead of roaming free to possibly kill again and again? What had really happened in that house in Newton, Kansas, ten years ago?

And why, after all I now knew about Trinity, did I still feel sorry for her?

Juan Carlos, Richard, and I pulled up in front of the convention center and paid the cab fare. Alex had stayed behind with James to work on getting Vivian released. He'd promised to call me with any new information.

We made our way into the lobby, stopping short to read a new sign that had been posted. There was to be a memorial service conducted by Dhane's partner, MacKenzie Todd, at nine that morning.

"What do you think? Should we go?" Juan Carlos asked.

"I think we should," I answered. "On TV the murderer sometimes goes to the funeral."

"But isn't Trinity our main suspect?" Richard asked.

"She's bumped up to the top of the list, but I'd also like to get a look at Dhane's partner. She has a very strong motive for wanting Dhane dead."

Juan Carlos considered it. "That's true. Hey, maybe Jerk and Shabby will be there too."

"Shorty," I corrected. "Jerk and Shorty."

"Who are Jerk and Shorty?" Richard asked.

"Come on," I said. "We'll fill you in on the way."

We walked down one of the halls that shot out from the main lobby to the conference room where they were holding the memorial. The room was large and already packed with mourners and gawkers. On the dais, a podium wreathed in flowers had been set up along with a half-dozen chairs. A large photo of Dhane from a Hjálmar product campaign sat off to one side. I frowned. It was all so impersonal, as though it were merely for show.

Juan Carlos managed to snag us some seats. As soon as I sat down, someone slid into the seat next to me and threw an arm over my shoulder.

"Fancy meeting you here," Kennedy whispered in my ear. "It seems my day wouldn't be complete without you in it."

"Jeez, do you always have to sneak up on people like that?"

"Who's your friend?" Juan Carlos asked, mashing me into Kennedy for a better look at him.

"Detective Kennedy, my friends Juan Carlos and Richard. Guys, meet the cop who arrested Vivian."

Juan Carlos bunched up his face and moved away. "What's he doing here? And why are you so chummy with him?"

"Nice meeting you, too," Kennedy responded.

"It's not like I invited him to sit next to me," I told Juan Carlos, trying to shake off Kennedy's arm. "He just sat down."

"Uh-huh." Juan Carlos turned away, angling his body toward Richard to shut us out.

"Great," I muttered to myself. Juan Carlos's cold shoulder could take hours to thaw.

"Don't worry, I'm used to it," Kennedy said, finally withdrawing his arm now that the damage had been done.

"I wasn't worried about you."

"I'm surprised someone as close to Dhane as you were isn't on the stage. Aren't you going to eulogize your, ah, what is it the kids call it? Hook up? Booty call? Date? No, not date—"

"Do you ever shut up?"

"Oh, I see. You were on the down low. Don't want your detective boyfriend to find out. Got it."

"He's not my... Oh, why do I bother? Don't you have an innocent person to lock up or something?"

"Nah, I already nabbed my quota for the day before breakfast." His gaze roamed the room, like a search beacon. "So, you come across any new info on our friend Dhane here?"

My bullshit radar beeped. Why was Kennedy being so nice? And why was he pumping *me* for information on the case? Unless…"You don't have anything, do you? You're stuck."

"It's just a question. Never mind."

He started to get up, but I grabbed his arm and pulled him back. "Wait. Maybe we can help each other."

"Help? No. See, you don't get it. I ask the questions and you answer." He motioned back and forth between us. "This here is a one-way street."

"Okay. Sure. If that's the way you want it…" I put on my best smug smile and batted my lashes at him. "I'm sure you already know about the fire ten years ago anyway." I examined my fingers. Dang it all if I didn't spot another hangnail. I was so getting a new manicurist.

I could feel his gaze on me, burning a hole in the side of my head.

"How about I buy you a cup of coffee after this little soiree?"

"I'd love to have a cup of coffee with you, Detective."

He eyed me uneasily as if trying to gage the level of my sincerity. "I'll meet you at that coffee-hut thing off the main lobby."

"It's a date."

"You sure are free with your dates." And with that parting shot, Kennedy got up and walked away.

I should have been annoyed at the implied insult, but I was too pleased with myself for having something over Old King

Kennedy. Plus it had the added benefit of helping to clear Vivian's name. If I had to, I'd let Kennedy insult me any old way he wanted to for that.

"I cannot believe you!" Juan Carlos's condemnation drew a few looks. "Fraternizing with the foe. Rendezvousing with the rival. Convening with the combatant. Associating with the—"

I held up a hand. "I get it. You're pissed."

"Pissed?" His voice rose. *"Pissed?"*

"Sshhh," Richard admonished, glancing around to bring our attention to all of the people staring at us.

I hugged Juan Carlos's arm and whispered, "He doesn't know about the fire and Dhane's parents. I'm meeting him afterward to try to negotiate some info out of him." Juan Carlos didn't look convinced. "The more attention is off Vivian and on to other people, the better for her, don't you think?" I tried to summon up any guilt I might have at throwing Trinity Kennedy's way, but what little I had was a pittance compared to my desire to prove Vivian's innocence.

"I suppose."

"Right. So, that's what I'm doing."

"Oh my God! You are totally crushing hard for the Irishman."

"I am not. I can't stand him. You think I would get the hots for the man who threw my best friend in jail? He's cute but not cute enough to overcome that kind of betrayal."

"You'd better not—"

The lights dimmed, cutting off Juan Carlos and signaling the start of the memorial service.

The crowd grew quiet. A petite brunette stepped onstage and then behind the podium.

"On behalf of Hjálmar and Dhane's family, I want to thank you all for coming. My name is MacKenzie Todd."

"That little mouse is Big Mac?" Juan Carlos whispered.

I put my finger to my lips and gave him my best kindergarten-teacher glare.

Several other people joined Mac onstage: Trinity, Tenchi, Sora, a woman I didn't recognize, and what did you know…Jerk and Shorty.

"See those two on the end?" I asked Richard and Juan Carlos. "That's Jerk and Shorty."

"I worked with Dhane," Mac continued, "We met a few years ago while I was employed at another company. When Dhane started Hjálmar, he asked me to join him. Of course I did. No one could resist Dhane." She said the last bit with a brittle half smile that said more than her words. "He steered Hjálmar through the rough seas of a fledgling business, navigating the waters deftly until he sailed it into the formidable ocean, turning it into the great conglomerate we know today."

"Gawd, this is awful," Juan Carlos murmured. "She makes him sound like a real Viking or something."

I bit the inside of my cheek. It *was* awful.

Mac's nautical-themed eulogy went on for another ten minutes. Other than that one hint at her real feelings toward Dhane, there was nothing special about what she said. I noticed Richard's chin had dropped to his chest and he snored softly. My own head had bobbed like a buoy on a rough sea more than a few times.

Finally, Mac wrapped it up. "Fare-thee-well, Captain. We'll miss you. And now I'd like to introduce Dhane's wife to say a few words."

I popped up in my seat.

Sora stood and approached the podium.

"Oh my God. Oh. My. God." I couldn't believe it! Sora was Dhane's *wife*?

Juan Carlos grabbed my forearm. "What? What?"

"I'll tell you later."

Sora looked glorious, her gorgeous red hair falling down her back like a crimson waterfall, shiny and breathtaking. I'd kill for a chance to work with hair like that. I noticed every other hairstylist in the place with the same covetous expression. Rarely do we get our hands on such brilliance. Frizzy, fuzzy frog fur…yes. Five hairs we're supposed to transform into a mass of splendiferous waves… yes. This shampoo commercial perfection…no.

Juan Carlos let out a pleasured sigh. Richard leaned into him. I found myself smiling despite the somber occasion.

Disney couldn't have concocted a more perfect princess.

"Thank you all for being here. It's comforting to know so many people loved Dhane as much as I did." She sniffed right on cue. "And I loved Dhane so much." She bowed her head, and that's when I noticed Ace standing to the left of the stage, staring up at her with such naked adoration he shook with it.

"You all have been so kind. I want you to know that his sister, Trinity, and I appreciate all of the support you've given us. It means more to us than you'll ever know." Sora turned to the photo of Dhane, her hand clutched over her heart. "We'll miss you, my love." Then she walked over and kissed the picture on the lips.

Ewww.

Richard embraced a snuffling Juan Carlos. Some sobbed openly, others sniffed and shifted in their seats, all obviously affected by Sora's words and actions. I felt eyes on me and turned to find Kennedy blatantly staring at me from the edge of the room as though he were gauging my reaction to Sora's words. He raised a brow as if to ask, *Well?*

I rolled my eyes in response and he nodded in agreement. So…Kennedy was mistrustful of the little wifey, too. Interesting.

Trinity remained fixed to her seat, petting her skunk harder and faster as the emotions in the room escalated. She looked lost, completely overset by her circumstances. I felt more sorry for her than ever.

The next to speak was the woman I didn't recognize. She had that hairstylist look to her, dressed all in black, her dark hair pulled back in a ponytail so sleek and tight it acted as a poor man's facelift.

"Hello. My name is Golda Gonzales." Her smoker's rasp was a sharp contrast to Sora's melodic voice. "I was Dhane's hairstylist and friend. We worked together for many years. He was a good man. I liked him very much. I will miss him." She clip-clopped her way back to her seat on sky-high heels.

So much for overblown sentiment.

Juan Carlos leaned into me. "*That's* who we need to talk to next."

He was right. Want to know a person's deepest, darkest secrets? Ask his hairstylist. We knew more about our clients' lives than their therapists.

"I'm meeting Kennedy afterward. Can you guys catch up with Golda?"

"Sure thang, darlin'," Juan Carlos said. "I'm Oprah. I'll get her to spill her guts like she's about to be given a car and a trip to Paris."

The last to speak was Jerk.

"Hello." He yanked at his collar. "I'm Hank Door, the new CEO of Hjálmar. Dhane recruited me right out of college. I started as an account executive and worked my way up the corporate ladder." The rest of Hank a.k.a. Jerk's speech was all about him and his incredible rise within the company. He earned his nickname with every word.

The memorial closed with a video montage of Hjálmar marketing-campaign photographs featuring Dhane in all of his splendid vivaciousness. It was hard to reconcile the images on the screen above the stage with the visions that had haunted my dreams, both waking and sleeping. He was so young, so attractive, so…gone. The finality of his death hit me harder than I imagined it would.

The lights came up.

"He was so beautiful," Juan Carlos blubbered. "Cut short in his prime. It's a crime against nature." He dabbed at his eyes. "It's true, only the good die young. Oh, why'd he have to die?" Juan Carlos threw himself at Richard, who caught him deftly, cradling him.

"We'll catch up with you later," Richard said over Juan Carlos's head.

For some, like Juan Carlos, the memorial made them wonder why. Why did bad things happen to good people? Why did only the good die young? To me, the memorial was a battle call. Who would do such a thing? What did they want that Dhane stood in the way of? What was worth killing for? And in the face of such an injustice, who would stand for Dhane? Who was willing to do more than just shake their head at the tragedy?

With the final onscreen image of Dhane burned into my memory and the anger at the unfairness of it all coursing through me, I made a vow right there, right then. If it was the last thing I would ever do, I would find out who killed Dhane. Not to satisfy my own curiosity, not even to clear Vivian's name, but to right a wrong and bring Dhane's killer to justice.

CHAPTER FOURTEEN

I met up with Kennedy at the coffee kiosk as planned. We ordered our drinks and found an out-of-the-way corner to sit down.

"I'm surprised you don't know about the fire," I said.

"Oh, I knew about the fire. And the parents."

Well, that popped my smugness balloon. "Then why'd you want to meet if you already know all there is to know?"

"I wanted to find out how you knew. And how much you know."

I just stared at him. Really, this was not going at all like I thought it would. This wasn't even a one-way street. It was a cul-de-sac.

"Well?" he asked.

"I'm smart enough to use a computer search engine, you know."

"No doubt. But what made you look it up in the first place?"

Here's where it got tricky. Vivian's story had seeded my curiosity and then Jun's made it take root. If I told Kennedy about Vivian's lies and half-truths…well, I wasn't sure that would be in Viv's best interests. So I decided to go with that measure-of-truth thing that had been working so well for me so far.

"I'd been hearing stories about Dhane's past and decided to do a little digging." I shrugged. "That's all."

"Uh-huh." He took a sip from his cup, eyeing me over the rim. "What else?"

"I did happen to overhear something that might be of interest to you."

"What?"

I told him about my eavesdropping on Jerk and Shorty's fight in the police station parking lot.

"Jerk's real name is Hank Door," I said. "He's the CEO who spoke at the memorial. Shorty was the guy who sat next to him. I don't know his name, though."

Kennedy narrowed his eyes at me. "You really need to stay out of this. You're a hairstylist, not a detective."

"I am out of it." Although I really wasn't. I was up to my gold hoop earrings in it and planned on keeping it that way.

"I'm not kidding. You don't know who you're dealing with here. Dhane didn't, and look what happened to him." He eyed my neck. "I like your pretty head right where it is. Stay out of it."

"I'm not in it. I'm way on the outside. I'm like Pluto."

"The dog or the planet?"

"Ha-ha."

"There's more, isn't there?"

"Maybe."

"Out with it. Or do I have to remind you that the sooner I find out who really killed Dhane, the sooner your friend gets out of jail?"

"You don't have to remind me, and you don't have to hold it over my head, either. All you have to do is ask." Then, because he brought out the contrary in me, I added, "Nicely."

He smiled for the first time and it completely changed his face, adding a spark to those seen-too-much green eyes of his. "Tell me what else you know...please."

He could pretend to be a human being all he wanted, but I didn't trust him as far as I could spit. I had a feeling he'd somehow take what I told him and twist it around to fit whatever theory it was that he had about Vivian killing Dhane. There was no way I was giving him any information that might help him achieve his goal.

"I gotta go." I grabbed my bag off my chair, knocking it into the table and spilling the rest of my drink in Kennedy's lap.

He stood up, coffee dripping from his crotch. "Wait!"

But I was already melding with the crowd, entering the convention floor. My last vision of Kennedy was of him muttering obscenities and dabbing at the front of his pants.

This was terrible. What was wrong with me, pissing off the cop who held the keys to Vivian's jail cell? At this rate she'd never get out. I'd be visiting her in a Nevada prison for the rest of her life, staring at her through a glass wall, trying to pretend that everything would be okay for her when it would never be okay again.

I closed my eyes and shook my head, trying to clear the image. And ran smack-dab into a wall of chest.

"You really ought to look where you're going."

Oh, no. This was just what I needed, the other guy who shook up my emotions like a can of soda. What an amazingly awesome day this was shaping up to be.

"What happened?" Alex asked.

"Everything and nothing. What are you doing here? I thought you and James were working on getting Vivian released."

"We did."

"You did what?"

"She's been released."

"*What?* Where is she?" I tried to peek around him to see if she was with him.

"She's back at the hotel with James. She wanted to shower and change. And I imagine they were going to do a little, ah, catching up afterward."

"Oh." I didn't care about her catching-up time. I really needed to see her.

"She told me to tell you to come to her room around three. She's dying to see you, too."

"Did she say anything else? Did she explain what all this is about? Why she confessed?"

"She didn't say much. I think she wanted to wait to talk to you herself." He pulled me over, out of the line of traffic. "She's had a rough time. Try to be understanding of that when you see her."

"*She's* had a rough time?" The resentment and anger at her that I'd been shoving down suddenly came up. "She created this rough time for everyone. She lied, confessed, and got herself arrested, leaving us scrambling to try and save her. I'll show her a rough time." I tried to push past him, but he wrapped his arms around me.

I struggled to escape his embrace, but he was too strong. And that's when I saw Kennedy, staring straight at us. I froze, stuck in the tractor beam of his gaze as he made his way toward us.

"Let her go," Kennedy said.

Alex turned toward Kennedy, releasing me except for the arm that fastened me to his side. His unexpected sense of protectiveness toward me was kind of thrilling—plus, I had to give him points for holding in the comments that must have been rattling around in his head about the coffee stain on Kennedy's crotch.

"We didn't finish our conversation," Kennedy said to me.

I adjusted my stance, folding my arms over my chest. I wasn't going to let him get to me. "Yes, we did."

"No. We didn't," Kennedy insisted.

"It felt done to me."

"We can do this the nice way or the Hagatha way. Your choice."

I pictured the burly police matron he'd threatened me with

earlier. That right there was why he annoyed the hell out of me. Always threatening. "Fine. The nice way it is."

"Go ahead, Kennedy. Ask your questions," Alex said.

The annoyed sternness of Kennedy's glare made me doubt the glimpse of human kindness I thought I'd seen in him just a few moments ago. Maybe it had been all in my imagination. Or, more likely, he'd been faking it to get me to spill my secrets. This man staring at me now was clearly annoyed with me. In fact, I thought he might hate me a little.

"I'm okay," I told Alex. "Why don't you catch up with Juan Carlos and Richard? I'm sure they'll want to tell you all about the memorial service this morning."

"Are you sure? He's looking hard for a new suspect now that the charges against Vivian have been dropped. You could be next."

"You dropped the charges?" I asked Kennedy. Of course he did. He was manipulating me to get what he wanted. How terribly, awfully familiar this all was.

"The DA dropped the charges," Kennedy said without a hint of shame or apology.

Glaring angry daggers at Kennedy, I shrugged off Alex's embrace. "Yeah, we're definitely fine. You don't need to stay, Alex."

Alex looked from me to Kennedy and back again, clearly picking up on the undercurrents between us. "Are you sure?"

"I'm sure." Boy, was I ever. Any softening I'd felt toward Kennedy, he'd blasted away with one betrayal and manipulation after another.

Alex gave my shoulder a squeeze and one last warning look at Kennedy before he left.

"You son of a motherless jerk!" I wished right then with everything I had in me that the coffee I'd spilled on him had been boiled in hell. "How dare you use Vivian's incarceration to get me to tell you stuff, all the while knowing the charges against her had been dropped?" My anger ratcheted up another twelve notches.

"You're a coldhearted bastard, you know that? I can't believe I thought for a minute that you… Oh! I'm so stupid. *Always* wanting to believe the good in people."

I got right up in his face, wanting to physically shove him like he'd been verbally shoving me around since the day we met. "You want to ask me any more questions, you're going to have to haul me in and do it in front of my lawyer." Shaking with the effort not to burst into hot, angry tears, I spun on my heel and wove my way through the crowd.

"Azalea, wait! I'm sorry. Azalea!"

But I didn't stop. I didn't turn around. I was so done getting jerked around by Kennedy. I plowed my way through to the other side of the convention floor and out through the back exit, right into a pack of smokers.

"Hey, man."

"Dude, watch it."

"Sorry, sorry," I mumbled, not looking back. If I had to, I'd walk all the way back home…or at least back to the hotel.

A hand grabbed my arm, yanking me back.

"I said I was… Oh!"

"I'm sorry. Did I frighten you?" Tenchi asked. "I saw you hurrying across the convention floor, but you didn't seem to hear me call you."

I was sure he'd scared at least three years off my being a natural brunette. "No, you didn't frighten me. I just wasn't expecting you." I eyed the distance between the smokers and myself just in case he tried to suck out my soul or something. "What can I do for you?"

"It's Trinity."

"What about her?"

"She wants to see you again."

"Oh, I don't know." How about *hells* no? The only person who freaked me out more than Tenchi was Trinity. And on the creep-o-meter they were both off the charts. There was no way I was going to be alone with the two of them ever again.

"Please? She insists," he said.

"I really can't."

"I see. Are you sure I can't change your mind?"

"No, I'm afraid not."

"Trinity won't be happy, you know."

"I'm sorry about that, but I just…can't."

He looked really unhappy, almost pained. "I'm afraid that's not acceptable."

"Like I said, I'm sorry, but I really can't." I glanced back at the smokers again. Only two were left, and they looked like they couldn't help me kill a short line of ants.

Tenchi moved toward me, his weird eyes boring into mine as if he were trying to do a mind meld with me or something. "You keep saying that, so I feel you must be sincere. However, Trinity wants to see you. So, you will come."

I felt a sharp pain in my side. "What—"

"I'm sorry. It would have been so much easier if you'd agreed."

I looked down at the knife pressed up against my left side. Although *knife* was an understatement—small sword would've been more accurate. "Don't ruin my shirt. It's vintage. Okay, fine. I'll go."

"I'm so glad you've agreed. I have a car waiting."

Of course he did. Because that was how my day was going. Kicked in the stomach by a dirty rotten detective and then thrown forcibly into a waiting car by a Comic-Con reject who was taking me to visit a mad murderer who probably wanted to kill me afterward.

My life was awesome.

A sleek black rental car pulled up just inches from us. I gave the smokers one last hopeful glance, but they were all gone. I was on my own.

"Please, get in," Tenchi said.

He'd put the knife away somewhere, but just knowing it was there and he'd use it was enough for me to climb into the back of the car. The door locks clicked, locking us in. I looked to the driver for assistance, but one glance from him in the review mirror and I knew there was no help there.

"I'm afraid I'm going to have to confiscate your cell phone. Trinity's rule. Do I need to go over them again for you?"

"No." Even if I had forgotten them, at this point I didn't care who I pissed off. I felt contrary enough to try to break them all just to see what happened. I gave him my phone. "Are you going to kill me?"

"What? No." He looked sincerely insulted. "What gave you that idea?"

I showed him the small hole he'd made in my shirt.

He looked like he was trying to frown, but his overly Botoxed face wouldn't cooperate. "That's unfortunate."

Unfortunate. Yeah, that's how I would have described it. "Where are you taking me?"

He gave me a pitying look and spoke slowly. "To see Trinity."

It was clear I was going to get nowhere with this guy. If he was the one holding all of the sanity in the Trinity/Tenchi relationship, I was pretty sure the bag he held it in had a serious rip.

I turned away and looked out the window. In the near distance stood the Raine Tower Suites. So we were going back to the scene of the crime, back to where it all began. A knot bunched up in the pit of my stomach. I really didn't want to go back to that hotel. Nothing good had happened there. I couldn't fathom why Trinity would want to stay mere feet from where her brother had died. Maybe that was part of the crazy.

Watching her during her brother's memorial, it was clear she was breaking apart. It was almost like watching a statue slowly crumble, a piece here, a chunk there. Again, I worried who would care for her. Going around kidnapping people at knifepoint,

Tenchi was obviously not in a mentally stable position to care for someone as ill as Trinity.

We pulled up to the front of the hotel. Tenchi gripped my elbow as soon as I got out of the car and hustled me toward the elevators. The lobby bustled with people checking out and more checking in.

I felt the coolness of Tenchi's blade through the fabric of my shirt. "It would be a shame to damage your shirt further."

So much for thoughts of escape.

We got out of the elevator and walked down the hall. The same hall where Dhane was killed in his suite, where Trinity's suite was, and where I'd first met Kennedy. I did not have good memories of this hallway.

Tenchi pulled out his key card and let us into the room. He ushered me through the living area and knocked on Trinity's bedroom door, then before she could answer, he opened it and shoved me through, slamming it closed behind me.

I felt like I'd been thrown into the lion pit.

It took a moment for my eyes to adjust to the dimness of the room. No candles were lit this time. The only light came from the peekaboo sunshine of the fluttering window drapery. I waited, anticipating Trinity to light her three bubble-gum-scented candles and, in her high, tinkling voice, repeat every insane thing she said three times.

Nothing.

I stepped farther into the room, expecting to find Trinity on the bed, but it was empty.

"Trinity?"

No answer. I moved toward the bed, thinking that maybe she'd left a note or something. A breeze blew the curtains up, illuminating the rumpled bed. Pillows were scattered around, the bedspread bunched and askew, as if someone had been tossing and turning.

I turned toward the nightstand and flipped on the light. A glass had been knocked over, spilling a dark liquid on the carpet. Wine, maybe? The false golden light exposed the corners of the room, allowing me to see it in full for the first time. I did a full three sixty, scanning the space for Trinity. Nothing else seemed out of order or disturbed. There was a closed door between the bed and the window, which I hadn't noticed before. I went over and put my ear against it. I couldn't hear a thing, so I knocked.

"Trinity?"

Again, no answer. I tried the knob and it turned easily in my hand. The bathroom was neat and exceptionally orderly, lotions and bottles lined up with the precision of a military unit. But no Trinity.

I returned to the bedroom, not knowing what else to do, and that's when I saw it, matted and worn, peeking out from underneath the bed. Curio. I rushed over and picked up the stuffed skunk as panic filled my chest. Trinity was *never* without Curio.

Something was very, very wrong here. And that was when it hit me. The last time I'd been here, the curtains had been drawn, the room closed up and chilly.

With Curio clutched to my chest, I turned to look at the window, the long drapes fluttering gently in the hot Vegas breeze. But it wasn't a large window. It was a doorway to a balcony.

"Trinity?"

Lifting the edge of the curtain out of the way, I stepped out onto the tiled terrace. I don't know what drew me to the railing. Thirty-eight floors was a long way up, and I was not good with heights. But the urge to look over was so strong, it was as if a string were attached to my chest and unseen hands pulled me closer… closer.

Don't look down.

The nearer I got to the railing, the more the view expanded around me. The mountains in the distance, so foreboding, stood guard over the masses of buildings spread out like a giant blanket on the desert floor, shiny and jagged.

Don't look down.

I was within reach of the railing now, my heart slamming so hard in my chest it hurt my ears. Reaching a hand out, I took the last couple of steps that brought me to the edge.

Don't look down.

But it was too late. My head bent automatically, drawing my gaze down until the world opened up below me.

Trinity lay on the rooftop of the portico covering the entrance of the lobby—her arms and legs bent at impossible angles, a pool of dark red spread out like a pillow beneath her head.

I gasped, my hands automatically going to my mouth, muffling my screams. Curio slipped out, following Trinity over the railing. Down and down until he landed with a silent bounce once, twice, before coming to rest next to Trinity's outstretched hand.

CHAPTER FIFTEEN

Trinity.

I paced the balcony, shaking my hands out in front of me. *Ohmygod, ohmygod, ohmygod, ohmygod, ohmygod.* Full-on freak-out loomed over me like a dark specter. I broke out in a flop sweat that left me flushed and weak. I bent double, gripping my knees to keep from heaving. *Oh, God.* Swallowing extra spit, I wiped my sweaty hands on my thighs.

Call someone. I reached for my cell phone but realized Tenchi had it.

Tenchi. Knife. Deranged.

Oh, God.

I wiped the sweat off my upper lip with a shaky hand and tried to think of my options. Thirty-eight floors down or the crazy, knife-wielding maniac in the next room. Not great choices.

This was a hotel. They had phones in the rooms. I went back into the bedroom and spied the handset on the bedside table. I reached for it, then snatched my hand back. Who was I going to call? The police? Hotel security? Kennedy? Alex? As much as I wanted there to be, there was really no choice. I sifted through my bag and came out with his card. I shook so hard, it took me two tries before I got the number right.

"Kennedy."

"It's Azalea. I need you to come to Trinity's suite. Right now."

"What's happened?"

"It's Trinity...she's dead."

"I'm on my way."

I replaced the receiver and went immediately to the bedroom door, locking myself in. Then I sank down, leaning my head back against the door.

The curtains continued their dance with no real rhythm or predictability. Kind of like this weekend. And life in general.

For the first time, I noticed the sounds from the street. Thousands, maybe millions, went about their everyday lives. Had any of them heard Trinity scream? Had they watched her body falling? Had she fought all the way down or had she been relaxed, resigned to her fate?

I rested my arms on my drawn-up knees and put my head down, trying not to cry and working hard to blank my mind and drive away the reappearing image of Trinity on that rooftop. A teardrop dripped off the end of my nose, then another. I sniffed. She was so young, so damaged. She'd lost so much in her young life. Poor Trinity.

I heard voices in the outer room and quickly got up and wiped my face.

"Azalea!" Kennedy's voice boomed.

That was all I needed. I threw open the door and came at him like a charging bull, knocking him back a step. He caught me, hugging hard.

"Hey. Are you all right?"

"Yes." I pushed to get out of his arms, suddenly feeling ridiculous for letting him comfort me. I didn't even like the guy. "She's in there." I gestured back to the room behind me, my arm shaking as badly as the rest of me. "Down there. She went over the balcony."

"What have you done?" Tenchi roared, coming at me like six feet of pissed-off boyfriend.

I edged around Kennedy. "Nothing. I did nothing. She was already gone when you brought me here."

"Gone? What do you mean gone?" Tenchi turned to go into the bedroom, but was stopped by a uniformed officer.

One of the detectives I recognized from Dhane's suite, Platt I think, came out of the bedroom. He adjusted his pants over his substantial middle and announced, "DB's on the roof of the hotel entrance. Probably a suicide."

"Oh, no. No." Tenchi collapsed, crumpling to the ground like a discarded costume after Halloween.

"She didn't commit suicide," I insisted.

"Something you want to tell us?" Platt asked, suspicion dripping from every word.

"How do you know?" Kennedy asked.

"Curio, her stuffed skunk, she always carries him around with her. I found him under the bed," I answered.

Platt looked at me like I'd taken a couple of laps 'round the crazy bush. "What the hell's she talking about?"

Kennedy pointed at Tenchi's still form. "Make sure he doesn't go in the bedroom." Then he strolled in, earning a long-suffering huff from Platt.

I followed somewhat reluctantly.

Kennedy walked around the bed. "Where is it?"

I motioned toward the open door to the balcony. "It went over the railing."

"All by itself?" Platt chuckled, but it wasn't a nice sound. "Next you'll be telling us it didn't commit suicide either."

"Of course not." I couldn't keep the annoyance out of my voice. "I dropped it…by accident."

Kennedy went out onto the balcony. I couldn't see all of him, just part of one leg, but I figured he was looking down at Trinity. When he came back in, his expression was a little starker, a little more worn around the edges. He started barking out commands at Platt and the two other uniformed officers he'd arrived with. Then he gripped my elbow, leading me back into the living room. Tenchi was still lying in a heap on the carpet.

Kennedy pushed me onto a couch and sat down next to me. He took out a notebook much like the one Alex had. "Okay, Azalea, I want you to tell me everything that happened, everything you can remember. Try to be as detailed as possible. All right?"

I nodded, twisting my fingers in my lap. It took some effort, but I told him everything that had happened since I'd seen him at the convention center, stumbling a little when I got to the part about finding Trinity.

I hadn't noticed Platt had taken up a station near the front door and was listening to everything I said. "That's the best story I've heard in a *long* time."

"It's not a story—it's the truth." I didn't bother to hide what a loathsome toad I thought Platt was.

"Your girlfriend's got fire," he teased Kennedy.

"I'm not his girlfriend, you tremendous ass."

"Wish I had a suspect with a rack like yours throw herself at me." Peeling himself off the wall, Platt shook his head. "But then I don't have Kennedy's looks or connections."

"Shut up, Platt. Go find out what's taking the crime scene team so long." Kennedy's patience for Platt was finally beginning to show cracks.

"Sure. Whatever you say, *Detective*."

Kennedy's gaze stayed on Platt's retreating form until he disappeared through the door. A random mix of anger, annoyance, guilt, and determination played across his face.

"What's going to happen now?" I asked, trying not to identify with how he felt.

"Now we're going to process the scene. I'm going to need you to come in later to give a formal statement." He jerked his head in Tenchi's direction. "Are you going to press kidnapping charges against him?"

I hadn't thought of that. I supposed I should, but there just didn't seem any point to it. Tenchi looked so stupid lying on the floor, his blond pageboy as perfect as ever.

"I just want my cell phone back," I answered.

Kennedy bent down and rummaged through Tenchi's pockets, coming up with my phone, the knife, and Tenchi's wallet. He handed me my phone.

"Should we throw water on him or something?" I asked.

"Nah, he'll come around." He stood and came over next to me. Moments ticked by where all he did was look at me, his watchful gaze taking in and cataloging everything about me. "Are you all right?"

I glanced at the bedroom doorway. "Not really, but I'll be okay." It seemed that even in death, Trinity needed someone to look out for her. Who was left to do it? "Does Trinity have any other family? I mean, who will take care of the, ah, arrangements?"

"I didn't come across any other family. The sister-in-law was all she had left."

"Will you let me know if there'll be a service or something?"

"Sure." He shoved his hands deep in his pockets, regarding me with a frown.

It was the wrong place and time, but I had to know. "Why did you manipulate me like that? I was cooperating, telling you everything you wanted to know. You didn't have to do that to me."

"I know. I—"

"Another one, Eamon?" A man with the rigid back of a soldier strode into the room, his green eyes sharp in his creased face, his white hair a little rusted on top.

Kennedy spun away from me and approached the man. The

pair exchanged a brief handshake that looked like it hurt.

Eamon?

"Yes, sir. The victim went over the balcony, landing on the roof of the hotel entrance. Would you like to see?"

The other man shook him off. "I've seen all the death I ever want to see till my own." He braced his feet and put his arms behind his back. "What have you got?"

"Possible suicide, although the witness"—Kennedy gestured toward me—"has given a statement that puts that in question."

The man noticed me for the first time. "Death is a terrible thing," he said to me. "Especially when it comes too soon." He held out a hand. "Chief Seamus Kennedy."

As I stood and placed my hand in the chief's, I gave Kennedy a questioning look. "Azalea March," I answered in return.

"Azalea. That a family name?"

"Something like that."

"I had an aunt named Heaven." The chief rubbed his chin, thinking. "Come to think of it, all of her siblings had unusual names. Orion, Calypso, Atlas." He smiled, and it was then that I could really see the resemblance. "Her ma'am fancied herself a bit of an astronomer, I suppose. Sweet lady."

Platt came in and spotted the chief. He gave King Kennedy such a hateful look, it was a good thing his back was turned. "Chief." Platt ambled over and put out his hand. "A pleasure to see you, sir."

"I don't think it's so pleasurable for Ms. March." The chief nodded toward the bedroom. "Or for that poor child in there."

Platt turned red. Adjusting his belt, he tried to backpedal. "Well, no, sir. I didn't mean it like that. We so rarely have the pleasure of your presence is all."

The chief clapped Platt on the arm. "Don't let me keep you from your duties, son."

I think I liked the chief. I think I liked him a lot.

"No, sir." Platt backed up toward the bedroom. "Not at all. Just making pleasantries. Thank you, sir."

Tenchi started to come around just then, making moaning noises.

"Sweet Mary and Joseph." The chief put a hand to his chest. "What is that?"

"My other witness," Kennedy answered, like he knew he was going to get majorly teased about this one.

"Just when I thought I'd seen everything," the chief muttered, scratching the tufts of his graying red hair.

Looking down at Tenchi, I felt kind of sorry for him. Not for the first time, I wondered what his relationship was to Trinity. Friends? Lovers?

Eww. Now I was picturing it.

Tenchi opened his eyes and blinked up at the three of us bent over him. "What happened?"

"You fainted," I answered.

I could see it all come back to him one link at a time. "Trinity." Her name sounded as if it had been ripped from his soul.

He leaped up, knocking us back. Then before we thought to move, he dashed to the bedroom. We ran after him, colliding in the doorway. Shouts rang out from the bedroom and there were grunts like scuffling. Kennedy muscled his way in front of us, pushing me into the chief.

The chief caught me. "Pardon me, miss."

Two uniformed officers came out, carrying a struggling Tenchi by both arms.

"We caught him just in time," the larger of the two officers said.

Kennedy followed close behind. "Take him in. I'm not sure how he fits into all this, but he's definitely involved. Better put him on suicide watch, too."

"Yes, sir," the other officer answered.

I watched them haul Tenchi out, which was not easy, as he'd gone completely limp, sobbing uncontrollably. Every couple of steps he threw himself backward, reaching a hand back and hollering Trinity's name. Streaks of black makeup ran down his face, making him look like he'd been attacked with a marker.

"Idiot tried to throw himself off the balcony," Kennedy said to no one in particular.

"Poor…" The chief looked like he was trying to solve a riddle. "Child."

"I think he's a man," Kennedy offered.

"He is," I said.

Kennedy turned to me as if he'd forgotten I was there. "Why don't you go back to your hotel, get some rest."

"Yeah, sure. Okay." I headed for the door, then turned back. "Call me if you hear anything, you know, about her service."

Kennedy looked like he'd say more if his father wasn't in the room, but instead he only nodded.

The hall was quiet and, for me, filled with ghosts. I couldn't wait to get out of there. But a noise coming from one of the nearby suites snagged my attention like a comb in knotted hair. I stopped and backed up a step. Suite thirty-eight forty-eight. Dhane's suite. I stood bracketed between the two doors, Trinity's and Dhane's. Being so close to where Dhane died gave me the sensation of spiders crawling up the back of my neck. I shivered.

There was the noise again. It sounded like…like moaning.

I leaned toward Dhane's door, afraid to get too close and be sucked into an alternate universe or something.

Mumbling, then a low, throaty groan. I sidestepped closer. It sounded like…like someone might be hurt.

I slid one foot closer, then the other, and pressed my ear to the door. My superdetective skills were really improving.

Something banged against the door. I jumped back. More low noises and then the moans turned to whimpers. I tiptoed back to the door and listened again.

It sounded like…like…sex! Ewww.

Who would have sex in the suite where a man had died? And right next to the door, too? I shuddered, trying to shake off the creepy-crawlies. I was half tempted to hide and wait to find out who it was. But what if it took hours? And the hotel could have filled the room with new guests. It might not even be anyone I knew. I considered listening again, but pathetically I was kind of jealous, which was annoying. And sad.

That was it. My life officially sucked. Jealous of two people having sex in a room I wouldn't be caught…better amend that. Jealous of two people having sex in a room I wouldn't enter if you handed me the formula for Hjálmar's new miracle product.

Hjálmar's new product.

Of course! I could almost hear the lightbulb in my head ping. If my instincts were right, there was more going on here than anime freaks and sex in a death suite.

A whole lot more.

I really needed to talk to Vivian and Juan Carlos. Right now.

Chapter Sixteen

On my way back to our hotel, I called Juan Carlos and told him to meet me at Vivian's room. It wasn't three o'clock yet, but I didn't care. We needed to talk. Now.

I knocked on Viv's hotel-room door. I could hardly control the anger mixed with joy, and the overriding sense of relief that she was safe. I'd held on by a thread, and now here I was, just feet away from her.

She answered the door wearing a thick terry-cloth hotel robe, her wet hair combed back from her face.

Anger pushed its way forward first. "We need to talk." I barged right past her into the room.

"Hello to you, too."

"I need you to tell me everything. No more lies, no more half-truths. Start from when you first met Dhane." I waved a shaky hand. "Go."

Vivian adjusted the lapels of her robe. "Can I get dressed first?"

"Talk and dress. We don't have much time, and you've already wasted so much of it."

"You're mad."

Hell, yes, I was mad—furious. I was caught between wanting to shake her until she felt half the panic and fear I'd been carrying around and hugging her hard enough to leave my imprint on her. I settled for sarcastic. It was what I did best. "Really? Ya think? Why ever would I be mad, Viv?"

She pulled some clothes from her suitcase, avoiding my gaze. "I shouldn't have lied, it's just…" She dropped down on the edge of the bed, her head bent toward the shirt she twisted in her hands. "I made a promise. And as usual, you asked too many questions."

"Nuh-uh, this one's on you. You're not blaming me for what's happened here. And it doesn't matter anyway, I already know Dhane's real name. I know about his parents and the fire, Trinity, all of it."

She looked up at me, surprised.

I folded my arms over my chest. "The police know about it, too."

"I guess they would." She got up and started to dress. "If you know that much, then you should probably know the rest."

James came out of the bathroom with nothing but a towel on. "Oh, shoot!" He immediately ducked back inside.

"Nice chest, James," I shouted.

"Hang on, let me get him some clothes." Vivian pulled a few items from another bag and gave them to James.

As she made her way back, relief slammed into me. I dove for her, wrapping my arms around her tightly. "You scared the crap out of me." My voice cracked and tears stung the backs of my eyes.

She hugged me just as hard. "I'm sorry," she whispered in my ear. "I'm so, so sorry."

Bending over her, I tucked my face into her neck. We'd always been close. Closer than I'd ever been to my own sister. "How could you lie to me?" I pulled back to look at her. "Why, Viv?"

She drew me over to the bed. We sat with our bodies angled toward each other. It was the first time she'd met my gaze since she'd told us that stupid story of how she and Dhane met. My chest hitched on a half sob.

"I missed you," I said.

She squeezed my hand. "I missed you, too. I'm sorry you had to see me hauled away like that."

"What happened? Why'd you confess?"

"You need to hear this from the beginning." She grabbed her pencil skirt and stood to zip it up. "Let's start with the night of the fire. Dhane was supposed to have been home that night, but he was out with me. When he got home, he found the house burned to the ground and his family gone. He didn't know what had happened. The next day he went back to the house. The police were there, and that's when they told him about his parents and their suspicions that Trinity may have started the fire."

"Why did they suspect Trinity?"

She pulled her arms through a black polka-dot blouse and buttoned it. "Trinity was...troubled. She'd been expelled from school and was in and out of juvenile hall—you know, rebellious teen stuff. I think they suspected her at first because she was the only one who'd escaped the fire. When the firemen arrived, they found her sitting on the curb two houses away, petting and talking to a stuffed skunk."

"Curio."

"You really do know everything, don't you?" she asked.

"No. I don't know why you confessed to a murder you didn't commit."

She tipped her head to the side. "First, tell me how Trinity's doing. Is she okay? Is Mac taking care of her?"

"Mac?"

James came out of the bathroom. "Is everything all right here?"

"Why don't you go down and get us something to eat? I'm starving," Vivian said.

I waited while they said their good-byes before I pelted her with all of the questions backing up in my brain. "By Mac do you mean MacKenzie Todd?"

"Yes, of course."

"What do you mean 'of course'?"

"Mac is Trinity's cousin."

"Trinity's but not Dhane's?"

"Dhane's father married Trinity's mother. Mac's and Trinity's mothers were sisters. Trinity and Mac have always been close—that's why she flew to Vegas as soon as she heard about Dhane. To be with Trinity."

"You mean Mac wasn't here when Dhane was killed?"

"No. Why?"

I took Mac out of the equation, and some of the pieces of this puzzle started to slide into place for me.

I hated to do it after all Viv had been through, but she had to know. "I need to tell you something about Trinity."

"What?"

"I'm so sorry… She's dead."

Viv's hand went to her mouth and her breath caught. "How? What happened?" She looked up at me, and I could see my reflection swimming in her brown eyes.

I took a breath to tell her this next part. "She was either pushed or thrown over the balcony of her hotel suite."

Viv didn't move. She just stared at me. "No."

"The police think it was suicide. But I'm not so sure." I told her about the state of Trinity's room and finding Curio under the bed.

"I failed him." She sounded so defeated, it made my chest hurt. "Dhane made me promise years ago that if anything ever happened to him, I was supposed to make sure Trinity was okay. He only ever asked one thing of me and I failed." The despair in her voice nearly cut me in two.

"How could you know?"

She got up and moved a couple of paces away. "Doesn't matter. I failed just the same."

"Stop it. This isn't like you. Would Dhane let you beat yourself up like this?"

"No."

"Then don't."

Some of the snap was back in her spine and her eyes were dry as she turned toward me. "Trinity wouldn't go anywhere without Curio. Somebody murdered her just like Dhane. But why?"

"Why did you confess to Dhane's murder?"

"I thought Trinity had killed Dhane. I was trying to protect her."

I called for a time-out. "Wait a minute. What made you think Trinity had killed Dhane?"

Juan Carlos banged on the door. "It's me, open up!"

I let in him and Richard. After Juan Carlos embraced Vivian about forty times and checked her for lice twice, he finally settled down enough for me to quickly catch them up to speed.

"Holy tragic family!" Juan Carlos paced the short hallway from the front door to the edge of the bed. "Poor, poor Skunk Girl." He stopped and looked at us. "Do you think they'll bury her with the skunk?"

"I don't know," I said. "Can we get back to why Viv confessed to Dhane's murder?"

"Oh, this *better* be good." Juan Carlos sat down in the desk chair and took up his I'm-listening pose with his legs crossed, an elbow on one knee, and his chin propped in the palm of his hand. "'Cause if it isn't, I may have to smack you."

Richard sat in the corner chair, silent as always. His presence was oddly comforting, like having our own private Buckingham Palace guard.

"Start from the beginning," I told Viv. "What made you go to

Dhane's suite and what did you find when you got there?"

"I'm glad James isn't here. He doesn't know about this part, so please don't say anything."

We all agreed we'd keep quiet, but I wasn't so sure it was a good idea to leave James in the dark. Somehow, some way, secrets never stayed secret. Just like Vivian's and Dhane's past with each other—oftentimes the keeping is worse than the secret itself. Once broken, trust was a difficult thing to earn back.

"Right after you left to go to your workshops, Dhane called and invited me up to his suite. He said he'd have a key delivered to me."

The key Jun gave me by mistake.

"The key never came, but I didn't care. I had to see him. I knew what he wanted and I went anyway," Viv said. "You have to understand, our pull was stronger than my ability to resist." She paused as if caught in the web of a memory.

I knew that look. I'd had that look. Seeing it on Vivian now instantly swept me away to a time not so long ago, when I'd felt that kind of deep gravitational pull toward Alex, more basic, more necessary than the need for breath.

Richard cleared his throat, shaking Juan Carlos, Vivian, and me out of our daydreams.

"I went to see him," Vivian continued. "When I got to his suite, the door was slightly ajar. I thought he'd left it that way for me, so I went in." She put a fist over her mouth and sniffed, her eyes filling with tears again.

I slid closer and put an arm around her. I hated that she would suffer through this next part, but it was important. I squeezed her shoulder in support.

"At first I didn't see him," she said. "I called his name, but there was no answer. Then I heard a noise coming from the bedroom. I thought maybe he was on the phone or getting dressed. I waited, but he didn't come out, so I went in. All I could see was his feet.

He was on the floor on the other side of the bed. I thought he'd fainted. And then…and then…"

I wrapped my other arm around her and she laid her head on my shoulder, her tears flowing freely now.

"I went to him, calling his name. Trinity suddenly stood up. Her hands were covered with his blood. I hadn't expected to see her. I hadn't expected all that blood. When I got around to the other side of the bed and saw…" Vivian turned in to me, clutching at my shirt.

"It's okay. You don't have to tell us what you saw. Sshh," I told her, rubbing her back, feeling completely inadequate.

"I almost didn't go in," she sobbed. "I thought about James and I got scared. I almost left. I should've left."

Juan Carlos joined us, hugging her from the other side. Crouching down in front of us, Richard put his hand on Viv's knee. He squeezed it in silent support and offered Viv a wad of tissues.

I hated to do it, but I had to press her. "What happened next, Viv?"

Blotting her eyes, she sniffed and straightened away from us. Even in her grief I could tell that she still had the resolve to want to help. "I thought Trinity had done it. At first she just stood there, her hands soaked, her eyes wild and crazy. You have to understand." Viv wiped her eyes. "After the fire Trinity was never the same. Whatever happened in the house that night totally took her over the edge. She was never right after that, unpredictable and sometimes violent.

"So when I saw her and Dhane and all that blood, I was afraid. I called the police and that's when Trinity flipped out. She started running around smearing the blood from her hands on everything. She was frantic. It was like the blood burned her or something. That's when I noticed Curio on the floor. I picked him up and gave him to Trinity. She immediately calmed down."

"So you confessed because of a years-old promise to protect

Trinity?" I asked. "Wouldn't it be better if she got the help she needed?"

"I wasn't thinking. I told her to go back to her suite and wash up. When the police got there, I told them I did it. Later, when they started asking me questions, I realized that Trinity couldn't have done it."

"The head." Juan Carlos shuddered.

"Yes, exactly," Vivian said. "She couldn't have done it for the same reasons I couldn't have, but by then it was too late. I'd confessed."

"Where does Sora fit into all this?" I asked. "I can kind of get why you would go and see Dhane, but I've never known you to look twice at a married man."

Viv tilted her head to one side. "What are you talking about?"

Richard, Juan Carlos, and I exchanged looks.

Viv looked around at each of us. "What is she talking about? Dhane wasn't married."

We all moved back a little, knowing what would come next.

"Um, he was. And, ah, I met her." I braced myself for the explosion.

"No, he wasn't," she insisted.

"Honey, pookie, lovey bear," Juan Carlos crooned, stroking her hair. "I'm so sorry, but he was. His little wifey spoke at his memorial. We were all there."

Vivian looked with narrowed eyes to Richard for further confirmation. Richard gulped and rubbed his palms on his thighs. Vivian could be terribly frightening for a pint-size pinup.

Richard nodded and Viv exploded off the bed, waving her arms around and shouting in Spanish at no one in particular. I was pretty sure most of what she said would result in a lot of confessing and Hail Marys for her later.

I looked to Juan Carlos for help, but he just shrugged. "You know I don't speak Spanish."

Neither did Viv really, but she knew *all* the swears and more gutter talk than a corner drug dealer. One of the few benefits of having two older brothers.

"I can't believe that *tramposo*! What was he doing calling me in when he had a wife? *Que un pendejo!*"

"I understood *that*," Juan Carlos said. "Hey, maybe the wife found out about you and gave old two-timing Dhane the ax." When he realized what he'd said, Juan Carlos backpedaled. "Oh my God. I'm so sorry." He drew a line across his throat. "I didn't mean she gave him the ax, ax. I just meant maybe she…I'm making it worse, aren't I?"

"Now would be a good time to shut up," Richard said.

"No, wait. He's right," I said. "If Dhane had a tendency to cheat and his wife got wind of it, that's a *real* strong motive. She could've been the one who killed him."

Viv got right up in my face—well, as much as she could, being about six inches shorter than me. She was such a shrimp without her high heels on. "Where's this wife? I want to meet her."

I thought about the sex I'd overheard in Dhane's suite. Who else could it be? "Ah, she might be busy."

Viv propped her hands on her hips. "What do you mean *busy*?"

"Whoa, ho, ho! Azalea knows something. Look at her blush. Come on, out with it, Zee," Juan Carlos said.

"I don't actually know anything, not really."

"You may as well tell them," Richard said. "They're not going to give up until you do."

He was right. There was no getting out of this one. "All right. I'll tell you what I *think*. These are not facts, just a lot of conjecture and gossiping on my part."

Juan Carlos clapped his hands. "I love gossip and conjecture!"

I told them about when I'd first met Sora in Trinity's suite and the way Ace had looked and acted around her. Then I told them about what I'd noticed at the memorial service. "If Sora isn't having an affair with Ace, it wouldn't be for lack of devotion on his part."

"That is just plain nasty. A man died. His ghost could be watching. Oh my God! If she got pregnant, I bet the baby would be cursed. You know, like that movie…" Juan Carlos snapped his fingers. "What was that movie?"

"I have no idea," Richard said.

"What the hell kind of name is Sora?" Vivian asked.

Juan Carlos tisked. "Easy, Jealous Jezebel. Tramps in glass houses shouldn't throw cheater stones."

"For that matter, Ace could have a very strong motive for killing Dhane," I said, thinking out loud. "Maybe he got tired of waiting for her to leave the marriage. Or, if they were having an affair, maybe he was tired of being second string and he wanted her all for himself."

"Yeah, but why would he kill Trinity?" Richard asked.

"Oh, I didn't think of that."

Conversation went on around me, but my head was so full of whys and what-ifs, I wasn't paying any attention. Who had both motive and opportunity to kill Dhane *and* Trinity?

Sora could have killed Dhane to get out of the marriage, but why kill Trinity? Ace could have done it to clear his path to Sora, but again, why kill Trinity? She wasn't a threat to anyone as far as I could tell.

Unless…

The new product the company had been developing would make millions for the owners. Dhane's death would've put a halt to any sale that had been in the works. I'd taken Mac out of the equation for the simple fact that she wasn't even in the state when Dhane died. But what if she'd hired someone to do it for her? Jerk and Shorty seemed like the kind of guys you'd hire to kill someone. There was only one catch… Why kill Trinity? No, it had to be someone who would gain from killing both Dhane and

Trinity.

So then who had the most to gain from the two siblings' deaths?

Either Ace or Sora could've killed Trinity or the both of them working together. Maybe they thought Trinity would inherit the company before Sora, depending on how Dhane's will read. Plus, that would leave them free to continue their romance out in the open. Mac wasn't listed in the corporation documents as a partner or even an officer in the company, but Dhane could have listed her as his beneficiary of the company.

Now all I needed to prove or disprove either of my theories was a copy of Dhane's will. Not an easy thing to get a hold of for sure.

This whole thing kept turning circles on itself. Just when I thought I might have a handle on what was going on, something happened to turn me in another direction. One thing I knew for sure: Dhane and Trinity hadn't deserved to die. Whoever killed them would likely kill again to get what they wanted.

I only hoped they wouldn't feel like they had to.

Chapter Seventeen

I took out my sparkly notebook and entered the new information along with my thoughts and guesses. There was a lot going on here. And it all made me so sad. Two lives had been lost, and for what?

I guessed that was the million-dollar question. If I figured out the *why* and *what for,* then I imagined the *who* would be as plain as day. On TV they were always talking about motive, means, and opportunity. When they went to court they often got a conviction because they could prove one or more of those things. So that was my new plan. I was going to go all *Law & Order* on this case.

To do that, I needed a lot more information from a lot more people. And I knew just where to start.

"Juan Carlos, did you and Richard get a chance to speak to Golda, the hairstylist, yet?"

"We did, but she wouldn't talk at the memorial. She gave me her number, which I was just about to call when you phoned and told me to meet you here."

"Call her. She, better than anyone, would know what was going on in Dhane's personal life. She might even know something more about how the company was run and what was happening there."

"You're still going to investigate?" Vivian asked.

All eyes fell on me, waiting for my answer. I'd been all in with this thing from the beginning. Vivian being released wouldn't change that. Whether I wanted to or not, I felt connected to Dhane's and Trinity's deaths. The note from Dhane, being there when his head had been found, visiting Trinity, finding her body—each of those events had pulled me further and further into this mess. There had to be a reason for that, right?

Vivian was free, but saving her hadn't been the only reason I'd gotten involved. And now my ragtag band of hairstylists turned detectives and I were the only ones who believed Trinity's death wasn't suicide. The thought of someone killing that poor girl and getting away with it punched all of my injustice buttons. I couldn't stand by and let her death go unavenged.

Plus, I wasn't 100 percent sold on the idea of Sora and Ace as killers. They just didn't seem...I don't know...smart enough to have pulled off two murders. Their bow-chica-wow-wow session in Dhane's suite pretty much proved it. Plus, if they'd been trying to hide their affair, they were really, really bad at it. I doubted they could pull off fooling the police.

"Yes." I punctuated my answer with a sharp nod. "With your help."

"Yay! I am so buying that fedora I saw in the gift shop downstairs," Juan Carlos said, clapping his palms together. "Very Sam Spade. We'll go all *Castle* on this case." He folded his fingers down, making a gun with his index fingers. "Book 'em, Charlie."

"You're mixing your TV shows," Richard told Juan Carlos. "Of course we'll help you, Azalea. Whatever you need."

"Thank you," I said.

"What about me?" Vivian asked.

James returned, letting himself into the room, his arms loaded with bags of food. He stopped when he saw the crowd that had accumulated in his absence. "What's going on here?"

"I think you're going to be too busy to help," I said with a wink. "But we'll let you know if we need anything."

James sought out Vivian, and when he spotted her pale, tear-streaked face, he lost it. "Out! Everybody out right now." He set the food aside and went to Vivian, crouching down on one knee. "Are you all right?"

She reached out a hand and stroked the side of his face. "I'm fine."

Watching them, my stomach twisted. They were so perfect for each other. Vivian keeping secrets from James was not right. I knew she was afraid of what would happen if she told him about her and Dhane, but keeping it from him had to be worse for them.

I showed Juan Carlos and Richard the hole in my shirt. "I have to do something about my clothes. Why don't you guys go back to Juan Carlos's room and I'll catch up with you in a bit?"

When the guys were gone, I asked for a moment alone with Vivian. James looked like he'd argue, but Viv put him at ease. "It's okay. I'll just be a moment. Why don't you get the food ready? I'm starved."

Vivian followed me to the door and we stepped out into the hall.

"Does James know about you and Dhane?"

"Just that we were friends. I couldn't—"

"Vivian…" I couldn't keep the surprise and disappointment from my voice.

"You don't understand—"

"No, *you* don't understand. That man loves you."

"I know he does."

"Vivian, secrets have a cost. And although I forgive you for lying to Juan Carlos and me, I have to tell you it hurt. You can't lie to people and always expect them to understand later why you felt you had to. You either have a trusting relationship or you don't."

"I don't like lying. I especially hated lying to you and Juan

Carlos. That's not who I am."

"I know it's not, but you still have to tell James about Dhane."

She looked for a moment like she'd argue further. "I really am sorry I lied to you."

"I know."

She dropped her head back and sighed. "This is going to be hard."

"I know."

"You're such a bitch, you know that?" she said with a wry twist to her mouth and no real heat. "I hate you." She gave me a hard hug and it felt so good, like we were finally getting back to where we'd been before Vegas. "Especially when you're right," she whispered in my ear. When she pulled back, her eyes were filled with tears. "I really am sorry. About everything. I had no idea it would lead to all of this."

"I know." I wiped the tear that had slipped down her cheek with the backs of my fingers. "Stop crying, or James is going to hunt me down and make *me* cry."

We laughed, and the link that had been missing between us slid back together. She gave me a small wave and went back into her room. Alone in the hall, I smiled. It was good to have Vivian back. As I walked to my room, I thought about the things that brought people together and the things that kept them apart.

What had brought Tenchi and Trinity together? On the outside they were more mismatched than Donald Trump and his horrible hair. But the opposite was true of Sora and Dhane. On the outside they'd seem like a perfect match and must have made a stunning couple. So what had made them seek out others? What had made Dhane go after Vivian and Sora give in to Ace?

Jun was my only link to Trinity, and although his information hadn't been all that accurate, he did seem to have an in with Tenchi, Trinity, Sora, and Ace. He might know more about Sora's relationship with both Dhane *and* Ace. But then again, he might start talking in circles and give me a headache.

I also needed to touch base with Alex. There was something nagging at me about the fire and Dhane's parents' deaths. Every version of the story I'd read or heard was completely different from the others. I needed to find out if Alex had connected with the detective who investigated the murders and what his account of events would add to or take away from what I already knew.

I slid my key card in the lock and opened the door to my room. As if conjured from my imagination, Alex sat at the desk, talking on the phone. He motioned for me to come closer, then put his cell phone on speaker so I could listen in.

"—the sister, but there wasn't enough to charge her," a sexy female voice said. If this was the detective from Kansas, she was wasting her time on police work. She could have made a fortune as a phone-sex operator.

"Was she your only suspect?" Alex asked her.

"We looked hard at the brother, but his alibi was solid. We also looked at a murder-suicide, but the evidence didn't support it."

I pulled out my notebook, wrote Alex a note, and handed it to him. He raised his brows at me. I motioned for him to ask her my question.

"Do you know what happened to the brother and sister?" he asked.

"The brother was of age, so the court awarded him custody of his sister. I do know they came into some money. Quite a bit actually, which is why we looked so hard at them. Money can be a powerful motivator for murder."

I wrote another note and showed it to him.

"Was the case ever solved?" Alex asked for me.

"A few weeks later we caught the guys who'd set that fire and a few others in nearby neighborhoods. B and E guys who thought setting fire to houses would cover their tracks. They might have gotten away with it if they hadn't pawned the goods they stole so close to home. Thank God for dumb criminals."

Alex chuckled under his breath. "I've caught a few like that myself." He raised his brows at me, silently asking if I had any more questions. I shook my head.

So the fire was a dead end. I didn't know what I'd hoped it would tell me about Dhane's and Trinity's deaths, but I did have a lot more insight into their past. It was interesting that they'd come into some money. That must've been how Dhane had started his company. He obviously hadn't gotten enough to go it alone and had to bring in Mac as a partner. What else had Mac brought to the table?

"Thank you for your time, Detective Leary," Alex said. "Hold on to my number so I can return the favor sometime."

"You got it."

Alex disconnected the call and turned to me, looking a little irritated and a lot relieved. "Where have you been? I called you at least twenty times."

I checked my phone. "Tenchi must have turned it off when I was with Trinity. Sorry."

"You went to see the crazy sister again?"

"I didn't set out to."

"What does that mean?"

I told him all of my misadventures since I'd last seen him. The more I talked, the darker his expression turned, like a low-slung storm moving over an open ocean.

"That's it. We're going home."

"You can go, but I'm staying. Your half of the room for last night should be about fifty bucks."

"You're going, too."

I parked my fists on my hips. I was really tired of people, especially men, telling me what to do today. "Go. Stay. I don't care, but I'm seeing this thing through."

He stood up, matching my attitude. "The hell you are."

"Who do you think you are telling me what to do?"

He leaned down until we were nose to nose. "Your friend. No, boyfriend." He shook his head and growled, "I don't know what the hell I am to you."

"What the hell do you want to be?"

"More."

"How much more?"

"More than you're letting me be."

We stared bullets at each other, our breath mingling. I inched closer, pressing for an advantage. He moved in too, our bodies so close now I could smell him and feel his heat.

"Azalea?" he whispered, causing fine shivers to race up my spine.

Short of breath, I licked my lips. "Yeah?"

"I want to kiss you."

"Why aren't you?"

He came at it slowly. And oh, sweet Jesus, he was good at it, taking his time as if he'd thought long and hard how he'd do it when he next got the chance. He pulled me up to sit on the desk and changed his angle, his lips soft and coaxing. I wrapped myself around him, shamelessly encouraging him to take whatever he wanted. I let down my defenses. It felt so good to be held and taken care of. Emboldened, I brought him closer, threading my hands through his hair. It was thicker and silkier than I'd imagined.

Somebody banged on the door, startling us apart. "Azalea! Open up."

Alex put his forehead to mine. "Can I kill him? I brought my gun."

I pushed him back and wriggled off the desk. "You can have your shot after I get mine." I padded to the door and opened it to find Juan Carlos with Golda, the hairstylist, and Richard.

"You'll never believe it, but Golda is staying right here in our hotel! Isn't that the most?"

"At least." I motioned them in. "Come on in. It's not like Alex and I were doing anything *fun*."

"I told you we should have called first," Richard said.

Juan Carlos put an arm around Golda. "Golda is the genius behind last year's Hjálmar campaign. You remember the one with the model whose hair color looked like a puddle of gasoline, all black with swirls of rainbow colors running through it?" At my nod he continued, "She's the one who did that color technique. Isn't that fabulous?"

"Totally," I answered. "It's nice to meet you, Golda. I'm Azalea and this is Alex. Thanks for meeting with us."

She checked her watch. "I have an hour before I leave for my flight. You get ten minutes of it." She settled herself on the bed and crossed her legs. "Go."

I pulled the desk chair over and sat across from her. Juan Carlos and Richard sat on the bed behind her and Alex edged a hip on the corner of the desk, his cop face on.

I started. "I'm so sorry about Dhane."

"Yes, it's terrible," she agreed, looking bored.

"Did you work closely with him? I mean, I know you were his hairstylist and you worked on last year's campaign—"

"This year's, too," she interrupted. "Just tell me what you want to know."

"Right." I was having a hard time getting a read on this woman and it put me off my game. "Can you tell me about Dhane's personal life, specifically his marriage?"

She let out a laugh like she'd heard a bad joke. "Such as it was."

"What do you mean by that?"

"I mean Sora is a conniving bitch who would sell her mother if it meant cash in her pocket."

"So theirs wasn't a love match, I take it?"

"Oh there was love—all on Dhane's part, at least in the beginning."

"What happened to change that?"

Golda cracked a smile that was far from nice. "He caught her flat on her back, feet in the air with that boy toy between her legs. That kind of thing tends to make a man fall out of love *real* fast."

That was the kind of thing that makes a woman fall out of love real fast, too, as I knew all too well. I'd caught my now ex-fiancé taking his lunch break between my assistant's thighs. That wasn't an image you could ever get out of your head. Alex had been the first guy I'd gone out with since that two-timing asshole, and as much as I wanted to unconditionally trust him, I was having a hard time believing his interest in me. Or maybe that was my insecurity cloaking itself in the protective blanket of that-rotten-jerk-cheated-so-all-men-are-untrustworthy.

"What did Dhane do?" I asked.

"Filed for divorce, but then she somehow talked him out of following through. I imagine she had to spend some more time on her back to bring him around to it. Or at the very least on her knees." She pulled a silver case from her purse. "Can I smoke in here?"

"This is a no-smoking room. Sorry."

She shoved the case back in her bag. "Figures."

"What about MacKenzie Todd?"

"What about her?"

"What was her and Dhane's relationship like? Were they close?" I asked.

"Now there's a piece of work. Were they close? As close as two people could be without banging each other."

"I'd heard she and Dhane were cousins."

"That would be news to me." She pulled the cigarette case out again. "Are you sure we can't just crack a window?"

"I think there's a fine or something."

"How did *you* feel about Dhane?" Alex asked, earning all of our attention.

She hitched a shoulder. "Depended on the day."

"What about the day he died?"

I could see where Alex was going with his questions. Something was off with Golda's demeanor toward Dhane's passing. Frankly, I was glad *he* was asking these questions and not me.

"He was in a good mood," Golda answered. "So that day I liked him."

"What was your real relationship with Dhane?"

Golda's brows dipped over her nose. "What do you mean? I already told you. I was his hairstylist and we worked together."

"Was that all?" Alex asked. "Or was there more between the two of you than that?"

Golda's gaze darted toward the door. "I don't know what you mean."

"No? Weren't you lovers?"

What? All four of our heads swiveled toward Alex.

"Lovers?" She gave a weak chuckle, her confidence waning. "Dhane and me?"

Alex looked at her hard, his cop eyes flat and unyielding. I wasn't even the recipient of that look and I already wanted to give up every single one of my secrets.

Golda shifted her shoulders. "Maybe once."

Whoa. Alex was good.

"Once? As in one time? Or would it be more accurate to say you and Dhane had been lovers for a number of years?"

"It was once. One time. Okay?" Golda looked like she could really use that cigarette now.

"Where were you when Dhane was killed?"

"What are you, a cop or something?" She popped up off the bed. "I answered your questions. The ten minutes are up. I'm leaving."

I leaped into her path. "Wait, please don't leave. I have just one more question. Please, just one more."

She looked like she didn't want to, but she nodded for me to go ahead and ask anyway.

"Who would inherit the company now that Dhane and Trinity are gone?"

She blinked, which was hard for her with her hair pulled back so tight. "What do you mean Trinity is *gone*?"

Uh-oh. Me and my big mouth. "Trinity died this morning."

"Died? How? How is that possible?" Golda seemed genuinely shocked to learn of Trinity's passing.

"The, ah, police found her body on the roof of the entrance to her hotel. She'd been thrown off her balcony."

"Trinity was *murdered*?"

"Yes, I believe so."

This news seemed to really rattle Golda. She dropped back down onto the bed and stared off at nothing.

"Are you all right?" I asked, sitting down next to her.

"Yes. No. That poor, sick girl." She pulled out her cigarette case and lit one with a shaky hand. No one bothered to stop her. She sucked hard on her cigarette, then let out a long stream of smoke on a sigh. "I suppose that bitch Sora would get it all."

CHAPTER EIGHTEEN

"How did you know Golda had slept with Dhane?" I asked Alex while we waited for Juan Carlos and Richard to return from escorting Golda downstairs to the lobby. She'd been shaken hard by Trinity's death, and I worried she'd accidentally veer into traffic or something.

"I didn't."

"Then what made you ask her that?"

"I knew she had feelings for him that probably weren't returned. It was a guess that he'd taken advantage of her at least once. It's what some powerful men do."

Boy howdy did I know that *way* too well. "Yeah, but how did you *know* her love was unrequited?"

"Perhaps I've had an unrequited love." He pulled his phone out and punched a few buttons.

"You?"

He looked up from his phone, frowning as if disappointed. "I need to make a call." He walked toward the door, stopping when he came even with me. Tilting my chin up, he kissed me, a soft caress. "Is that so hard to believe?" He stroked my chin with the pad of his thumb. "Maybe someday I can stop pining away for someone who hardly knows I exist." He gave me one last kiss, then walked out to make his call.

Mouth hanging open, I turned to watch the door close behind him. My knees gave out and I caught the edge of the bed, nearly tumbling onto the floor. I couldn't have been more stunned by his kiss and declaration than if a whole troupe of anime freaks rode through the room right now on the backs of pink elephants. I knew he was attracted to me but this... Holy freakin' jeebus. I'd had no idea.

I wandered over to the window, trying to squelch the excitement that wanted to bubble up inside me. Touching my forehead to the cool glass, I looked out over the strip.

Heat waves blurred the horizon. Down below, the Las Vegas Strip was alive, people buzzing about like bees on a hive. There was something oddly disquieting about this city in the daytime, like the inside of an amusement-park ride with the lights on. All of the magic was on hold, waiting for nightfall.

I turned away from the window and rubbed my forehead. I needed to stop thinking about Alex and start thinking about something that wouldn't get my hopes up to unreasonable heights. Like why had Trinity wanted to see me? Tenchi had seemed quite desperate for me to visit with her and quite devastated by her death. I wished I'd thought to ask him, but at the time I was too afraid he'd use that knife on more than my shirt.

My shirt! I unsnapped the front of my top and slipped it off, examining the damage up close. It was mendable...barely. I took out my travel sewing kit and went to work on it, thinking all the while about Trinity. Her words about "red" and "dead" kept coming back to me. Something like the red makes dead and dead makes red and then she talked about dead wanting red so dead was red.

It was hard to tell with all the wacky rules and Trinity's odd behavior if she was just speaking gibberish or if she'd really been trying to tell me something. I'd assumed "red" was referring to Vivian's flower, but what if Trinity was talking about Vivian's flower *and* Sora's red hair? And if Dhane was the "dead" she referred to, then substituting their names, she might have been saying Dhane wanted Vivian so Sora killed Dhane.

Or, more likely, I'd caught crazy off her and now my mind was fully infested with it. What was I thinking trying to make sense of her mad ramblings? Although…what if I were right? What if Trinity was trying to give me some kind of message?

Maybe Jun would know.

I tied my thread in a knot and bit it off. I was no Suzie Homemaker, but the tear was repaired and I could wear my shirt again. Slipping my arms into the sleeves, I thought about Jun. Did he know about Trinity yet? I hoped so. I didn't want to have to break that news a third time.

I grabbed my phone and dialed Jun's number. Alex walked into the room just as I closed the last snap on my shirt.

"Who are you calling?"

"Jun."

"Who's Jun?"

I put up a finger to tell Alex to wait as Jun's voice mail picked up. I left him a message, then gave Alex the rundown on Jun's role in this whole mess and why I wanted to talk to him.

"I really think Trinity was trying to tell me something."

"There's nothing you could have done to stop what happened to Trinity, you know."

And didn't he just hit the nail right on the guilt-ridden head. The front part of my brain knew Alex was right, but the back half carried the burden of *what if?* What if I'd understood what she'd been trying to tell me? What if I could have done something to prevent what had happened to her? What if it was my fault she died? What if? What if? What if?

"I know." But I didn't, not really.

"I'm going to let you in on a little secret. Right now Kennedy and every other cop on this case is wondering if there was something he or she could have done to prevent Trinity's death. Hell, I'm wondering if I'd gotten here sooner, gotten involved earlier, if *I* could have prevented her death. And we're professionals. There's nothing you could have or shouldn't have done that caused this." He laid his hand on my shoulder. "Do you believe me?"

"Yes." *No*.

My cell phone buzzed in my hand. I looked at the screen. "It's Kennedy."

"Put it on speaker."

"Why?"

"I don't entirely trust that guy."

I didn't, either, so I did as Alex suggested. "Hello?"

"Am I on speaker?" Kennedy asked.

"Yes. What do you want?"

"Take me off speaker."

"We either talk on speaker or not at all. What do you want?"

"You need to come down and give a formal statement about Trinity's death."

I looked up at Alex. He nodded.

"All right. When?" I asked.

"Now would be most convenient."

Alex nodded again.

"I'll be there in about twenty minutes." I clicked off without waiting for Kennedy's response. "Well?" I asked Alex. "What do you think?"

"It's procedure, but I wouldn't go in without representation."

"Now you tell me. How in the world am I going to get a lawyer in twenty minutes on a Saturday?"

"Let me make a call."

While Alex talked on the phone, I touched up my makeup. And what a scary mess I was. My crying jag from earlier had washed away most of my mascara and blush. I repaired what I could, adding a nice thick layer of fuchsia lipstick. I did my best with my hair, twisting and pinning it into something resembling a style. Sometime during the day I'd lost my flower. Damn. I really liked that flower.

"I got you a lawyer," Alex said. "She'll meet us at the police station."

"How'd you manage that?"

"An old friend who owes me a favor."

Someone knocked on the door. I exchanged looks with Alex. It wasn't Juan Carlos. He usually beat the door down and shouted my name. I was surprised none of my hotel neighbors had complained yet.

Alex peered through the peephole. He looked back at me with an odd expression on his face. "Are you expecting a singing telegram?"

"A what?"

"Could be a Cirque du Soleil performer."

Jun.

"Let him in."

"Are you sure?" He looked through the peephole again. "He kinda looks like a mime. I hate mimes."

"Oh, for crying out loud." I pulled Alex away from the door and looked through the peephole. "It's Jun." I opened the door to a very sad-faced boy.

"Trinity's dead and they…they locked up Tenchi!" Jun threw himself at me, nearly knocking me over. He clutched me as though he'd drown if he let go, sobbing, like a child with hiccups and too much snot.

I patted his back. "It's okay. It'll be okay." Over Jun's shoulder I gave Alex a help-me look.

Alex grabbed a fistful of Jun's shirt and plucked him off me. "Easy, pal. Here, have a seat." He deposited Jun on the end of the bed.

My heart ached for Jun. He'd lost so much in such a short period of time. I sat down next to him and put my arm around him. "I'm so sorry about your friend."

Jun curled into me like an oversized baby. "Why is everybody dying?"

"I don't know what's happening or why. But you're going to be okay."

Alex bent down to our level. "Hey, buddy. How did you find out about Trinity and Tenchi?"

"W-what?"

"Who told you about what happened to your friends?"

"Oh. Ace." Jun wiped his nose with his sleeve. "He called and told me."

"Do you know how he found out?"

Jun blinked, leaving long black marks from his lashes on his cheeks. "I don't know. Maybe Sora?"

"What did he say when he called you?"

"He said that Trinity had committed suicide and that Tenchi got taken to the hospital because he wanted to kill himself, too... because of Trinity."

"Did he say how Trinity committed suicide?"

Jun tilted his head to the side. "How?"

Alex nodded.

"He said she jumped off her balcony, which doesn't make any sense."

"Why doesn't it make sense?" I asked.

"Curio is afraid of heights."

At Alex's questioning look, I said, "Curio is the stuffed skunk Trinity used to communicate with others." I turned my attention back to Jun. "Did Trinity often say Curio didn't like things that Trinity didn't like, either?"

Jun bobbed his head. "Especially broccoli. Curio really hated broccoli and so did Trinity."

"Was there anything else Curio didn't like?"

Jun thought for a moment. "Raisins."

"Uh-huh. What else? And it doesn't have to be food."

"He didn't like crowds, the color yellow, or having his picture taken. He also hated clear drinks and too much light. Especially sunlight."

Well, that wasn't very helpful. I already knew most of that. I decided to change tactics. "Tell me about Dhane and Sora."

Jun rubbed his nose again. "What about them?"

"What was their marriage like? Were they happy? Had they been married long?"

"They fought sometimes. Dhane could yell very loud."

"What did they fight about?"

"Sometimes Dhane would get mad at Sora for spending too much time with Trinity."

"Why would he get mad about that?"

"I don't know, because one time he got mad at her when she wasn't even with Trinity."

"Oh? Where was she?"

"With Mac."

That threw me off. I had expected him to say Ace.

"When was this?" Alex asked.

"The night before Dhane died. I was there with Trinity, Ace, and Tenchi. We were playing mah-jong. Trinity won like she always does…did." Jun put his head back on my shoulder. "I keep forgetting she's dead."

Alex checked his watch. "We need to get going."

"I know. Hang on." I had one more question. "Jun? When you spoke to Trinity, how did you understand what she was trying to tell you?"

Jun sat up. "That was easy. I listened when she talked to Curio."

"Yes, but how did you have a conversation with her and

Curio?"

Jun angled his head and a crease appeared between his brows. "Same as you and me."

I forgot it was Jun I was talking to. Straight questions wouldn't get me straight answers. "If you were talking to Trinity about Dhane and she said 'dead wanted red so dead is red,' what would that mean?"

"I'm not sure. What was the rest of the conversation?"

I told Jun what I could remember about my visit with Trinity, including Tenchi's reaction afterward.

"Oh," he said.

"What do you mean, 'oh'?"

"It's never good when Trinity is happy…I mean was happy. I keep forgetting."

"Why wasn't it good?"

"Trinity did bad things when she was happy."

"What kind of bad things?" Alex asked.

"One time Tenchi walked in and found her sitting on a shelf in her closet. She'd turned all the furniture in the room upside down and had rolled up the wall-to-wall carpet. Another time she wrote 'gladness' all over her walls. Every inch was covered with the word in big and small print. Just the word 'gladness' over and over.

"And sometimes she'd get obsessed with people, follow them around, steal their stuff." His gaze dropped to his finger picking at the skin next to his thumbnail. "I know she did worse, but Tenchi never wanted to talk about it."

"That is bad." I felt even sorrier for that poor, tragic girl, and I couldn't help but hope she found some measure of peace wherever she was now.

"Red is for sure Sora," Jun said. "That part you said about the red mixing with red and making more red sounds like Sora was doing something that might hurt her."

"What about 'The red makes dead'? What could that mean?"

"Oh, no."

"What?" Alex and I said together.

"I think Trinity might have been giving you a warning."

"About what?"

"I think maybe Sora's in some kind of trouble."

"What kind of trouble?"

Jun squinted his eyes and his mouth moved to one side. "I don't know."

"We really should go," Alex reminded me again.

"Okay." I turned to Jun. "I want to talk to you some more, but I have to take care of something first. Where are you staying?"

"Excalibur, room twenty-six fifteen."

"I'll call you when I'm finished, probably in a couple of hours. Keep your phone on, okay?"

"Okay."

I stood in the hall, watching Jun leave, his steps heavy with the weight of grief. I knew he'd never again be that man-child, so guileless and eager to please. His world had changed with the deaths of his friends. I couldn't help but be sad to see his innocence lost. It was like the pang I got in my chest when my niece confessed to me that she knew there was no Santa Claus. She'd lost a part of her childhood she'd never get back.

"You can't take every puppy home from the pound, you know." Alex said from behind me. I hadn't heard him come out into the hall.

"I know."

He wrapped an arm across my shoulders. "It's a good thing you're a hairstylist and not a cop."

"Why's that?"

"You get too involved."

"How can you help it?"

His smile was a mixture of sadness and resignation. "You have to. Or you can't do the job." He handed me my bag. "Here." He started off down the hall, taking me with him.

"Doesn't it ever get to you? The depravity? The senselessness?"

"No."

I knew he was lying. Maybe to protect me, or more likely himself. I let it go. Sometimes it wasn't good to look too hard at your feelings. The enormity of it all just might swallow you whole.

• • •

Alex and I arrived at the police station, rolling up in a cab with a driver who had greased the steering wheel so liberally when he'd sneezed we'd ended up three lanes over. I had to sit on the curb for a moment or lose my lunch.

"Are you all right?" Alex asked, standing over me. "You look a little green."

"Why are you not sick from Mr. Cabbie's Wild Ride?"

"From many years at sea."

I looked up at him. The sun gave him a halo, lighting up his blond hair like he was the second coming. "I never figured you for a seaman."

"There's a joke in there, but since I'm here with my lawyer hat on, I should probably pass." I turned to see a blond woman, all Marilyn Monroe curves and hair extensions a high-class stripper would kill for. She looked at Alex like she knew what he looked like naked and had examined every inch of him. Up close. With a magnifying glass and her tongue. "Hello, sailor," she purred. Actually purred like she was Eartha freakin' Kitt or something.

"Hey." Alex wrapped her in a hug, which she ended with a kiss, transferring half of her Tramp Red lipstick to him. "Thanks for coming down on such short notice." He cleared his throat and tried to peel her fingers from the buttons of his shirt. "Meet your client, Azalea March. Azalea, this is Amber Hooker, your attorney."

I laughed. This was a joke, right? He couldn't be serious. Must have been the cab ride.

By the twist of Amber Hooker's lips, I could see he was serious. Terribly, horribly serious. I scrambled up from the curb, wiping the gutter dust from the seat of my jeans. This was just great. I could already see the look Kennedy was going to have on his face when I walked in with Burlesque Barbie as my lawyer. And her name... I looked to the heavens. What had I done in this life or any of my past lives to incur this level of perverseness? I mean, come on! Who names their kid Amber Hooker?

I rubbed the dirt off my hand onto my thigh, then offered it to Amber to shake. To her credit, she didn't so much as hesitate in taking it. "Nice to meet you," I said, trying to squelch my embarrassment.

"Likewise. Alex already filled me in on your little predicament. Anything you want to add before we go in?"

"I don't think so."

I glanced at Alex. He looked both ridiculous and pretty in Amber's red lipstick. I made a wiping motion over my mouth. "Can you...?"

"Oh. Sorry." He had the good sense to look embarrassed as he pulled a handkerchief from his pocket and rubbed the lipstick off. "Better?" His lips were still red, but it was more from the handkerchief than the lipstick now.

"Much."

"Let's go," Amber said, spinning around on her platform heels. Her hips swayed like a metronome. In my seasick state, it was not good.

"She pay for law school in singles?" I mumbled to Alex out of the side of my mouth as we followed Amber into the police station.

"She's an excellent attorney and a good friend," he warned.

Message received.

Just how *good* a friend was little Miss Amber Kissy-face

now? For sure they'd been more than friends in the past. The question was just how much of that past was leaking right on into the present, and exactly what *kind* of favor did she owe Alex? I suddenly realized that burning in the pit of my stomach was not churned-up stomach acid from the cab ride. It was flat-out, plain, old, ordinary jealousy.

Huh.

I'd been so wrapped up in freeing Vivian and finding Dhane's and Trinity's killer that I hadn't been paying attention to what was in front of me. And I wasn't talking about Amber's fantastic backside. Alex had all but sketched me a picture of the way he felt about me, and while I'd tried to maintain my distance, it seemed my stupid old heart had gone ahead and decided it liked him without even discussing it with me first.

And now here I was getting jealous over a guy I'd convinced myself I didn't want.

My life was well and truly awesome.

I had to jog a bit to catch up with Alex and Amber, who was already working her magic to get us into the fortress. It was a good thing Juan Carlos wasn't here to see this. He'd hurt himself coming up with one snarkalicious comment after another.

The door Jerk and Shady had come through the last time I was here opened. A uniformed officer approached our little group. "Ms. Hooker? Detective Kennedy asked me to escort you back."

Amber turned her sparkly veneers on the policeman. "Thank you, Officer…?"

"Hodgkins, ma'am. This way please."

We followed Officer Hodgkins through a maze of half cubicles. Double, triple, and one very conspicuous quadruple take rippled in our wake. Just about every male with a pulse—and a couple of rogue females—dropped what they were doing to get a gander at Amber. She must have been used to it because she didn't even break stride or show any of the nervousness I felt for her.

We were led to a room off a short hallway at the back of the building. Your basic interrogation room with a table, seating for four, and what I assumed was a two-way mirror. It looked like it had been ordered straight from the Police Show Drama catalog or something.

"If you'll have a seat in here, Detective Kennedy will be with you in a moment," Officer Hodgkins informed us.

"Thank you, Officer," Amber replied, putting a little lip pout and boob tipping into it. Honestly, this woman didn't even try to dispel the stereotype.

I was so screwed.

I tried to get Alex's attention to tell him that maybe I didn't need a lawyer after all. For sure I didn't need one that looked like she'd break into a lap dance at any moment.

But Alex's eyes were all for Amber. I clenched my teeth together with a snap. Right in front of me. Um, hello! Girl you said you wanted more from sitting *right here*.

"What's your plan?" he asked her.

Amber turned, doing that hair-tossing thing that made men's tongues fall out of their mouths like a rolled-up rug. "I plan on protecting my client." Sliding gracefully into the chair next to me, she finally gave me her attention. "From here on out, you run everything by me before you say it. If you have to sneeze, I want to know about it first. You let me do the talking for you. Got that?"

I nodded, stuck between being impressed and wanting to rip her extensions out.

Alex took the chair on the other side of me and grinned at Amber like he'd created her. "I told you she was good."

She hadn't *done* anything except sway her hips and exploit her cleavage. Hell, I could've done that and I didn't have a law degree. *Men.*

The door opened, framing Platt's massive bulk. "Well, my day just went from shit to shine. Hello, Ms. Hooker."

"Hello yourself, Detective Platt." Amber leaned an elbow on the table, arching her shoulders forward, deepening her cleavage so much it looked like it could swipe credit cards. "Have you been working out?"

Sucking in his considerable girth, Platt blushed and preened. "Well, I've been lifting weights some."

"I don't think quarter-pound burgers count as weights," Kennedy said, edging his way into the room. "My, my *Ms. Smith*, you do keep the best company, don't you? Hello, Ms. Hooker, pleasure to see you again." Kennedy dropped into the last empty chair. "Shall we get started?"

"Who's Ms. Smith?" Amber asked me.

"It's a long story," I whispered to her. "But basically, it's a nickname for me."

She narrowed her eyes at me. "Is there something there I need to know about?"

"No." Not really.

The only one without a chair, Platt stood, looking like the loser in a game of musical chairs. He gave Kennedy a nasty look, then stormed out of the room. He came back with a chair and plopped down with so much force the chair groaned.

Kennedy opened a folder and leafed through it as if he were paging through a magazine in a waiting room.

Amber flipped her hair over her shoulder, drawing Platt's leer. It seemed to have no effect on Kennedy. He continued to turn page after page, skimming each one as though he had nothing but time to kill.

Finally he came to the last page and closed the folder. He pushed it away from him and looked straight at me. "We know you killed Trinity. What we don't know is why."

CHAPTER NINETEEN

Amber clamped her hand on my arm. If it hadn't been for that anchor, I would have leaped out of my chair and smacked Kennedy's smug face.

Releasing my arm slowly, Amber leaned back, causing the buttons on her blouse to gape. "Do you have a question for my client, Detective Kennedy?"

Kennedy was either very self-disciplined or a eunuch, because his gaze never left me. Platt, however, was having trouble sitting still in his chair.

"I have several," Kennedy said. "We'll start at the beginning and work our way through, shall we?" He didn't wait for an answer. "Why did you remove Dhane's head and leave it in that bin of doll heads?"

Fear expanded in my chest, leaving me no room to breath. I couldn't hear for the whooshing in my ears. I must have made some kind of sound because both Alex and Amber turned toward me, concerned.

Amber put her hands on my shoulders. "Azalea, are you all right?"

I couldn't breathe. The room narrowed, blackness zooming in.

I tried to speak but could only gulp air.

Amber shook me. "Azalea!" She patted my cheek, then shook me again. "She's hyperventilating."

There was some scrambling. People were all talking at once. I gripped the edge of the table, trying not to collapse.

And then Kennedy came up behind me and put a paper bag over my nose and mouth, his other hand on the back of my head. "Breathe, Azalea. That's it."

Alex came into my line of vision. "Just breathe. You'll be okay. Just breathe." He rubbed the top of my thigh. "That's my girl."

My breaths came a little easier.

"Should we call an ambulance?" Platt asked.

"She's catching her breath. She'll be fine in a moment," Kennedy said. "That's the way, Azalea. Better?"

I bobbed my head as best I could with it clamped between Kennedy's hands. The room brightened for me, the blackness receding. I could take in more air now that I wasn't suffocating.

"Okay. I'm going to remove the bag," Kennedy said. "Breathe easy. Not too deeply. Nice and easy. How's that?"

"Better."

Kennedy leaned over me to see my face. "Would you like some water? Platt, get her a cup of water."

Platt made a huffing sound that reminded me of a tire losing air.

"You can let go of her now," Alex said, glaring at the way Kennedy stroked my hair.

Kennedy dropped his hand but didn't move away.

Amber regarded me through narrowed eyes. "I want a moment with my client. Alone. Now."

Platt returned and placed a cup of water in front of me.

"You heard the lady. Everyone out," Kennedy said, swiping the folder off the table.

Alex made a move to sit back down in his chair.

"That includes you," Amber said to him.

"Why can't *I* stay?"

"Because you're not my client." Amber pointed a red-tipped finger at the door. "Out."

Alex gave me a long, worried look before departing. Kennedy closed the door behind him, leaving Amber and me alone.

"I've obviously not been properly informed. We're going to remedy that right now. Start at the beginning and I mean the *very* beginning. You landed in Las Vegas on what day?" Amber asked.

"Thursday."

"You got off the plane," she prompted. "And then what?"

"You want me to fill you in on every minute?"

"Every single one. I want to know when you peed, what you ate and where, who you met, what you did and said. *Everything.*"

I took a sip of water and began by picturing it all in my mind. The airport, waiting for our luggage, Juan Carlos making us take a picture at the baggage carousel with the WELCOME TO LAS VEGAS sign in the background, everything I could remember from the moment we landed until I met her in front of the police station. She took no notes, which worried me. I'd lived it and could hardly keep it all straight. How was she going to manage it?

When I finished rehashing my trip, Amber looked at me for a long time, and then she asked, "What's between you and Detective Kennedy?"

"*What?* Nothing. Absolutely nothing. Less than nothing."

"Uh-huh. And I'm Lady Gaga."

"I'm not sure what you're talking about."

"Let me put it to you this way…are you sleeping with him? Because I'd need to know."

I stared at her, my jaw gaping. Was she serious?

"I take that as a no," she said. "Interesting." She looked off for a moment, tapping a long red nail on the table. A slow smile kicked up one corner of her mouth. "This is good. I can use this."

"Use what? What are you talking about?"

She looked me up and down. "Not my look, but it certainly works for you." She smiled. "Yes, I can definitely use this." She reached into her briefcase, pulled out a compact, and handed it to me. "Fix yourself and touch up your lipstick if you have it with you."

"What does this have to do with Kennedy thinking I killed Dhane *and* Trinity?" Oh, I shouldn't have said that. Just saying it made me woozy again.

"Nothing whatsoever." Her grin was so calculating it reminded me of a wicked stepmother.

I did as she asked, applying another layer of fuchsia lipstick and swiping a light dusting of powder over my face.

"Do you have any blush?" she asked. "Maybe a little eyeliner?"

"No. What's going on here?" I handed her the compact back and she clicked it shut.

"You'll see. Now sit up straight. That's good." She walked to the door, hesitating for one more up and down look at me. "Remember, let me do the talking." She opened the door, leaning against the frame like she was posing for a cover shot. "Come on in, boys."

The three men shuffled into the room. Platt had gotten himself a cup of coffee and a big fat bear claw. It looked kinda good until he took a giant bite and chewed with his mouth open. Weight Watchers had nothing on this guy. He was a human binge deterrent.

When everyone was seated around the table again, Amber spoke. "In answer to your earlier question: my client is saddened by the tragic deaths of both Dhane and Trinity."

Kennedy turned his bad-cop stare on me. "What were you really doing in the hallway after Dhane's death? The real reason."

"My client had been invited to the suite of the deceased by the deceased. As I'm sure you've already verified with the witness who gave her the note and the key card to the suite." Pretending to pat her mouth over an exaggerated yawn, Amber rolled her eyes. "Let me know when you get to the part where you have real evidence against my client."

Kennedy's mouth pinched. "I find it odd that Ms. March was there at every turn of this case." He ticked off points on his fingers. "When Dhane's head was found. When Dhane's body was found. At Dhane's memorial service." He opened the file in front of him. "She visited Trinity the day of Dhane's death. And she was the one who found Trinity's body."

Amber examined her nails. "Do you have a question, Detective?"

Kennedy slammed the file shut, directing his anger and frustration at me. "Why are you so involved with this case? Why can't you stay out of it?" He got up and paced, running a hand through his hair. Catching sight of himself in the mirror, he pulled up. He took a deep breath and turned back to me. "How's this for a question: why did you kill Trinity?"

I gasped. He truly believed I could've done such a horrible, violent thing. The edges of my vision began to darken again and their voices got very far away.

"I'm sure you're being ridden like a pony at a kid's party to find the person or persons who committed these terrible acts." Amber leaned across the table, her shrewdness sharp enough to cut the steel table. "You know my client is innocent. What you want to know is what she knows. So why don't you just ask?"

Kennedy glared hard at me, popping me back from the edge of hysteria. "I did."

"Yes, but you didn't do it nicely. A lady likes to be asked, not threatened. My client is more than willing to assist the Las Vegas police department in any way she can."

"She can start with answering my question." Kennedy turned his attention back to me. "Why did you kill Trinity?"

Again with the tunnel. All of this zooming in and out was making me nauseous. I fisted my hands so hard my fingernails bit into my palms. The pain seemed to ground me, but if Kennedy accused me of murder one more time, I was sure I'd keel over onto the floor.

Amber sighed, her enormous chest rising and falling like a groundswell. "Really, Detective? I thought we covered this."

Kennedy rifled through his file and pulled out two photographs. "Maybe this will relieve your boredom."

He placed the photos side by side in front of me, watching me closely. The first one was a picture of Trinity lying on the rooftop. The pool of blood under her head was dark and sticky-looking, but her face was unmarred. In the stillness of death, her features softened, her beauty perfect and fragile. Curio rested next to her outstretched hand as if she were reaching for him or had just let go. My chest hitched and I clasped a hand over my mouth to catch the sob before it escaped.

Kennedy tapped the second photo, drawing my attention to it. It was a close-up of Trinity's hand. Nestled in her palm was a small pink flower. I looked up at Kennedy, confused.

"Recognize it?" he asked.

"I—"

Amber interrupted with a hand on my arm. "What is your point here?"

"If Ms. March didn't kill Trinity, then how'd the flower from her hair end up in Trinity's hand?"

Oh, God.

Picking up the two photographs, Amber examined them for herself. "Looks like a flower anyone could purchase from any craft store." She stacked the pictures and handed them back to Kennedy.

"Certainly. But how many of those flowers will have strands of your client's hair on them?"

Platt let out a we-got-you-now chuckle and I started to sway a little in my seat.

"That may or may not be my client's flower. Either way, it doesn't really matter, does it?"

"It'll matter to a jury," Platt said, finally getting in the game now that it looked like it might be a win.

"Still doesn't matter," Amber said.

Kennedy focused all of his attention on Amber for the first time, a frown lining the space between his brows. "Is that so?"

"Evidence or no, the way I see it, you've got a major problem with your theory." Amber's mouth curved into the kind of smile that sent men into battle. "And you know it."

Platt glanced back and forth between Kennedy and Amber, trying to sort out what they were talking about. For the first time since I'd met Platt, I found myself identifying with him. Which made me want to gag.

"And just what is it you think I know?" Kennedy asked.

"My client couldn't have possibly killed that poor girl because she has an alibi."

Platt glared at Kennedy. "What is she talking about?"

Kennedy leaned against the wall next to the mirror and regarded his reflection as though he were looking through it to someone on the other side.

With no answer from Kennedy, Platt turned his question on Amber. "What are you talking about?"

Amber's gaze met Kennedy's in the mirror. She arched a brow.

"I'm her alibi," Kennedy answered.

My lungs finally filled with air and I could almost feel my limbs again. I had an alibi!

"You?" Platt looked like he'd need a bypass.

"What's he talking about?" Alex asked me, speaking for the first time.

Amber held up a hand to silence him. "That's correct,

Detective," she said to Kennedy. "Whoever killed that girl went out of their way to frame my client for it. I don't envy you." She shook her head, casually rearranging her hair. "You not only have to solve two murders, but you also have to protect my client. There's no telling what kind of danger she might be in."

Amber's words spread a strange coldness through me. I might be in danger? I reached for Alex. He wrapped my hand in both of his, sealing it in warmth. I couldn't look at him, afraid I'd see my own worry and panic reflected back at me. I stared down at the blunt shine of the table, allowing the conversation to go on without me. Whoever had killed Trinity and possibly Dhane had now set their sights on me. I'd inserted myself into the case, so why was I so surprised now to find myself at the center of it all?

The image of Trinity's hand holding my flower like she'd just picked it swamped me with guilt. Was it my fault Trinity was dead? Was the flower supposed to be a message for me? Had I gone too far, pushed too hard?

Would the murderer kill again? And if so, was I next?

CHAPTER TWENTY

Platt looked like someone had just snatched away his favorite donut and left him with a whole-wheat bagel instead. "I don't like this."

Amber winked at him. "Don't worry, big guy. I'll explain. The last time anyone saw Trinity was at Dhane's memorial service. My client met with Detective Kennedy directly afterward. Then she was abducted and taken to the Raine Hotel where she discovered that Trinity had died. She called Detective Kennedy and your handsome self to the scene." Amber turned to Kennedy, her smile dropping from warm and flirty to arctic and cunning. "So why all the theatrics, Detective? I thought you were better than that."

Kennedy peeled away from the mirror and shoved his hands in his pockets. "Your client has been involved in this case from the very beginning. Every time I turned around, she was there. It wasn't too far a leap to assume she had *something* to do with Trinity's murder, either directly or indirectly."

I gasped. He blamed me for what had happened to Trinity. Alex squeezed my hand. I remembered his words from earlier about blame and wondered if we had been smarter, faster, better, could we have prevented Trinity's death? I could see it on Kennedy in the way his jaw set, the overbrightness of his eyes and the brackets around his mouth: Guilt weighed on him like a leaden coat. And he was looking to shove some of it off onto me.

Maybe he was right. Maybe I was to blame. The flower in Trinity's hand was a clear message I wasn't going to ignore.

"Can I say something?" I asked.

Amber answered, "No" at the same time Platt and Kennedy said, "Yes."

"I think our time here is done." Picking up her briefcase, Amber pushed to her feet. "Let's go."

Alex stood, too, leaving Platt and me the only ones sitting.

"Dhane's wife was having an affair," I blurted out.

"Azalea!" Amber plopped back down into her seat. "Are you sure you want to do this?"

"Yes." I looked at Kennedy. "I have to."

Amber put her hand on my arm. "Give me a moment first." She directed her attention to Kennedy. "I want immunity and protection for my client. In writing. I don't care who you have to pull out of the swimming pool to get it, but she doesn't say another word until she gets it."

"Done," Kennedy said. "But the best way to protect her is for her to go home."

"I agree." Alex didn't look happy about having something in common with Kennedy.

"I'm not leaving. I came here for a fun weekend with my friends and to go to the hair show." I had to try to salvage *something* from this trip. "Tomorrow is the last day and tomorrow night is the awards ceremony. I have a couple of friends who are up for awards. I'll just go to the show and the awards and that's it. I promise." And I meant it. I really did. I turned to Alex. "You'll be with me. That's all the protection I'll need."

Alex shook his head. "I won't. I have to fly back tomorrow. I really think you, Juan Carlos, James, and Vivian should go home with me."

"I'll go if they go." But I knew they wouldn't. They'd been looking forward to this trip more than I had. Especially Juan Carlos.

Three frowns and a glare were directed at me.

"Why don't I believe you?" Kennedy asked.

I held up a hand, trying hard to convey how serious I was. "I swear I won't ask any more questions, snoop where I don't belong, or look up anything on the Internet."

"Speaking of..." Kennedy turned his angry stare on Alex. "From now until you leave Vegas, you won't interfere in this case. That includes calling Kansas, Washington, or Timbuktu."

Alex's blue-eyed gaze stuck on me. "Now that Vivian's clear, I'm not going to do anything else to encourage Azalea. You've got my word."

Washington? Wait. What was in Washington?

"Uh-oh, she's got that look," Alex said.

I browsed the faces in the room, confused. "What look?"

Narrowing his eyes, Alex pointed at me. "That look you get when you're trying to figure something out. What's going on?"

"I hate that look," Kennedy said.

"Nothing's going on. I swear."

I could tell I hadn't convinced anyone.

"Platt." Kennedy addressed him with his eyes on me. "You're her guard tomorrow."

"What? Why me?" Platt whined.

"Yeah, why him?" I whined, too.

Kennedy moved his focus to Alex. "What time does your plane take off?"

"Ten. I leave at eight thirty," Alex replied.

"You'll be at her door by eight fifteen," Kennedy told Platt. "And you'll do it because it's our job to protect and serve."

Platt looked like he was trying to sneer at me, but he ended up looking more constipated than mean. Great. What was I going to do with this boat anchor dragging along behind me all day tomorrow?

It took twenty minutes to get the paperwork Amber wanted and another forty for me to tell them everything I'd found out, speculated on, and supposed about Dhane's and Trinity's murders. When I finished, Kennedy gave me one last "Stay out of trouble," combined with a fierce warning glare before he strode out with Platt riding his heels.

Alex, Amber, and I walked out of the police station and into the oven-hot Vegas afternoon.

Alex put an arm around Amber. I really wished he'd stop doing that. "I owe you, and so does Azalea."

"I thought this made us even." Amber fingered a button on Alex's shirt like she was thinking of popping them all. "But if you insist we're not, then I can't wait to collect."

I mentally rolled my eyes.

"Azalea, thank Amber."

I looked at my sex-kitten attorney. She sure had flummoxed all of the men in the room. She'd played to the stereotype, but there was definitely a brain under all of those bleached-blond extensions. She wouldn't ever be NOW's poster girl, but she had definitely come through for me in a pinch. And it sure had been fun watching Platt make a drooling fool of himself.

"Thank you, Amber." I went to her for a hug that caught her off guard. "If you're ever in Southern California with a hair emergency, you give me a call." I handed her my card. Whatever might have been between her and Alex, I was positive it was firmly in the past. He liked her, but he didn't look at her the way he looked at me. Even if I didn't have all of her *attributes*.

My offer of friendship seemed to touch her. I could have sworn she had tears in her eyes. I guessed she didn't have many female friends.

"Thank you. I will. Call me if you need any more legal help." She gripped Alex's chin and gave him a quick kiss on the lips. The spark of jealousy was still there, but not as sharp. "Take care of this one," she said to me, patting his chest. She gave us a small wave and spun on her heel.

Alex put his arm around me and gave me a half hug. "I told you she was incredible."

We watched Amber sway away until she rounded the corner of the building, then we strolled out onto the main street to try and catch a cab.

"Alex?" I asked with a smile.

"Hmm?"

"Are you going to wear that lipstick all day?"

CHAPTER TWENTY-ONE

Platt knocked on my door at eight nineteen the next morning, interrupting Alex's lecture on promises and meddling. I never thought I'd live to see the day when I'd be glad to see Platt at my door. My vision of a lengthy, lusty good-bye scene with Alex had long since been replaced by a twenty-minute rant on the dangers of inserting myself where I didn't belong—glossing over his role in the whole escapade, of course. Like he needed to tell me anyway. Visions of my flower in Trinity's hand had haunted my dreams, making it impossible to sleep.

Platt's Neanderthal brow lowered, casting an even deeper shadow over his eyes. I guessed that was his way of saying good morning.

"I'm not any happier than you are about this," I said, waving him inside. "You may as well come in."

Alex handed Platt his business card. "Call me if anything goes wrong. *Anything*."

Platt took the card without looking at it and shoved it in his pocket. "Sure you can't stay?"

"I would if I could. I appreciate the help." Alex's words of thanks sounded more like he'd signed an IOU than a simple gesture of gratitude. He grabbed the handle of his suitcase and took my hand. "Step into the hall with me."

I slid my keycard into the back pocket of my jeans and followed him out into the hall.

"I'm going to miss you," Alex whispered, stroking the side of my face with his thumb. "I think I'm already used to sleeping next to you and that little snorty, wheezy sound you make."

"At least I don't kick you and pretend I'm asleep so I can cop a feel under the guise of sleep groping."

He backed me up against the wall, his hands moving to my hip and the back of my neck. "I *was* sleeping, and I'm not the only one with wandering hands, you know."

"Yeah, well, I was going to let you get to second base when we said good-bye this morning, but you wasted all of our fondling time with your lecture."

He put his forehead to mine. "Damn."

I looked into his baby blues and wondered if he were for real, if what was happening here was all my imagination, wanting it to be real. It felt real and scary and oh so thrilling. I closed my eyes, trying to control the hope that wanted to bloom.

"Azalea?"

I pulled away and opened my eyes. "What?"

"I'll call you tomorrow and we'll set up that date you owe me. Okay?"

He said and did all the right things, so why was I still having a hard time trusting him? "Sure."

He looked for a moment like he'd say something else, then changed his mind. Instead he tipped my head back and gave me the kind of kiss that made me forget everything that had happened this weekend, my fears, hell—even my own name.

"Uhhh," Alex said, breaking the kiss. "If we're not careful, we'll give the guys in security something to post on the Internet."

"It's your own fault."

"I know. I wish I didn't have to go. Be careful. I mean it."

"And you didn't the last fifty-nine times you said it?"

"Be good," he scolded. "I'll call you tomorrow."

"All right."

He gave me one last kiss, pressing his lips hard to mine as if branding me, then he walked off down the hall, towing his suitcase behind him.

I turned to go back into my room when a thought struck me, snagging my attention. I looked up at the ceiling, noting the small black half globe at the end of the hall. A security camera. If my hotel had them, surely a hotel as swanky as the Raine had them. They would have picked up anybody going in or out of Dhane's and Trinity's rooms. And if so, why hadn't the police looked at them? They'd know their approximate times of death, cross-reference that with the cameras, and you'd have an image of the killer on video.

I let myself into my room. Platt had parked himself at the end of the bed and was flipping channels like a champion.

"Hey, Detective Platt?"

He grunted.

"I'll just be a couple of minutes, and then we'll go down to the convention center."

He might have mumbled something rude, but thankfully the TV drowned it out.

I finished drying my hair, smoothing it straight and bumping it at the ends with a round brush so it curved toward my face. I brushed bronzer on my cheeks and a matte coral lipstick on my lips. A thin line of black liquid liner on my top eyelid and lots of mascara completed the look. I'd chosen jeans again for comfort and topped them with a striped T-shirt strategically ripped and worn inside out for that I-paid-a-fortune-to-look-like-a-bum look. Five chain necklaces looped down at different lengths, matching my tassel chain earrings. I pulled on black Converse All Stars and examined myself in the mirror, feeling very punk-rock chic.

"I'm ready," I called out to Platt, grabbing my bag and cell phone.

He flipped off the TV and trudged out into the hall after me.

With as innocent a face as I could muster, I asked, "Hey, what are those black globey things on the ceiling?"

Platt glanced up without tipping his head back. "Security."

"Oh, wow, really? Do all the hotels have them?"

"Sure."

"Huh. And they're on all the time? I mean, they're, like, taping every second? Day and night?" I punched the button to call the elevator.

"They ain't Christmas ornaments. Of course they do."

"How fascinating." I put in as much enthusiasm as I could, channeling Amber. "Your line of work must be so interesting, getting to investigate crimes and all." I tried to bat my lashes, but it made me kinda dizzy, so I stopped.

He adjusted his belt over his belly, tucking his thumbs into the waistband. "It can be. I get to lock up some major asswipes."

The elevator arrived. Thankfully it was empty.

"Really?" I was quickly nearing the end of my ability to shovel bullshit while pretending to be impressed by anything Platt did other than not walk with his knuckles dragging the ground. I had a new appreciation for Amber. It must have taken her years to perfect her skills. "You must have gone through scores of footage in your career. I bet you've seen some pretty strange things."

He snorted, and I had to resist the urge to check him for a curly tail. "This is Vegas. What do you think?"

"Gosh." Mental head slap. Did I just say "gosh"? "I guess with technology these days, you could have cameras everywhere and they'd never fail."

"You'd think that, but believe me, they do. Like this case I'm working on... Hey." Platt's face scrunched up. "You're not supposed to ask questions."

"Oh, sorry. I just get so curious. It's a fault, really. I blame my mother. She questions *everything*."

"That and you don't shut up."

The elevator reached the bottom floor, letting us out.

"Right. Sorry." I headed off ahead of him, trying to hide my smile. So there *was* something wrong with the tape at the Raine. Interesting. Except I wasn't supposed to be involved with this case anymore. Conflounded! And I wasn't supposed to speculate about who would have the technical knowledge and skill to go around Raine security. *Or* how they would do it.

I got in line for a taxi, with Huff-n-Puff wheezing behind me from the short walk to the front of the hotel. Honestly, that man was one cheeseburger combo away from a gazilliondruple bypass. Some protection he was. I would have been better off with Jun in a fight than Platt.

Finally a cab pulled up and we climbed in. I was meeting Vivian, Juan Carlos, and Richard at the convention center. I had already missed most of the workshops, so I was really looking forward to going to some today. And I had a really cool outfit for the awards tonight. It had taken me weeks to put it together and I couldn't wait to wear it. I loved dressing up.

We pulled up to the convention center and Platt got out, leaving me to foot the full cab fare. That Platt, always the gentleman.

I traipsed into the convention with my very large, very surly shadow and found Juan Carlos and Richard.

"Where's Viv?" I asked.

"She's not coming. She and James are spending the day together to see the sights." Juan Carlos rolled his eyes so far up I thought they'd drop inside his skull. "Please. The only sights she's likely to see are her ankles and the ceiling above the bed."

Platt chuckled.

Juan Carlos jerked his head at Platt. "Who's the *Grimace*

clone?"

"My bodyguard."

"Seriously?" Juan Carlos scrunched up his nose. "Where'd you go, Cheap Charlie's Discount Security? Was he marked down? Is he paying *you*? Wait! Why do you need a security guard?"

Platt waved a hand. "Hello? I'm standing right here." He patted his side. "And I have a gun."

"Sorry," I said to Platt. "He tends to talk about people like they aren't there. He's harmless." I gave Richard and Juan Carlos the rundown on what had happened at the police station yesterday and why I was saddled with the world's least-intimidating bodyguard.

"Holy shitake mushrooms! That's it. I'm not doing any more investigating for you." Juan Carlos made a motion across his throat. "You're cut off." He froze. "Oh my God. I did it again. I can't believe I did it again."

"Come on, Sensitive Sally," Richard said. "Let's go look at the scissors. I need a new pair of channeling shears. Unless you want us to stick with you, Azalea." He gave Platt a concerned once over, clearly doubting his ability to protect me.

"I have a gun," Platt reminded him, patting his side again.

"I'll call you if I need you, but I'm sure I'll be fine," I told him.

"Sensitive Sally is right," Platt mumbled as we walked to the part of the convention center where the workshops were being held. "That guy's more than a little light in the loafers."

I rounded on him. "If we're going to spend the day together, you're not allowed to disparage my friends and I won't mention the blob of jelly on your tie. Or your awful hair."

Platt touched the top of his head. "What's wrong with my hair?"

"That color is too ash for your complexion and the hair over your ears makes your face look wider, more block-like. And we should really discuss your manscaping. You could braid the hair from your ears with your eyebrows."

He put one hand to his ear and the other to his brow, frowning.

"If I had my shears and trimmer with me, I'd fix it for you. But I couldn't bring them on the plane. Hey, I know. When my workshop on updos is over, we'll go into the Expo and I'll pretend to try out all the scissors on you. How does that sound?" I couldn't walk around all day with Platt's hair looking like that. People would think it was *my* work.

"What the hell's an updo?"

I grinned. "You'll see."

Forty-five minutes later, we emerged from the updo class. I thought Platt would have nodded off or made fun of the presenter, who made Juan Carlos look butch, but he sat there watching like he'd take what he'd learned and use it.

"That wasn't so bad, was it?" I asked. "You looked like you might have enjoyed it at least a little."

"My daughter's into that hair stuff."

I whipped my head toward him so fast I nearly gave myself whiplash. "You have a daughter?"

He gave me a look, daring me to make a crack so he could use his gun.

"How old is she?"

"Nine. Her mom passed a year ago." He shoved his hands in his pockets and fixed his eyes to the floor.

"I'm sorry."

"Yeah, well."

We entered the main Expo floor. The noise level here must have been about a million decibels, but it had a fun, circus-type atmosphere. I couldn't wait to do some shopping!

"Let's see if we can't find her some pretty barrettes," I said to get him out of his funk. "Oh, I know. I bet she'd love some clip-in hair extensions. I got some for my niece. What's her favorite color?"

"Pink."

Like my flower, I thought, then quickly pushed it out of my head.

"What's your daughter's name?"

"Phoebe."

"What a pretty name."

"Her mom picked it out."

Ugh. Okay. Note to self: Don't bring up anything having to do with the mother. I couldn't take the way Platt's jaw firmed, like he was fighting emotion. It made me think of his poor motherless daughter and another less-than-fortunate girl who'd died with my flower in her hand.

"Hey, look. This is what I was talking about." I dragged him over to a booth with clip-in extensions.

Half an hour later, Platt had a bag full of pink clip-in hair, pink nail polish, and pink barrettes. I had even trimmed him up enough so that he almost looked attractive. Well, maybe attractive was a stretch, but at least I didn't have to watch his ear hair move with the breeze anymore.

"Come over here," I told Platt. "My friend Devin was looking for hair-color models the other day. I bet he'd fix your color right up."

Sure enough, faster than you could say midlife crisis, Platt was sitting in a styling chair with Devin applying color to his hair while he pitched the product to the crowd. Platt was a very good sport, even allowing Devin to put in a few foiled highlights.

I watched for a while, but then I got bored and my gaze wandered. The Hjálmar booth was just a row over. I thought for a moment about going to see if Juan Carlos's friend Mateo was still there, until I remembered all of my promising and swearing to not investigate anymore.

I stood on my tiptoes but couldn't see over the crowd. Taking a reverse step, I arched my back to see if I could look up the row. Nothing. There were too many people in the aisle. I took another step. Then another. Before I knew it I was in the aisle. The booth wasn't far. If I could see it from here, then I could see Devin's booth from the Hjálmar booth, right? I'd just be a second. I'd be right back.

I reasoned my way up the row until I stood at the Hjálmar counter. It was packed. They must have somehow shipped more product overnight and it was flying off the shelves. I spotted Mateo.

I jumped with my hand in the air. "Mateo! Mateo!"

He saw me and made his way over. "What's up, Azalea? Crazy, huh?" he said, indicating the counter.

"Insane. I can't believe you guys restocked so quickly. I thought you would have been cleaned out by now."

"Nah. The corporate office is in Washington, but we have a distribution center here in Vegas."

Washington?

"Is that where Dhane lived?" I asked.

"Of course."

"Is that where research and development is, too?"

"Yeah. I gotta go before I get in trouble. See you around?"

"Sure. Thanks, Mateo."

Kennedy had scolded Alex for calling Kansas, but he had also mentioned Washington. Had Alex called Washington and not told me? And if so, what did he find out? What *other* information did Alex have that he hadn't shared with me?

I turned away from the counter, so deep in thought I went the wrong direction and ended up two rows over from where I was supposed to be. I hustled double time back to Platt, panic clawing at my throat.

Someone tapped me on the shoulder. I turned around to find the last person I expected standing in front of me, face flushed and mad as hell. My heart leapt into my throat, making it hard to breathe.

"Oh, crap," I croaked out.

CHAPTER TWENTY-TWO

"Where's Platt?" Alex asked, scanning the area around us with a scowl. He huffed a little, as though he'd run laps around the convention floor. I could almost see little puffs of smoke wafting from his ears.

I pointed up the aisle. "He's over there, getting his hair done. What are you doing here? I thought you left."

"Getting his *what*?" He shook his head. "Never mind. If he's over there, why are you over here?"

"Well, see, I was just gone a second, checking out the Hjálmar booth and saying hi to Juan Carlos's friend Mateo…"

"I knew it. I knew you couldn't stop. All that promising."

"It's not like that." But it kind of was *exactly* like that.

"You were just saying hello." I could tell he didn't believe me for a second. He knew exactly what I'd been doing and why.

I nodded, mentally chastising myself for giving in to my overactive curiosity gland. If only there were a pill I could take to control it, or have it surgically removed or lasered or something.

Blowing out a breath, he moved closer. Some of his mad melted into relief or exasperation. It was hard to tell with him. "What am I going to do?" He framed my face in his hands, pressing his forehead to mine, his tone softening. "It's crazy. You're crazy. Or maybe I am, but I swear to God the only time I feel calm is when I'm at the center of your tornado."

I closed my eyes against the sensations his whispered words sent crashing through me. Fisting my hands in his shirt, I brought him closer. His heart beat strong and steady and maybe a little too fast under my hands. I wanted to tell him not so say those things to me. They were just the words I wanted to hear, and yet they scared me right down to my manicured toes. I so badly wanted to believe him.

He raised his head to look at me. "What the hell am I supposed to do with you?" He seemed as baffled as I was at his feelings toward me. His cool blue eyes told me more about his intentions than his words had. And suddenly I did more than want his words to be true. I started to believe them.

"Azalea!" Platt lumbered over to us, foils flapping. The color cape was wrapped over his shoulder, fluttering out behind him. He stopped when he reached us and bent over, gripping his knees. He wheezed like an asthmatic grizzly bear, his face flushed. "You... dis...appeared... Couldn't...find..." He lifted a hand off his knee, greeting Alex. "Hey..."

"Are you all right?" I asked, leaning over to see his face.

Keeping his head down, Platt nodded.

Alex lifted one of the foils in Platt's hair with a finger. A corner of his mouth twitched. "You weren't kidding."

I pushed Alex's hand away. "Leave him alone. Can't you see he's having trouble breathing?" I returned my attention to Platt. "Are you going to be okay? Should we call an ambulance or something?"

Platt waved a hand at me. "No...no...I'm fine. I'll...be fine."

"Do you want some water?" Alex asked.

Platt waved away Alex's question without answering. After another couple of minutes where Alex and I exchanged shrugs and what-should-we-do? glances, Platt stood up. His face was redder than an Englishman on vacation. I was seriously concerned for his welfare. His daughter had already lost her mother—it would be awful if she lost her father, too.

"You should really take better care of yourself," I told him. "Think of Phoebe."

"You sound like…my doctor."

"Who's Phoebe?" Alex asked.

"Never mind," I said to Alex. "Not to be a nag, but your doctor's right, Roy."

Alex got a funny look on his face. "I've been gone barely two hours and there's a whole new cast of characters. Who's Roy?"

I gestured to Platt. "He's Roy."

"You're on a first-name basis? I thought you hated each other."

Platt gave me a *meh* look. "She's all right when she keeps her yap shut."

"He's not so bad when he's not being a raging jackass." I winked at Platt and he winked back.

Alex looked back and forth between Platt and me. "I've dropped into an alternate universe."

"I thought you left," Platt said to Alex.

"I was just about to board the plane when I had a sudden vision of Azalea up to her pretty little neck in trouble."

Platt snorted. "Ain't that the truth."

"Don't you two go ganging up on me." I spotted Devin waving at us from his booth. "Oh, shoot. Let me check your foils, Roy." Platt bent over a little. I opened one of the foils and scraped away some of the color with a fingernail. "Yep, you're done." I wiped my finger on his color cape. "Let's go get you rinsed."

As soon as we got back to Devin's booth, Platt was whisked away to have his color washed out.

I looked up to find Alex grinning down at me. "Azalea March, making friends and making over enemies."

"Yeah, well, he needed it."

Alex kept smiling at me in that goofy way. It made the space between my shoulder blades itch.

"What are you grinning at?"

"You."

"Stop."

"Come here and give me a proper hello." Alex drew me into his arms and hugged me.

"I thought you had to get back to work."

"I called in sick."

"Cops can do that?"

He pulled back to look at me, keeping me in his arms. "We get sick."

"Huh, I guess so. I never thought of it before."

"Hairstylists get sick."

"Yeah, but we work through it. Have you ever tried rescheduling a woman's hair appointment? She'd rather put up with you heaving in a waste basket than wait a day to have her roots touched up."

"Tough business," he teased, stealing little kisses.

"Speaking of business…"

He nibbled at my ear, sending fine shivers through me. "Hmm?"

"What did you find out when you called the Hjálmar corporate offices in Washington?"

He stopped nibbling and gave me a fierce, disapproving frown. "What makes you think I called the corporate offices? And even if I did, I wouldn't tell you. You're. Not. Involved." He tapped my nose with each word. "Remember?"

"I'm *not* involving myself. What you found out isn't new information. You called before we went to the police station so there's no harm in telling me what you found out because it predated my promise. See?"

He shook his head. "Your logic somehow makes a circular kind of sense."

"Thank you." I plastered on my most serious face, the one I used to bargain with our vendors at the salon. The one that said *I'm a professional, take me seriously.* "So? What did you find out?"

Alex's brow lowered. I could tell I was having some kind of effect on him. I just hoped it was the one I wanted. He grabbed my hand and towed me to an out-of-the-way corner without a word. I took it as a good sign.

"I didn't call Washington State," he said. "I called a friend in the State Department in Washington, DC."

"What? Why?"

"Something seemed off to me from the start so I decided to follow up on my hunch."

"And?"

He got that determined look in his eyes again. "And nothing."

"Nothing as in your friend told you nothing, or you're telling me nothing?"

"I shouldn't have told you that much."

"So what's a little more?"

"This is a bad idea," he mumbled to himself. "I expect you to keep your promise." At my eager nod, he continued, "He wouldn't tell me why, but Dhane and his company were under investigation. They were about to file charges when Dhane was killed. His death may put an end to the investigation."

"Why?"

"Their informant on the inside isn't cooperating anymore."

"Interesting." So Dhane's death might end the investigation. Huh. That may have been exactly what the killer was after when he or she murdered Dhane. Who was the inside informant and what was being tattled about? I wished I could talk to Alex's friend in DC. I had so many questions...

"Not that look again. I knew I shouldn't have said anything to you."

"Just because my wheels are spinning doesn't mean I'm going anywhere. I made a promise. I intend to keep it."

"Uh-huh."

"Skepticism is very unattractive. Come on." I waved for Alex to follow me. "Let's go see if Roy's done. I'm hungry." I swiveled my head up at him. "You're buying me lunch to make up for your lack of faith in me."

He caught my hand in his. "Okay, but this doesn't count as the date you owe me for getting you in to see Vivian."

"Fine. Do you think the restaurant here serves lobster and caviar? Mmm, maybe they'll have some champagne, too."

We found Platt sitting in Devin's styling chair getting his hair blow-dried. He looked curious and uncomfortable, like a caveman being exposed to modern technology for the first time. I couldn't believe the transformation in him. The new hair color made his eyes look more green than hazel and gave him a healthier-looking complexion. Devin handed Platt a mirror. He looked at himself so long I got twitchy.

"Do you think he likes it?" I asked Alex.

"I think he doesn't recognize himself. I don't and I *know* it's him."

Platt thanked Devin and climbed down from the small dais. He walked over to us and grabbed me in a hug, trapping my arms at my sides. "Thank you," he whispered.

"You're welcome," I murmured against his chest.

Platt released me and looked away, coughing into his hand. I could have sworn his eyes were a little misty. I pretended not to see, giving my attention to the other side of the convention floor.

"Alex is buying us lunch. Are you hungry?"

"I could eat," Platt replied with a shrug.

On our way to the little café where I'd met with Kennedy after

Dhane's memorial, I kept sneaking looks at Platt. I got that special little tummy flutter I get when I'm proud of my work. I wanted to pat myself on the back, and him, too, for letting me make him over.

Just as we got in line to order, Platt's phone rang. "Excuse me."

I watched Platt walk away, thinking maybe I'd take a crack at his wardrobe next. "Where do you get your clothes?" I asked Alex.

"What?"

"Your clothes. You always dress nicely. I just thought maybe I could help Roy with his clothing."

"Leave the guy alone." Alex scanned the menu board above the cash register. He shook his head and turned to me. "On second thought, that's a very good idea. You should concentrate on making Platt over. Head to toe."

"You're not very tricky, you know that?"

My phone beeped. I pulled it out of my purse and read a text from Jun. He wanted me to meet him, but I knew if I did, Alex would think I was investigating again. Which I would be. *If* I met Jun and *if* I told Alex about it.

I shouldn't meet Jun. Even though I wanted to. Badly. I tucked my phone back in my purse without replying to the text. My restraint truly bordered on miraculous.

We were next in line when Platt came back. "I have to go. I told Kennedy you decided to stay," he said to Alex. "You can watch her, right?"

Alex nodded. "Like a hawk."

"Or a two-year-old," I grumbled.

"Okay. Thanks," Platt said, looking like he wanted to hug me again. Instead he gave me a half wave and jerk of his head before he lumbered off.

Darned if I didn't miss the big lug already.

We ordered and ate, talking about nothing in particular. My phone beeped three more times, all Jun. His incessant texting made it hard to concentrate.

His last text had been sad and pouty. He didn't understand why I was ignoring him. I could hear the hiccupping and sniffling in his messages and that pitiful, plaintive tone in his voice when he'd talked about Trinity. I felt bad. He'd lost two friends in a matter of days. And now here I was ignoring him. He might think something bad had happened to me, too. Maybe I should text him back to let him know I was okay.

Alex didn't say anything as I pulled out my phone for the fifth time and punched out a quick text: *Having lunch*. There — that should calm Jun down. But it didn't. My phone rang. I looked at Alex, but he only smiled back, making me feel like a jerk.

"Hello?"

"Azalea! Where are you? Why didn't you answer my texts?" he half sobbed, half yelled. I had to hold the phone away from my ear. "I thought you were dead!"

"No, Jun, I'm fine."

Alex's brows jumped up. I guessed he heard Jun.

"I'm at the police station. They made me come here, then left me all alone. Why did they make me come here? I don't know anything. I'm all alone, Azalea. What am I going to do?"

"Calm down. You're fine. They just want your help finding out who killed Dhane and Trinity. I told them what you told me — that's probably why they want to talk to you."

"You *told* them? Everything?" His voice reached a pitch only bats or dolphins could hear.

"It's okay, Jun. You're going to be okay."

He started babbling, spouting gibberish mixed in with an occasional coherent word. I tried to calm him down, but all my efforts seemed to make him worse. Then I heard Kennedy shouting at Jun. There were some scuffling noises and more shouting, then the line went dead.

"Jun? Jun!" I clicked my phone off. "We have to go help Jun," I told Alex. "I think he's in trouble."

"Why do we have to go? That's what the police are for."

"He's *with* the police."

Chapter Twenty-Three

When we got to the police station, Alex used his charm and badge to get us access into where they were holding Jun, which was a room down the hall from where I'd been taken the day before. Kennedy stood in the hallway waiting for us, arms crossed, attitude blasters up.

He made a show of checking his watch. "It's been thirteen hours and twelve minutes since you've meddled in this case. I wonder who won the pool. It sure wasn't me. I had four hours. Platt had nine. I guess he had more faith in you than I did."

"You're as funny as ever, Kennedy. You really should try stand-up." I made a show of looking at my watch, too. "It's been three days and two deaths and you still haven't solved the case." I made a tsking sound. "Maybe you should spend more time investigating and less time betting on me."

"Azalea," Alex warned. "Antagonizing him isn't going to help anybody."

"But she's so very good at it," Kennedy said. "It's my favorite thing about her."

I could tell Alex was putting a great deal of effort into ignoring Kennedy's barb. "Azalea got a call from a friend of hers named

Jun. He said he was here and it sounded like he was in trouble. Azalea insisted we come down and check on him."

"He's here all right, and nuttier than squirrel sh…excrement," Kennedy amended. "We had to restrain him. I came out to see about getting him signed up for a *hold*"

"What's a *hold*?" I asked.

"Psych hold," Alex answered.

I gave Kennedy an accusatory glare. "Psych hold? He's that upset? What did you guys do to him?"

"Nothing. We hadn't even talked to him yet. All of a sudden he went crazy, started knocking things over. We restrained him for his own protection. And ours." Kennedy folded his arms over his chest. "What's this guy's story anyway? Why's he dress like that? Is it some kind of costume or cult?"

"It's anime," I answered. "You know, Japanese cartoons. He's as harmless as a child. He probably just got scared." I couldn't help but feel guilty. If I'd answered Jun's texts, he might not have freaked out. "Can I see him? I might be able to calm him down."

Kennedy looked at me, like he was thinking of putting *me* on a psych hold. "I don't think that's a good idea."

"She's got a way with him," Alex said. "He's got the emotional capacity of a five-year-old, but he responds to her."

Kennedy's face was an impassable mask. "I don't like this."

"He's one of the few people who knew both Dhane and Trinity very well. You want to know what he knows? Then let me talk to him." I mentally crossed my fingers.

"All right. But you can't stay. You calm him down, then step out. Got it?"

I nodded. "Got it." Kennedy opened the door and followed me in, while Alex stayed in the hall.

I wasn't prepared for what I saw. Jun's hands were cuffed in front of him and tethered to his shackled feet. He sat in a chair in the center of the room, a stern, square-faced officer standing behind him. Jun's eyes were blank, his mouth slack.

I rounded on Kennedy. "Did you drug him?"

"Had to Tase him. He should have come out of it already. His vitals are steady. We can't figure out why he's pretending to be comatose."

I turned back to Jun and inched closer. "Jun? It's me, Azalea. Are you okay? I'm sorry I didn't come sooner. If I'd known you were in trouble, I would have answered your texts right away. Jun? Come on, answer me." I turned to Kennedy. "Can I touch him?"

"Be careful."

I placed a hand on Jun's shoulder. "Jun? Are you all right? Talk to me." I gave him a gentle nudge. "Jun?" Kneeling down, I shook him harder. "Jun! Come on, buddy."

Jun turned his head so fast, I jerked back.

"Azalea?" he whispered, searching my face.

"Yes, it's me. I'm here."

"Azalea." He tried the word out, bunching his face up. "What happened?" He looked down at himself, then around the room, spotting Kennedy by the door and the uniformed officer's reflection in the mirror. "Where am I? Why am I tied up?"

"You're at the police station. You got upset, so the officers had to restrain you. But you're okay." I ran a hand up and down his arm. "They just wanted to talk to you about Trinity and Dhane. They need your help. Remember how I asked you for help?"

He nodded, his gaze wandering the room again, not focusing on anything in particular.

"The police need your help, too. Will you help them as a favor to me?"

"Yes. I guess."

"Good. That's good, Jun. And will you stay calm, not get upset again?"

He looked at me and blinked. I could see him gradually return to himself, his focus fixed on me. "I'm not upset."

"No, you're not. You're doing really well."

Jun lifted his hands. The metallic chime of the chains rubbing together seemed to puzzle him. "I can't move my hands."

"Can you take the chains off?" I appealed to Kennedy.

He shook his head. "Not a good idea. He's stronger than he looks. It took five of us to secure him and he put one of my guys out of commission with an ice pack on his, ah…private area."

I could hardly believe what Kennedy was telling me. Jun must've been so frightened to have acted out like that. Again I wished I'd answered his texts. I might've been able to calm him down and prevent him from hurting anyone.

"What if he promises to behave himself?" I turned back to Jun. "If they take the chains off, will you be good and not hurt anyone?"

"I hurt somebody?" He blinked at me, tears filling his eyes.

"You did, but you won't do it again, will you?"

Jun shook his head, emphatic. "No. I don't want to hurt anybody."

"You see?" I said to Kennedy. "He's calm now."

Kennedy moved forward. "I'll take the chains off, but the handcuffs and ankle restraints stay on. You so much as twitch wrong and they go back on, got it?" he said to Jun.

"Yes, sir."

"Step out, Azalea," Kennedy said.

"No! Please don't go, Azalea. Please don't make her go. I'll be good. I'll be real good," Jun begged.

"If you don't behave yourself, I'm leaving," I said to Jun before Kennedy could protest.

Kennedy gave me a warning glare to stay put. Officer Burly in the corner took out a weird looking device and stood, braced to use it, while Kennedy removed Jun's chains.

"Better?" I asked Jun.

"I guess so."

I gestured to Kennedy. "This is Detective Kennedy. He's going to ask you some questions about Dhane and Trinity. Answer him as best you can, okay?"

Jun swallowed and bobbed his head.

Kennedy leaned against the wall, the mirror over his right shoulder. "What is your full name?"

"Jun. It means obedient." He smiled, looking like he expecting Kennedy to be impressed.

"Is that your real name? No last name?"

Jun tilted his head and squinted. "Doesn't it sound real?"

Kennedy gave me a look like it was my fault Jun had answered a question with a question. If he wasn't happy with Jun's answers now, I couldn't wait to see how he felt after another five or ten minutes of this.

"Moving on," Kennedy said. "How did you come to know Dhane and Trinity?"

"Playing Mah-jong with Willow at Tenchi's party. Trinity loves Mah-jong." Jun moved his gaze from Kennedy to me and sighed, his mouth bent down. "Loved. I keep forgetting."

Kennedy cleared his throat, getting Jun's attention back. "When was this?"

"Well, it would have been right after FanimeCon because that's when Tenchi told me about the party."

"How long ago?"

"Oh. Two…no, three years ago last March." He gave an affirmed nod. "Yes, March. FanimeCon is almost always in March."

"How well did you know Dhane?"

"I knew he liked spinach, but not lettuce. He had a mole on his neck shaped like a coin, and his hair wasn't real."

I stared, gape-mouthed, at Jun. Dhane's hair wasn't real? I could have sworn… Wow, that was a really good weave. I pictured all of the times I'd seen Dhane, and not once had I noticed his hair wasn't real. I itched to call Golda, his hairstylist, to find out how she did his hair.

Without missing a beat, Kennedy pressed on. "Did you know anything about his business? How it was run? Maybe you overheard him say something about it?"

"One time when I was playing Mah-jong with Trinity, he yelled at somebody on the phone."

"What did he yell?"

Jun concentrated real hard, his face squinching up with the effort. "He said, 'You effed it up for the last time. You're fired!' Only he didn't say effed, he said, you know, the F word."

"Yes, I know. Do you know who he was talking to?"

"I'm not sure."

"Okay. What about Dhane's marriage to Sora?"

Jun bobbed his head, eager now. "Dhane was married to Sora."

"That's right. Did Dhane and Sora ever fight? Would you say their marriage was a good one?"

"Mostly. But this one time Sora got real mad. She didn't like that Dhane left his socks on the bathroom floor. She yelled and yelled. Dhane yelled back, saying if he could put up with her playing leapfrog all the time, then she could put up with his socks on the floor."

Leapfrog. I rolled my lips in and looked at the ceiling to keep from giggling.

"Who did Dhane say Sora played leapfrog with?"

"He didn't."

"Who do you think Sora was playing leapfrog with?"

"I don't know. I was never invited to play."

A laugh caught in my throat. I smothered it, spraying the side of Kennedy's neck with a fine mist of snot.

Kennedy wiped his neck, keeping his focus on Jun. "If you had to guess, who do *you* think she played with?"

Jun's gaze veered off toward nothing. "Well, Trinity once told me she saw Sora playing hide the bone with Ace, so maybe she played leapfrog with him, too."

Clamping both hands over my mouth, I spun toward the wall, my body shaking with the effort to not burst out laughing.

Kennedy coughed. Then coughed again. "Did Sora know that Trinity saw her playing…games with Ace?"

"I don't know."

"Did Sora and Trinity get along?"

"All the time."

"What about Ace?" Kennedy asked. "Was Ace nice to Trinity?"

"Of course. Everyone was nice to Trinity. Curio, too."

"Curio the stuffed skunk, right?"

Jun bounced in his chair a little. "Yes! Have you met him?"

"No. I never met him." Kennedy's patience with Jun was impressive. I should have been taking notes.

"What about Dhane?" Kennedy continued. "How did Dhane and Ace get along?"

"I don't know. I never saw them together."

"How long have you known Tenchi?"

"A long time."

"How did Dhane get along with Tenchi? Did they like each other?"

"For a while."

Kennedy pulled away from the wall and took a step closer. "Did something happen to change that?"

My super suspicious alarm dinged. Kennedy had asked a question I hadn't even thought of.

"I don't know."

"How do you know they didn't like each other anymore?"

"Dhane told Tenchi he had to leave."

Whoa.

"When was this?"

Jun's gaze wandered off again. A long time passed without

him answering. I made a move to go to him, but Kennedy put an arm out, stopping me.

"Jun!" Kennedy said sharply, earning Jun's attention, interrupting whatever random thoughts were tumbling through his mind. "When did Dhane tell Tenchi he had to leave?"

"The day he died." Jun's voice was hollow, as if Dhane's death had carved a chunk out of him.

Double whoa.

"How did Tenchi handle that?"

Jun blinked up at Kennedy, his eyes wet. "He left."

"But he came back after Dhane's death, right?"

"Yes."

"What was Tenchi's role in Trinity's life? Were they friends or something more?"

"More?"

"More as in a romantic relationship."

Jun tilted his head from one side to the other, but I didn't think he was weighing his answer. He seemed confused.

"Detective Kennedy wants to know if Trinity and Tenchi were boyfriend and girlfriend. If they ever kissed and held hands, or if they were just friends like you and Trinity," I explained, earning a scowl from Kennedy that should have dropped me where I stood. "Sorry. He didn't understand."

"You're quiet, or you're out," Kennedy warned.

I made a key-turning motion over my mouth and threw the invisible key over my shoulder.

Kennedy returned his attention to Jun. "Were Trinity and Tenchi boyfriend and girlfriend or not?"

Jun shook his head so hard and fast he nearly unseated himself. The guard came up behind him and gripped his shoulders, pressing him down. Jun stopped shaking his head; his eyes went wide and fearful, his breaths short and shallow.

"Stop! Stop touching him." I moved forward and bent down,

trying to draw Jun's attention. "You're okay, Jun. Calm down."

"Where's Tenchi? Where'd he go?"

I looked to Kennedy for an answer. I hadn't seen Tenchi since the police had dragged him away after he'd tried to throw himself off Trinity's balcony. He motioned me over.

"Hospital. He tried to kill himself again," Kennedy whispered so Jun couldn't hear.

I put a hand over my mouth. "Oh, no. Is he okay?"

Kennedy gave a curt nod and jerked his head toward Jun. "I think he should join him."

I looked back at Jun. He watched us with an intensity I hadn't seen in him before. I debated whether or not to tell him the truth about Tenchi. He'd lost two of his friends already. I wasn't sure he could handle the possibility of losing another one so soon.

"Let me answer. Follow my lead," I told Kennedy.

I knew he didn't like following anyone's lead, but he agreed with another nod.

"Tenchi's okay," I told Jun. "He was very upset about losing Trinity. He just needs to be alone for a while. Okay?"

"But he's coming back, right?"

I wasn't sure how to answer. I didn't want to make promises that were out of my ability to keep. So I went with generic and pat, two characteristics I ordinarily despised. "He's your friend and he's going to need his friends to help him cope with losing Trinity."

Jun bobbed his head slowly. His grief etched lines in a face too young to have known such pain. I wanted so much to hug him and tell him it would all be okay, but I knew it wouldn't. His life, like so many others, had been irrevocably altered by the deaths of Dhane and Trinity.

Kennedy continued to gently prod answers from Jun. Watching him work was like having a front-row seat to the greatest show of patience on earth. Did this case have Kennedy's head spinning as wildly as mine? If so, he didn't show it. But then he had a lot more experience at this sort of thing than I did.

Like a dog chasing its tail, it seemed the more answers there were, the more questions there were to ask. I had the strongest sensation of a clock counting down, the hands moving closer and closer to the time when questions weren't enough and the answers painted a picture no one wanted to look at.

CHAPTER TWENTY-FOUR

When Kennedy had gotten all the answers he was likely to get from Jun for the time being, I followed him out into the hall.

"You were good with him in there," I told Kennedy.

He leaned in. "I don't like how close to this you are."

"I didn't set out to be."

"I suppose you didn't, but here you are." He inched closer, his gaze roaming my face. I could smell him—a combination of woodsy cologne and bad-ass cop—could see the shadow of his auburn beard and the light dusting of freckles on his cheeks. His gaze snapped to mine. "Be careful," he whispered, brushing my arm with his to open the door behind me. He swept past, close enough that I could feel the hard ridges of his body as it came into contact with mine.

That man confused me more than anyone I'd ever met. Just when I thought I had him nailed down, he'd throw me a curve ball that sent my thoughts spinning. Half the time I wasn't sure if he liked me or not, and the other half I was positive he didn't. And then there were times like now, when everything between us felt warped and out of balance. Whatever Kennedy's motives were I knew one thing for sure, it was all about the endgame with him. I'd be smart to remember that.

I let out a breath, slapped on an all-purpose smile, and followed him into the room. Alex and a couple of other cops I didn't recognize were there, watching Jun through the mirror. They were examining and discussing him as though he were a specimen in a jar.

I looked through the mirror, trying to see what they saw. Jun sat perfectly still, his head tilted to one side, eyes closed. I saw a boy, hurt and afraid. Sure, he dressed strange and acted funny, but really he was just so very sad and all alone. Didn't we all put on a façade we hoped the world would accept?

Platt came in with a sheaf of papers, grinning ear to ear. "Got him." He saw me and pulled up short. "Oh, hi, Azalea. I didn't know you were here." His cheeks flushed at the catcalls and whistles from his fellow officers about his new look.

"Don't tease him." I pointed at one of the officers. "You're not fooling anyone with that comb-over. And you—" I turned my finger on the other cop. "There's this really great new product… it's called shampoo. Check into it." I switched my attention to the third officer, the one who had interrogated me after Dhane's death, Detective Weller. "As for you"—I gave him the once-over—"nice hair. You should give the number for your stylist to Roy and these other two."

Detective Weller winked at me. I could almost hear the ping off his toothpaste smile.

"Who did you get, Roy?" Comb-over asked with a smirk, showing off less –than-stellar dental hygiene.

Platt jabbed a thumb at Jun. "I got a name for the clown in there."

"What'd you get?" Kennedy asked.

"Real name's Hideki Komatsu. American citizen. Orphaned at the age of eight." Platt frowned over that bit of knowledge. "In the system until it kicked him out at eighteen. He's got a clean record. No warrants. No arrests."

I kept my eyes on Jun as Platt read off a few more tidbits about him. He hadn't gotten much of a break in life, losing both parents and being thrown in the system at such a young age. Was it any wonder he had tried to recreate a family for himself and a new identity to go with it?

"He's a grown-up," Alex said next to my ear. "He doesn't need a mother."

"Doesn't he? Doesn't everyone?"

"You can't fix what's broken inside him."

"No. I can't." And that made me sadder than I had words for.

Alex sighed. "All right. We'll take him back to the hotel with us. Make sure he's okay. But when we leave tomorrow, you're going to have to say good-bye."

"Thank you."

"Don't thank me just yet. There could be charges against him for injuring that officer. Or Kennedy could decide to throw him in the hospital with his friend."

"Or I could cut him loose," Kennedy said from behind us.

I turned away from the image of Jun in the mirror. "Really? You would do that?"

Kennedy's frown could have anchored a boat. "Yeah. I would do that."

"Thank y—"

Kennedy cut me off with a hand. "Don't thank me, just keep him out of trouble and out of my sight."

"Done. When can he leave?"

"We'll take the restraints off and see how he does. If he's calm, he's out of here."

"Tha—"

Kennedy put his hand up again, then made a shooing motion. I got the hint: don't let the door hit you on the way out.

Alex and I went into the hall. I turned back to say good-bye to Platt, and I saw Kennedy lean over and whisper something to him. Platt nodded solemnly. Kennedy looked up and caught me, his eyes hard and flat. Reaching up, he grabbed the edge of the door, shutting it in my face.

My hinky radar went off. Something wasn't right here. I stared at the closed door a moment, trying to get a sense for what was off. Replaying the scene in my head, it suddenly hit me that Kennedy had *let* me hear the information about Jun's life. Why would he have done that after he made me practically swear a blood oath to stay out of his investigation? He must have wanted me to have that information, but why? And what had he whispered to Platt? What was he planning?

I walked to where Alex waited outside the room Jun was in. I considered telling him my suspicions, but he'd probably just wave it off, teasing me about my overblown curiosity. I gave the door Kennedy had closed one last considering look. The detective was definitely up to something.

The other door opened, and Jun came out, followed by the uniformed officer.

"Azalea!" Jun threw himself at me, knocking me back against the wall. He squeezed me tight, rocking me side to side. "I'm so glad to see you."

I patted him on the back. "Good to see you, too."

He pulled back. "He said I could leave. I didn't have to answer any more questions."

"That's right."

"Where are we going?" Jun looked at me with that wide-open expression, as if he hoped I'd answer Disneyland or something.

"The hair show?"

"Oh, yes." He bobbed his head up and down. "Let's go there."

We walked down the hall toward the entrance. Behind us a door opened. I looked back to find Kennedy standing in the hall, arms crossed, watching us. His clinical detachment had morphed into something hard and calculating. The fine hairs on my neck and arms lifted. I couldn't help feeling as though I was walking into a carefully laid trap. One designed specifically for me.

The chill stayed with me as we walked into the oven-parched afternoon. I rubbed my arms.

Alex noticed the gesture. "Something wrong?"

"Yeah, but I'm not sure what."

"What do you mean?"

I gave a quick glace back at Jun, who strolled behind us, his head bopping to a beat only he could hear. "Kennedy made a big show with Amber about me not being involved in this case," I whispered. "He was very clear about that. So why would he let me stay while he questioned Jun? And why did he let us hear all about his life? It's like he wanted us to have that information. Or me specifically."

Alex gave that some thought as we stood at the curb, trying to hail a cab. "You did calm Jun down."

"I know, but he could have told me to tell Jun to cooperate and then make me leave. It didn't occur to me at the time how quickly he gave in to my staying during questioning. Don't you find it odd?"

Alex threw a look at Jun, who was busy touching a finger to the spikes of a cactus and giggling. "Define odd."

"You know what I mean."

Alex slipped an arm over my shoulders. "Odd has become so commonplace for me in the last couple of days that normal now seems strange."

I gave him an elbow to the ribs. "Be serious."

"I am, but yes, now that you mention it, it was unusual."

"I think he's up to something."

"What?"

"I wish I knew."

"Not everything is a conspiracy. Sometimes things really are how they appear on the surface."

"Shh," I said. "Don't let my mother hear you say that. There's a conspiracy for every theory and ulterior motives behind every action. I was raised on suspicion and doubt. It coated my cornflakes and was stirred into my milk. I call it curiosity because it sounds cuter, but really I'm just a chip off the old block."

"Come on. You're not as cynical as all that."

I wasn't so sure. Life hadn't exactly proven itself to be fair and danger-free. I looked back at Jun, who was staring up at the sun as if he couldn't quite figure out what it was. Maybe that's why I'd taken to him. He reminded me a little of myself once upon a time, before life had smacked me upside the head with reality. What was so wrong with a little escapism?

A cab finally pulled up to the curb, illegally picking us up off the street instead of at a taxi stand. We'd have to tip extra for that…again. If I had to pay for another taxi ride from the police station, I'd have to find a way to deduct it from my taxes.

We all climbed in, with me riding the hump, wedged between Jun and Alex.

The ride to the convention center was blissfully short. Jun scrambled out of the cab with the speed and grace of a young giraffe, all knees and elbows. Placing a hand on the seat, I slid over to get out on Jun's side. My finger caught the edge of something. I pulled it out from between the seats. A hotel key card.

Alex had come around to my side of the car and gave me his hand. As soon as I was on the curb, I turned to pay the fare and slipped the card into my pocket.

"I already took care of it," Alex said, closing the door and waving the driver off.

"Thanks. You're much better to ride with than Roy. He didn't even offer to pitch in for the tip."

I moved to follow Jun into the convention center, but Alex

held me back. "I've been giving some thought to what you said about Kennedy. And I think maybe you're being a little paranoid, wanting to see some kind of conspiracy that doesn't exist."

"Paranoid?"

"You asked my opinion."

"My mistake."

"If you wanted someone to agree with you, then you should have taken your concerns to Juan Carlos or Jun. You asked my opinion. I'm giving it."

"Well, you're wrong."

"If I'm wrong, I'll be the first to admit it. But I think you should look at the possibility that your emotions are clouding your judgment." He put his hands on my shoulders, pulling me toward him. "I'm worried about you." He traced the dark circle under my eye with a fingertip. "You've been through a lot and you haven't been sleeping well."

"So in my sleep-addled state I'm manufacturing conspiracies, is that it?"

"Don't get mad. I'm just concerned about you."

"Then stop saying things that make me mad."

He released me and threw up his hands. "Fine. I'll do nothing but agree with you from now on."

"There you go again, saying stupid, patronizing things that make me mad."

"There's no winning here, is there?"

"You want to win?" I cracked a self-deprecating smile. "Won't happen. You can't beat a paranoid, sleep-deprived conspiracy theorist who only wants a yes-man in her life."

"For a minute there, I thought we were having our first fight."

"Oh, you'll know when we have our first fight." I eyed him as though he might not measure up. "I hope you're good at ducking."

"Don't worry about me. I'm a dodge-ball champ from way back."

Gosh, he was cute when flustered to the edge of annoyance. His cheeks were a little flushed, his eyes sharp and snapping. But mostly I liked that he could go toe-to-toe with me. It didn't hurt that he was sexy as hell and could kiss the clothes off a nun. I could get in real trouble with this one.

He moved into me, dipping his head for a quick kiss, proving his ducking skills and a whole lot more. *Yeah, I could get into some real trouble here*, I thought as he shifted back to meet my gaze. And there was the other thing that set Alex apart. He elevated eye-to-eye contact to an art form. I could almost feel my resolve to take it slow melt, along with a few other things, like my heart and virtue. If I weren't careful, my panties would be dropping faster than coins from a slot machine.

"Come on," Jun whined, dancing from foot to foot. "The Goth Hair for Emos class is just about to start."

Alex twined his fingers with mine and we followed Jun into the convention center. "The what for what?" he asked.

"Goth. You know, black hair, lots of black eyeliner, black fingernails, pale skin, old-fashioned black clothing. Think macabre, pagan, erotic, and dark."

"Uh-huh. And what's the other?"

"Emo. Cutters, long bangs, studded belts, bright colors, and tight jeans. You know, sad, angst-ridden teens who write really deep, emotional poetry and cry a lot," I said.

"And cutters?" he asked.

"People who cut or hurt themselves to feel physical or relieve emotional pain."

"Huh. I don't know whether to be impressed or depressed that you know all that."

"Me neither."

We reached the classroom where the workshop was being held. Glancing around, I felt like the only one not dressed for the costume party. The Emos looked like peacocks among the

Goth crows. Jun fit in just fine, since his style was a tweaked conglomeration of both groups.

"Hey, there's Trent, Emily, and Raven," Jun said. "Come meet them."

I eyed the tattooed, multipierced, black-garbed group he pointed out. "Yeah, that's okay. You go be with your friends. Alex and I will sit in the back."

When Jun was out of earshot, Alex leaned in. "Are we really staying? I've been made as a cop by half the room. The other half can't get their eyes off their toes. Or if they could, they wouldn't be able to see through all that hair in their face."

"Come on, Grandpa." I took his hand, steering him toward the exit. "I've got something in mind that might be more your speed."

"Does it involve a dark, out-of-the-way corner?"

"No. It's a class where they use five shears at once to cut hair."

"How the hell do you do that? You only have two hands."

"No, silly. They bind five or more shears together to make a multiblade shear, which isn't all that special on its own. That's been done for years." We were crossing through the lobby on our way to the other classroom. "What's so cool about this workshop is that you use two sets of multi shears, one in each hand."

"Like Edward Scissorhands?"

"Kinda like that, yeah." I stuttered to a stop in front of the memorial that had been set up the day Dhane had died. Something was very wrong.

Someone had drawn on the poster of Dhane, a jagged line right across his throat. Real-looking blood dripped from the gash, creating a puddle on the floor as if the wound had actually bled. I shuddered and curled into Alex's arms.

With a hand to my mouth, I whispered, "Who would do such a horrible thing?"

Holding me, Alex bent to get a closer look, then leaned to inspect the back of the poster. "Someone rigged it. See here."

I unfolded myself from him and peered at where he pointed. Someone had attached a bag of blood-like stuff and a small battery-operated pump that dribbled droplets onto the front side through a small hole. Pretty ingenious and majorly disturbing.

Alex had his phone out and punched in numbers.

"Who are you calling?"

"Kennedy."

"Why would he care about vandalism?"

"This may be the work of the killer. Kennedy'll want to see this, maybe take some evidence." He turned away a little, talking into the phone. "Kennedy? Alex Craig here. I found something you may want to have your guys get a look at." He described what had been done to the poster. A couple seconds later he disconnected the call. "He's sending somebody down."

"Good. Let's go. The farther away from that thing I get, the better."

"Can't. Someone might tamper with it and destroy evidence."

"If they haven't already. Who knows how long it's been here like this. I'm not sticking around." I hugged myself, rubbing my arms. "That thing gives me creep bumps."

"I told Kennedy I'd stay till his guy shows up."

"You're on your own, then. I'm going to watch my Edward Scissorhands workshop. It's the last session of the convention and I'm not missing anything else." I pointed in the general direction of the room I'd be in. "I'll be in N245 down that hall. Join me when you're done, or if I'm done first, I'll meet you back here."

"I don't like the idea of you being on your own, Azalea."

"Look at all these people. I couldn't be alone here if I tried. Besides, what could happen?"

"To you? What hasn't happened?" He started ticking off items on his fingers. "You found a decapitated head—"

"I didn't find it, Juan Carlos did."

"You were there. Then you were there where the body was

found."

I propped both hands on my hips. "That was by accident. I didn't *know* there would be a body in that suite."

"You managed to find *another* dead body."

"That wasn't my fault either. I was kidnapped!"

"Yes, kidnapped." He ticked off an extra finger. "Then you were questioned by the police—"

"Voluntarily."

"—your flower was found in the hand of the second murder victim."

"I *lost* that flower." I cut a hand through the air. "Totally not my fault either."

"As I'm sure the next terrible thing that will happen to you will be. Totally. Not. *Your*. Fault."

I huffed and I puffed and dang it all, I couldn't come up with a rebuttal.

Alex pointed a finger at me. "Face it. You're a trouble magnet. So pardon me if I think of a thousand and one things that *could* happen to you when you ask me what could happen. And of all those things I can come up with, I'll bet I don't come up with the one thing that actually *will* happen."

"Maybe I should have asked what *else* could possibly happen, because I should have more than reached my quota. Don't you think? I mean, really, what else *could* happen?"

He gave me the same why-I-oughta look Moe used to give Curly. "Your logic." He shook his head slowly. "It defies logic."

"Yes, but it makes a perfect kind of sense." I started to back away from him toward my workshop. One step, then another. "Don't you think?"

"Azalea," he warned.

I took another step back. "I'll be fine." I held up my cell phone. "See, I have my phone." Another step. "I'll call you and keep the line open. Then you can listen in." I was about ten paces away now.

"This is not a good idea." He reached for his ringing phone and frowned at the display before answering, *"Azalea."*

"Hello?" I said as I backed up a little more. "See, this will work," I assured him over the phone.

"Azalea," he growled into his phone as I spun and jogged away.

"You can watch me by listening in," I told him. "You can't see me now, right?"

"No."

"But you can hear me. I'll leave the phone on in my lap during the workshop. I'll be fine."

He didn't answer, and I got the feeling I wouldn't be fine when he caught up with me later.

I slipped into a seat toward the back of the classroom. The workshop had already started. "Alex?" I whispered.

"I'm here. I still don't th—"

The line went dead. I hit the end button and redialed. Nothing. No bars. Ah, cripes. I'd forgotten all about the spotty reception in the convention center.

CHAPTER TWENTY-FIVE

I kept checking my phone for reception, totally missing the explanation on how to hold the shears. After about the fiftieth attempt, I gave up. If by some miracle I managed to get more than one measly flashing bar and Alex was able to get through to me, I didn't want to miss his call. So I slipped my phone into the front pocket of my jeans and came up against the hotel card key I'd found in the cab. I pulled it out and flipped it over. Of all the rotten, mocking luck! The pearlescent, metallic logo of the Raine Hotel twinkled up at me like a warning beacon under the fluorescent overhead lighting. What were the odds? What were the mother-loving odds?

Of all the hotels in all of Las Vegas, I find a key card from the Raine? My luck. It sucked. So very, very bad. And my idiotic, suspicious, conspiracy-crazy mind automatically clicked to the possibility that this key card…from *that* hotel…could have fallen out of Jun's pocket during the cab ride.

No. Jun was staying at the Excalibur not the Raine. Someone else must have lost it. It could be anyone's.

But what if it wasn't? What if it was the key to either Trinity's or Dhane's suite? And what if Jun had used it when he killed one or both of them?

No. Not possible.

But…he could have. He had means…the key. It was possible that either Dhane or Trinity could have given him the key to their suite. Opportunity…I had no idea where he'd been when either one of them was killed. Motive? What would've been his motive? They were his friends. They were the family he'd created in place of the one he'd lost. He'd been devastated by their deaths. Especially Trinity's.

I sucked in a breath. What if the killer had planted it on him? Tried to set him up? The police wouldn't have searched him when they'd brought him in for questioning, but they probably would have when they restrained him after his breakdown. They might not have given a second thought to finding a hotel key card on him. Or maybe they didn't find it at all.

I fretted until I broke out in a sweat, my mind spinning one possible scenario after another. I'd worked myself up so much that I began to imagine the key card had been planted in the cab or on Jun for me to find like my flower in Trinity's hand. It might be another message. Maybe somebody, maybe the killer, was watching me right now to see what I'd do with it.

I spun in my seat, looking over my right, then left shoulder. All I saw was a sea of anonymous faces focused on the teacher of the workshop, not on me. Facing front again, I couldn't shake the feeling of being watched. My paranoia soared until my armpits and palms were moist and tingly and I was positive that the murderer had me in his or her sights.

Suddenly the thought of standing next to a bleeding poster with Alex was much more appealing than sitting here with eyes, maybe the eyes of a killer, on me. Watching…waiting.

I jumped up out of my seat and excused my way down the row until I hit the door at a run. I kept on running back down the hall, through the lobby, and straight at Alex.

He caught me, pulling me in and away. Turning his body to protect me, he made a motion toward the gun he'd normally be carrying if was on duty, prepared to battle whatever or whoever was chasing me. "What happened? What's the matter?"

I clung to him, shaking like a drug addict in her third day of detox.

"Azalea, answer me."

"I…" I what? I found a key card and freaked out for no reason? In the presence of Alex's practical solidity, I felt completely stupid. I'd let my paranoia run away with my reason, conjuring up one ridiculous scenario after another. I was losing it for sure. It was bound to happen, really. I'd endured maximum exposure to some major whack jobs and now insanity had me in its insidious grip. Or maybe I was just overly stressed and sleep deprived.

I decided to go with option two.

"Nothing," I said. "I'm fine. Just a little tired and stressed out, I guess."

"I don't think so. I know panic when I see it. What happened?"

"Nothing outside my own head. I'm fine, I promise. How much longer until Kennedy's guy shows up?"

"Could be five minutes or an hour." He searched my gaze, maybe looking for the truth or something less definable, like my sanity. After a few moments, he seemed satisfied. Relaxing, he released me from his embrace but stayed tethered to me by our joined hands.

Twenty minutes later, Kennedy's guy showed up, asked us a few questions, then did his thing with the poster, taking it with him when he left. It was all very anticlimactic and rather boring, not at all like TV.

"What now?" Alex asked.

I checked the time on my phone. "We've got a few hours until the awards show. Let's grab some food and take it back to the room. I'm going to need all that time to get ready."

We headed toward the front of the convention center to grab a taxi.

"*All* that time?"

I propped my hands on my hips. "You've never lived with a woman, have you?"

"I have three sisters."

"Three? Wow. Older or younger?"

"Older."

"How much older?"

"There's eleven years between me and my youngest sister. I was kind of a surprise."

"I bet you were. Well, that certainly explains it."

"What?" He seemed genuinely perplexed.

"Why you have no idea how long it takes a woman to get ready for a special occasion. There's hair time, makeup time, getting dressed time, getting undressed time, getting redressed time, trying on multiple pairs of shoes time, and primping and posing time followed by last-minute changes time. Plus you have to account for forgetting and going back for something time."

"I'm glad I'm a guy," he mumbled as he climbed into the cab with me.

"Speaking of, what are you wearing tonight?" I eyed his button-down shirt and slacks, doubting he'd brought anything more fancy than that. "It's formal."

"I have a dark suit. Is that formal enough?"

"You brought a dark suit to Las Vegas?"

"I always bring a suit," he defended with a shrug. "You never know."

"Huh."

"What?"

"I bet you pay your bills as soon as you get them."

"What does that have to do with anything?"

"You probably fold your underwear, too."

"So?"

"Let me guess, you change your oil every three thousand miles and never have less than a quarter of a tank of gas. You change the batteries in your smoke detectors on the same day every year. You don't cheat on your taxes. Your mother gets flowers every Mother's Day. And you're never late to an appointment."

He glared at me like I'd caught him under the covers with a Victoria's Secret catalog. "Is that a crime?"

"Nerd alert."

He folded his arms over his chest and huffed. Apparently, I'd deeply offended him, when in reality I found his nerd status kind of sexy.

"If you have a well-worn library card in your wallet and could get rid of the thousand and one viruses on my computer, I'd probably jump you right now."

His smile crept in slowly, getting wickeder and wickeder as it grew. He pulled his wallet out and handed me a library card so worn it was nearly transparent. "And the answer is yes, if the motherboard isn't shot, I could probably fix your computer."

"Oh my God, that's so hot," I breathed, edging closer until I had him pressed up against the door. I toyed with a button on his shirt. "Um, how many majors did you have in college?"

"Three."

I bit my lip and let out a whimper.

"I speak four languages."

I leaned in, running a hand up his leg. "Tell me more," I whispered in his ear, then bit his earlobe.

"I, uh, my IQ is one forty-three."

"Oh, God." I crawled up into his lap, my hands fisting in his hair. *More.* I licked the edge of his ear and rubbed up against him.

"Uh…yeah…I, mmm, qualify for, ah, Mensa."

That snapped it. I dove in, kissing him with a hot, hungry

abandon I hadn't felt in forever. Maybe never. He lowered me down on the seat, kissing me back. We rolled around and some clothing may have gotten dislodged, hands seeking the feel of flesh on flesh.

"You want me to drive around a little more, or you wanna take that upstairs?"

Breathing hard, Alex and I turned our heads to find the cab driver watching us over the back of the seat. Alex levered himself off me and fumbled around for his wallet, which must have gotten lost during our mad make-out session. I scrambled to sit up, yanked my clothing back in place, and opened the cab door, hoping for a quick exit.

Finally locating his wallet on the floor, Alex lifted my foot to grab it, nearly sending me out the door headfirst. He reached for my hand and tugged me back upright. "Sorry."

He paid the driver and we found ourselves standing on the curb in awkward silence, watching the taxi drive off.

Alex ran his hands through his hair, smoothing it back into place, his gaze everywhere but on me. "We, ah, forgot to get food."

I rubbed at my forehead. "Oh, yeah."

"I can go get some." He glanced around as though he were unsure how to accomplish the task. "I'll just go. Find food." He strode away, leaving me to gape at his retreating back.

Had he just walked away? Oh my God. I covered my face, mortified. What was wrong with me? I'd backed him into a corner and threw myself at him. He probably hated me now, couldn't wait to get away from me. I whirled around and walked into the hotel, embarrassment burning my cheeks.

I half jogged to the elevator bank and jabbed a finger at the call button.

"Just so you know…" Alex said from behind me, causing me to jump and spin.

Flattening myself against the elevator doors, I looked at him with wide, unblinking eyes.

"I'm not leaving because I didn't like what happened in that taxi," he said, frustration and anger deepening his voice.

"Okay."

He began to pace. "I thought… With everything that's happened to you I thought…" He stopped and glared at me, all rumpled and sweaty, his brows lowered. "I think it's best if we don't get carried away just yet. Understand?"

"Uh-huh. Okay." No, I didn't understand at all. Not at freaking all.

He nodded as if some great decision had been made. "Okay. I'll go get the food, then." He turned and marched away.

The elevator pinged, and before I could think to move, the doors opened. Losing my balance, arms pinwheeling, I fell back, taking out an older couple. We landed in a pile of twisting, grumbling bodies. Coins from their gambling cups flew everywhere, pelting us, as we lay sprawled on the floor. The other occupants tiptoed around us and off the elevator. I thought I saw one guy scoop up some coins on his way out. Jerk.

I rolled to the side and assisted the couple to their feet, helping them pick up as many coins as we could find. The man complained about the ones that had likely fallen down the elevator shaft, so I gave him a twenty and wished them luck in their gambling.

Trudging down the hall to my room, I was so busy trying to decipher what Alex had said that I didn't notice the man walking toward me from the other end of the hall until we were almost even. He watched me, blatantly staring, but not in a sinister or sexual way. He looked at me like you would a palm tree or office art.

We came even. He didn't smile or speak, just stared. I turned as he passed, not trusting enough to put my back to him. He maintained eye contact for another moment or two, then turned away and continued on. I stopped and watched him until he disappeared down the corridor to the elevators.

Weird.

My curiosity piqued, I jogged after him, holding my big bag to my body so it wouldn't rattle and give me away. Peeking around the corner, I was shocked to find he'd disappeared. The elevator dinged and the doors opened. After a moment they closed and the elevator was on its way again. I tiptoed around, trying to figure out where the man had gone, and came upon another hallway. I held my breath and peered around the corner. Nothing. Just an empty hall dotted with doors.

I headed back to my room, questioning my mental faculties. Hello? Paranoid much? I'd just made the turn down the hall to my room when…there the man was again! Still staring, headed my way. We passed each other as we'd done before, but this time after he passed, I hightailed it to my room, swiped my key card, and ducked inside.

I leaned against the closed door, clutching my chest, trying to calm myself down. What was that man doing, patrolling the halls? Walking off energy? Maybe he had a strange kind of OCD. I looked through the peephole of the door and waited. There he was again, looking right at my door as he went by!

I flipped the lock on the door and made a beeline for the mini fridge. I pulled out one of the juice-box-sized wines I'd sneaked onto the plane, punched a hole in the top, and drank straight from the container. Who needed a glass when you had the finest fermented grapes ever packaged in cardboard? I glugged a little more, then gave the door a sideways glance, completely positive the man wasn't just out for a stroll.

My phone rang, keeping me from indulging my curiosity. Juan Carlos.

"Hello?" I answered.

"What are you wearing tonight? It'd better be good because we're going to be bridesmaids. I can't be documented for posterity standing next to you decked out in one of those lacy, vintagey dresses you think look Victorian, but really look like you wrapped yourself in my aunt Mabel's good tablecloth. And do something with your hair for once. Wait! Never mind. I'll be right over."

He hung up before I could ask him what the hell he was talking about. A minute later there was a knock at my door. I checked the peephole before opening the door to Juan Carlos.

I started to speak, but before I could get a word out, Juan Carlos brushed past me, mouth running like a legislator midfilibuster.

"You're not dressed? We're going to be late! Look at you. Oh my God. We've got *so* much work to do." He ran his gaze over me. "You look like you got into a hot and heavy backseat tumble."

I put my back to him, trying to hide my flaming cheeks. Dang Juan Carlos! Why did he always have to be so observant?

He went to my closet and started sliding hangers, making comments on everything he came across. "Ugly. You look hippy in this. Always hated that color. You spent money on *that*? I bet the dead presidents cried. Well, well, well. What do we have here?" He pulled Alex's suit from the closet. "Holy moley, mother-loving designer! *Prada*," he said on a pleasured sigh, rubbing a sleeve across his cheek. "Detective Dreamy has the best taste. Can I have him when you're done? I promise to be good to him. We can dress in matching Prada. We'll be the Pradettes. No, the Pradettos."

"Gimme that." I took the suit and returned it to the closet. I fished around in the closet some, then pulled out the dress I intended to wear. Although now in light of Alex's Prada—and who brings a Prada suit to Las Vegas?—I wasn't so sure it was right. "I'm wearing this." I held up the dress, blocking his face from my view. He went stone silent. I lowered the dress, afraid he hated it so much he'd passed out from too much ugly. "Well?"

"It's gorgeous," he whispered hoarsely. I could have sworn he had tears in his eyes, too. "Who picked it out for you? It's perfect."

I yanked the dress away from his sight. "I picked it out."

"Gawd, where'd you get it? Can I touch it?"

"You really like it?"

"Totally. I wish I could wear it. Lemme see."

I handed the dress over, still not sure it was right.

Juan Carlos took it to the window where the light was better. "Real vintage. The lining, the boning, the construction…they don't make them like this anymore." He held it against his body, shaping it to fit his nonexistent curves. "I think for the first time ever I wish I were a girl just so I could wear this. Where ever did you get it? Do they have more? Change that. Do they have men's clothes?"

"I got it in this little vintage clothing store off the Orange Circle. They have a separate store for men." I remembered what I wanted to ask him about his phone call. "What were you talking about on the phone about us being bridesmaids?"

"Oh my God! Okay, so I got this phone call from Vivian and you'll never guess what." He waved a hand at me. "No, let me tell it. So Richard and I were…well never mind what we were doing. Vivian calls me and she's all out of breath, squealing like a teenager at a concert, going on about being in Vegas and what you do in Vegas—"

"She's getting married?"

"Well, now you spoiled it. But yes! Viv and James were headed down to the courthouse to get their license, and after the awards we're all going to a chapel to get them hitched. Can you believe it?"

I shook my head.

"That's not the best part. She wants us to be bridesmaids!"

"Why didn't she call me?"

"She said she did and you didn't answer. Anyway." He held up the dress. "This is so perfect. We're going to match!"

I must have missed Viv's call at the convention center. Stupid bad reception. I couldn't believe it. Vivian and James were getting married. I was so happy for her. "I have to call her."

"No time. If we're going to fix you up to look good enough to stand next to me, then we'd better get busy." He clapped his hands. "Chop, chop. Out of those ratty, old clothes. Put on a robe so you won't mess up your hair and makeup getting dressed later." He gave my dress one last lingering caress before hanging it back up. "Gorgeous. I promise you I'll have her looking good enough to deserve you," he told the dress. He sighed and turned back to me, eyeing me critically. "You brought, like, eight pairs of Spanx, right? And a good bra? Never mind." He made a shooing motion. "Go. Change. I have half-a-dozen miracles to perform and not nearly enough time."

I zipped into the bathroom, stripped down to my bra and panties, and threw on my robe. By the time I came out of the bathroom, Juan Carlos had set up a station, using the desk chair and full-length mirror. He sat in the chair, examining his eyebrows up close in the mirror while talking on the phone.

"That catty little mouse," he said with some astonishment. "Who knew Plain Jane had it in her to double cross a double cross. Good for her." He noticed me and held up a finger for me to wait. "I know you're a genius," he said into the phone. "That's why we get along so well. I can't do anything with the intel, but I still owe you. Okay. Later." He clicked his phone off.

"What intel?" I asked.

"Oh, nothing." He stood up and waved me into the chair. "Sit. I have a minor miracle to work and primitive tools to work it with. Would it kill you to get a proper eyelash curler?"

Hmm. I knew that shifty-eyed look of his. "You learned something about the murders, didn't you?"

His gaze slid away. "Me? No. I don't know what you're talking about."

"You're a terrible liar."

"All right! You beat it out of me. I'm a broken man." He perched himself on the edge of the desk, settling in to spill all.

"You'll never guess what ole Big Mac did!" I opened my mouth to speak, but he beat me to it. "She two-timed the two-timer. She out tricked the trickster. Foiled the foibler—"

I put up a hand to stop him. "Got it. What did she do?"

"She patented her new product in her own name, not the company's! Can you believe it? She *owns* the formula to that incredible new hair color."

I dropped down into the chair, my thoughts doing backflips and somersaults. MacKenzie Todd *had* outtricked the trickster. "So it didn't matter whether or not Dhane sold the company. Either way, she owned the product. She really is a genius." Even on the slight chance Mac might've paid someone to kill Dhane while she sat in Washington with the perfect alibi, she had no motive. There might have been a lengthy court battle between her and Dhane, but then again maybe not. If Dhane was keen to sell the company, he might not have cared what MacKenzie did with the patent.

"Uh-oh. You're doing it again. You're thinking about investigating, aren't you?" Juan Carlos asked.

"MacKenzie's out because she lacks both motive and opportunity. That leaves Ace and Sora. Either one of them could have killed Dhane and Trinity." My thoughts were spinning like a roulette wheel, the little ball popping around, looking for a place to land. "My money's on Ace. That kind of devotion would make him do anything. Plus, I can't see somebody like Sora getting her hands dirty."

"You promised! Detective Dreamboat is going to have *my* head for getting you started on this again."

"I'm not getting started again." You can't start something that you never really stopped. I mentally patted myself on the back for that little gem. "I'm just thinking about…things."

"I don't like this."

"You don't have to. You just have to keep your mouth shut. I promise I won't do anything to put myself in danger. I'm not investigating. I'm just thinking things through."

"I still don't like it."

"You've made that abundantly clear."

He got up from the desk and squirted some foundation on a sponge. "I care about you, girl. I just want you to be careful."

"I will."

Half an hour later, Alex walked in with bags of food that smelled so good I almost passed out from inhaling so deeply.

He stopped with a jerk at the sight of Juan Carlos applying liquid eyeliner in long strokes across my eyelids. "I only brought enough for two."

"That's okay," Juan Carlos said. "If she eats, she might not fit into her dress. Smells good. What'd you bring us?"

"Burgers. I meant I didn't bring enough for you. Just for Azalea and me." Alex set the bags on the desk and handed me a soda. "You want to eat now or wait?" he asked me.

"I'd better eat before he puts on my lipstick."

Alex pulled a burger and fries out of the bag and handed them to me. He glanced around, like he didn't know what to do with himself. "I think I'll go downstairs." He looked at me as if he expected something from me.

There was still a whiff of awkwardness in the air between Alex and me that was almost tangible. We glanced at each other, but there was no real eye contact, as if we might see something in each other that we didn't want to see. I wasn't entirely sure what had happened back in that cab and what Alex had meant about not getting carried away. He was the one who had pushed for a date and then had hung around to keep me safe. So why was he pulling back just when I was starting to get comfortable with the idea of moving forward?

CHAPTER TWENTY-SIX

"Look at your boobs. Look at them! Can I touch them?"

I swatted Juan Carlos's hand away. "No, you can't touch them." My breasts were so high I could practically rest my chin on them. They sure didn't make dresses like this anymore. All the boning and stays carved curves in the figure I hadn't known existed.

"So you think I look good?" I turned to the side, trying to see what the back of me looked like in the full-length mirror.

"I think Detective Delish is going to have a hard time fitting into his slacks. Get it? *Hard* time." He snickered at his own joke.

I had to resist the urge to roll my eyes so I didn't dislodge one of my false eyelashes. "I got it. You really think I look good?"

"Honey, you look so good *I'm* almost having a hard time fitting in my slacks. Speaking of. I'd better go and get myself dressed." He kissed me on the cheek. "You're beautiful. Perfect. I'll meet you in the hall in ten minutes. Be ready."

After he left, I smoothed my hands down the front of the dress. The midnight-black satin was cool and smooth beneath my touch. In the classic fifties style, the dress fit snugly down my hips, then flared at my thighs. The sweetheart halter framed my bust, leaving my back bare. A built-in sash wrapped across my hips, tying where the dress began its flare. It was feminine to the extreme. Taking advantage of the skin left exposed by the dress, Juan Carlos had pulled my hair into a simple French twist with a low sweep of bangs off to one side.

Sitting down, I slid my feet into a pair of black-satin stiletto evening sandals. Just as I buckled the last one, Alex walked in. Surprised, I jumped up.

He froze when he saw me, his mouth slack, eyes glazed over. He stared at me so long I grew nervous, twisting my fingers behind my back. His eyes were everywhere, taking in every detail, from the top of my sleek twist to the tips of my silver-painted toes and back again a dozen times.

"Wow." He infused that one word with so much heat, my heart skipped a beat and I got that warm, tingly feeling he'd generated in the cab.

"Yeah?"

He swallowed hard, his eyes twinkling in that way that could make a good girl go bad. He nodded. "Oh, yeah."

"So we're okay?"

"What?" He looked confused, like his brain couldn't quite make the subject leap.

I motioned back and forth between us. "You and me."

His brows bunched, and he shook his head.

Disappointment washed over me and it took all my strength to act like I didn't care. "Are you still going?"

"What?"

"To the awards? We're leaving in ten minutes. After that I assume you'll be at the wedding."

"Wait a minute." He put his hands up in a stop gesture. "Back up."

"To where?"

"To right after I came in and we started talking."

I grabbed my earrings and evening bag. "Why?" I brushed

past him and pulled my white faux-fur wrap, which was more for show than warmth, out of the closet. "What's the point? If you're going, you'd better get dressed. We're leaving—"

"I know, in ten minutes. What did I miss? What just happened here?"

"Are you kidding me?" I spun around and tried to open the door.

He reached over my shoulder and slapped his palm on the door, preventing my escape. "Azalea, talk to me."

Tipping my head back to glare at the ceiling, I huffed out a frustrated breath.

He dipped his head. His breath whispered over the contours of my neck, sending shivers through me. "Mmm, you smell as good as you look."

I spun around and found myself pinned between his big body and the door. "Stop it!"

"What? What did I do?"

"It's what you're doing. Hot, cold, hot, cold, hot again. I can't keep up."

"Please tell me what you're talking about." He brushed his thumb over the pulse in my neck.

"Alex, stop."

Taking a step back, he raised his hands in surrender.

"I can't think when you do that. Stop it. Stop giving me go-ahead signals and then pushing me away. And stop looking at my breasts!"

"But they're so—" He made a helpless gesture. His voice deepened, sending little vibrations through me. "There. So very, very there." He tipped his head to one side. "What do you mean pushing you away? When did I push you away?" It took him a moment while I stood there fuming at him, forcing him to maintain eye contact with me and not let his gaze drop, for him to come around to it. "You're talking about what happened after what happened in the cab?"

I nodded.

"You said you were okay with taking it slow. Although seeing you in that dress sure makes a liar out of you."

"You did not just call me a liar."

He started to say something, shook his head, and started again. "That was a badly timed joke. Sorry."

"Apology accepted."

"Back to what happened earlier. Vivian told me a little bit about your past."

I narrowed my eyes at him. "She shouldn't have done that." I couldn't believe Vivian talked to him about me.

"Don't be mad at her. She only told me as a warning. I won't get into the ways she threatened to disembowel and dismember me if I ever hurt you." He shuddered. "For such a small thing, she sure is violent."

"What did she say?"

"She said you'd been through a lot. She didn't tell me exactly what, but I could guess from what little she said."

Shifting from foot to foot, I averted my gaze. I didn't like anyone talking about me behind my back. I especially didn't like Alex knowing about my past. It highlighted all of the defects I'd been so carefully trying to conceal. But most of all, I didn't want his pity. I folded my arms over my chest, hugging myself.

"I've been cheated on, too."

That brought my head up. Who in their proper mind would cheat on Alex?

"It's easy to cheat on a cop. We work lousy hours and aren't always attentive. At least I wasn't."

"I told myself that, too. That it was my fault. He was very convincing on that point."

"Yes, they can be very convincing."

I rubbed the spot on my finger where an engagement ring

once sat. There were times when I thought I could still feel its weight. Every once in a while I'd have a brief moment of panic, thinking I'd left it somewhere or had lost it. And then everything would come crashing back down around me.

"We obviously have something going on here. Between you and me. And setting aside Vivian's castration threats, *I* don't want to hurt you. Or scare you off."

"Okay."

"That's what I meant. You know, before." Now it was his turn to look uncomfortable. "I like you, Azalea. A lot. And I want you to like me."

"I do."

"Do you?" He took a step toward me, his face breaking into the grin that got me every time. "Really?"

I bobbed my head, not trusting my voice.

"So if we take it slow, you're okay with that?"

I nodded once more. I needed slow and cautious, but mostly I needed a reason to trust again.

"You're killing me with that dress."

"Do you really qualify for Mensa?"

"Yes."

"Then I suppose we're even."

He took a couple more steps that brought him right up against me. "I really want to kiss you."

I lowered my gaze to his lips. "So why aren't you?"

He eased his arms around my waist as I slipped mine around his neck. We were millimeters from kissing when Juan Carlos banged on the door.

"Azalea! Time to go."

Alex dropped his forehead to mine. "I hate him. I really, really hate him."

"He's the one who made me look like this."

"I suppose I can forgive him just this once."

We broke apart, and I went to answer the door, while Alex took his suit into the bathroom to change.

"Your timing sucks," I told Juan Carlos.

He examined me, touching a finger to his lips. "Not one hair out of place. You should be smudged, smashed, and thoroughly smooched up by now. He's not smooshing you right. I had him pegged all wrong. I figured him for the type that takes his time, wrecking everything in his wake. Very disappointing."

"We weren't... We're not... What the heck is smooshing?"

"Bumping uglies, knocking boots." He made a rude gesture. "Smooshing."

I slapped a hand to my forehead. "Gah." I couldn't come up with a more coherent response than that.

"Where are your earrings? You're not even all the way ready."

I held out my palm, showing him my earrings. "Come in a minute while I put them on. Alex is changing. Where's Richard? Isn't he going, too?"

He waved my question away. "He's watching some sport with tight pants—football maybe. I told him he had some time because I knew you wouldn't be ready." He did a little pirouette for me. "How do I look?"

I scrutinized his appearance. He'd gone for classic with a charcoal suit, cut very close, reminding me what a great body he had. His snowy-white shirt brought out his olive complexion, while the deep gold stripe on his tie was very nearly the color of his eyes. Funny, when you see a person every day you forget to really look at them. Juan Carlos was a very handsome man.

I brushed an imaginary speck of dust off his shoulder. "You're gorgeous." Winking at him, I put a little flirt in my voice. "Sure you don't want to come over to my side?"

Alex came out of the bathroom and I forgot to breathe.

"Ab-so-freakin-lutely not," Juan Carlos murmured, fanning himself. "Gawd, why can't I look like that in a suit? Those shoulders, that waist, the way it tapers right on down to... Honey, if you don't jump him tonight, I just might." He jiggled his leg. "I need a cold shower. I should have worn bigger pants."

I smacked Juan Carlos in the arm.

"Thanks, Juan Carlos," Alex said. "Are we ready to go?"

We all filed out into the hall. I glanced up and down, expecting that man I'd seen earlier to still be making his rounds. Thankfully, he didn't make an appearance. Alex and I waited while Juan Carlos rounded up Richard. I kept sneaking glances at Alex. I couldn't help it. It was wrong for him to be prettier than me.

"What's the matter?" he asked.

"What do you mean?"

"You keep looking at me, but not really looking. I thought we were okay."

"You're like the sun."

"The sun?"

"Yeah, I can't look too long at you. Your beauty...it blinds."

He tucked his hands into his pockets and rocked back on his heels. "I don't think I've ever been called beautiful. Or been compared to the sun." His mouth kicked up and he gave me a look that filled my head with visions of sweaty bodies and twisted bedsheets.

I blew out a breath. This was going to be a long night.

"Azalea." Richard grabbed my hand and twirled me around. "You're stunning. Absolutely breathtaking." He held his arm out for me. "May I?"

The taxi line was long, but it moved quickly and before I knew it, we were pulling up to the Raine Hotel where the awards were being held. Juan Carlos gawked like a backwoods hick, his head swiveling side to side like a pendulum.

Alex leaned down to me. "Are you all right? I know it must be difficult being back here."

"I'm fine." But I wasn't really. That feeling of being watched sat like a Circus elephant on my shoulders.

I glanced around, pretending to look for someone I might know. If I was being watched, they were invisible, blending in with the other hairstylists, which was difficult to do. A woman—no, a man—dressed in a jumpsuit made of peacock feathers stood next to a woman wearing a skin-colored dress anatomically painted to make it appear as though she were nude. They were chatting with a man in a kilt and a woman in a tuxedo complete with top hat and cane.

"Oh, there's Black Jack," Juan Carlos said. "Let's go say hello."

We followed him across the room where a very large black man leaned an elbow on the bar, looking bored.

"I'm constantly amazed at how he gets away with saying the things he does," Alex whispered to me.

"I know what you mean, but in this case that man's name really is Black Jack."

We chatted with Black Jack and a few other friends who wandered over. Everyone was libationaly lubricated yet somber, speaking in hushed tones about Dhane's and Trinity's deaths. From aliens, to cults, to a murder-suicide, to a hoax that they'd faked their own deaths, theories abounded, each one more bizarre than the next. By the time the doors to the awards ballroom opened, my head spun. Somewhere in there, amongst the crazy speculations, assumptions, and downright manipulations was the truth about what had really happened to Dhane and Trinity.

I looked up from swirling my straw in my piña colada to see Sora slip into the ladies' room. I suddenly had the urge to use the facilities.

"I'm going to go freshen up," I announced.

Thankfully Alex only nodded and didn't offer to escort me. I pushed through the door, nearly colliding with another woman on her way out. Sora wasn't at the mirror or the sinks, so she must have gone into a stall. I jockeyed for position at the mirror with two other ladies and pretended to take great interest in the minutia of my appearance just as they did. Finally Sora came out and bypassed the sinks for the mirror. Eww. I made a mental note to never shake hands with her again or eat at her house.

She edged into place beside me, dislodging another woman in the process. My opinion of her slid another couple of notches.

I affected a happily surprised expression and turned toward her. "Oh, hi, Sora."

It took her a moment, where I imagined she weighed the options of admitting she knew me or pretending she didn't. Fortunately recognition won out. "Azalea, right?"

"Yes. I was so sorry to hear about your husband and now Trinity. My condolences. How are you holding up?"

Sighing, she returned her attention to her reflection. "Barely."

Yeah, she looked a frightful mess. Was that a hickey on her neck?

"How's Tenchi doing?" I asked. "I heard he was so distraught he had to be taken to the hospital."

"He took Trinity's death hard, as we all have."

Right. "How's Mac taking it? She and Trinity were cousins, right?"

Her gaze snapped to mine in the mirror. "How'd you know that?"

How would I know that if Vivian hadn't told me? I was so leaving Viv's name out of this. "I, ah…think I heard somebody say something about it at Dhane's memorial."

"No they didn't."

"In the crowd. I was sitting near a group of Hjálmar employees."

"Gossiping monkeys," she muttered.

"It must be difficult for Mac…and for you, losing two relatives so close together."

"I suppose."

O-kaaay. "Is Ace helping you with the funeral arrangements?"

She angled her body to face me. "You sure do ask a lot of questions. You writing all this down to sell to the tabloids?"

"I'm a hairstylist, not a reporter. Also, my curiosity borders on pathological."

"Just a curious hairstylist?"

I decided to go for broke. "I noticed that Ace seems to have a...fondness for you."

She dropped her lipstick in her bag and snapped it shut. "We're done."

She walked away from me, but not before I'd seen the way worry crinkled her brow and flattened her lips. I got the feeling she was afraid, but not for herself. Could she be covering for Ace?

If I had to place a bet on who killed Dhane, I'd bet on Ace. His relationship with Sora gave him a motive, which would also give him the means and opportunity. Wouldn't a wife have a key to the suite she shared with her husband? Wouldn't that same wife cover up the fact that her lover killed her husband?

Sora could've even helped him afterward. Putting Dhane's head in that bin of doll heads was a particular bit of genius by someone who knew how important Dhane was in the hairstyling world. It would've been a very effective way of demeaning him in front of his peers. Yup. My money was on the Ace and Sora combo.

I waited another moment before I made my way out of the bathroom, in case Alex had been watching the door. When I reached his side he put his arm across my shoulders and bent so he could whisper in my ear.

"What did Dhane's wife have to say?"

I batted my eyelashes up at him. "Dhane's wife?"

Juan Carlos came over to us with Richard trailing behind. "Let's go before all the good seats are taken."

"You're going to tell me what happened in there," Alex warned as we followed them into the ballroom.

I pretended I didn't hear him.

We found our seats and the awards ceremony began. The MC this year was that guy from that show about fashion nightmares who get made over in the style of their favorite star or famous person. *His* face had been made over so many times it looked as though the last time they'd forgotten how all the pieces went back together.

"He needs bigger veneers," Juan Carlos whispered. "Where'd he get those, a party store? They come with a fake nose and glasses? Were they left over from his Austin Powers costume? I bet horses get jealous when they see *his* teeth."

I bit the inside of my cheek to keep from laughing.

"Don't even get me started on the hair. Didn't his agent tell him he was hosting a *hair* awards show?"

I felt Alex chuckle next to me.

"Shh, I want to hear this," I told Juan Carlos as the room grew dark and the video tribute for Dhane began.

It started with an interview Dhane had done on a morning talk show. His face filled the screen. His lightly accented voice rolled over me, and his piercing gaze speared me to my seat.

The interviewer asked him how fame had changed him.

"Fame is the bridge that delivers my work to the people. It shifts, crumbles, gets rebuilt, but it stands. The work?" Dhane turned fully to the camera to deliver the punch. "It is everything."

I felt the energy of the crowd change. Dhane's power and passion came through on video every bit as much as it had in person. He had been made for the spotlight, for fame and fortune. He'd had that intangible star quality that couldn't be taught or bought. Knowing he was gone too soon, cut down so cruelly, shifted something in me. I got angry. I fisted a hand in my lap, wanting to strike out at something, do something to change what couldn't be undone.

But all I could do was sit in that darkened ballroom with all the others, watching Dhane prowl the stage in the video taken on the opening morning of the hair show. His pale hair flowing out behind him, he delivered what no one else could: the bridge that brought his work to the people. It was his last performance on the last day of his life.

My phone vibrated inside my evening bag as the screen went black, only to relight with a Hjálmar publicity photo of Dhane and the words REST IN PEACE. I took out my phone and looked at the display. Vivian. I clutched my phone to my chest, glad she wasn't here to see this.

I leaned to whisper to Alex. "It's Viv. I'm going to step out and take this."

"I'll go with you."

"No, I'll just be outside. I'll be fine."

I edged past him and answered the phone as I made my way out of the ballroom.

"Viv. I'm so glad you called."

"I tried you earlier. Did Juan Carlos tell you? Oh, what am I saying? Of course he did. I'm getting married!" she squealed. "Can you believe it?"

Hearing the excitement in her voice had me grinning, too. She deserved her happiness. "Oh, Viv. I'm so happy for you. And James, too. Where are you?"

"In a limo. We're on our way to get the license!"

Music from the ballroom drifted out, making it difficult to hear. I wandered away, finding a small hallway to duck into. "Did he get you a ring?"

"We just came from the jeweler's. Wait till you see it."

"I can't wait."

"Thank you for what you said to me about telling the truth. It was hard, but we worked through it and now here we are, getting married. I still can't believe it." She sniffed a little and I heard James mumble soothing words to her. "Azalea? I wanted to ask you something. Will you be my maid of honor?"

"Oh, Viv. I'd love to. I'm so happy for you. I really am."

"Thanks. We're here. I have to go. I'll see you at midnight at the Little White Chapel. I'll be the bride in the red dress and black veil."

We clicked off and I had to laugh. Leave it to Vivian to do things her way.

I turned to head back to the ballroom, feeling genuinely happy for the first time in days, and froze. Tenchi stood a couple of feet away, blocking my exit. At first I was glad to see him because of Jun, and then I realized he wasn't standing right, leaning a hand against the wall to steady himself.

"You," he snarled.

I blinked. The hatred poured off him, scorching hot, obsessively loathing. I put my hands up in defense and took a step back. He matched my move, but his stride was longer, so when we came to a stop he was even closer than before.

"You couldn't stop. Didn't stop. And now she's dead. My Trinity's dead."

"I know you're upset, but it wasn't me, Tenchi." I shook my head. "It wasn't."

He inched closer, his hand dragging along the wall, leaving a red smear in its wake.

"You're bleeding. Let me get you help," I pleaded, making a move to go around him.

A low sound rumbled from deep in his chest, part growl, part moan. He continued to advance, backing me farther down the hall. I took in everything about him, trying to gage my next move, and that's when I noticed the knife in his other hand, tip down, resting against his thigh.

"I loved her." His knife hand twitched, the point catching on the material of his pants, cutting cloth and skin. There was blood there, too, on the knife and running down his leg. "She was everything," he whispered, the words wrenched from him. "Everything."

I weighed my options, which were quickly running out. Reasoning wouldn't work here—the look in his eyes told me that. I wouldn't get past him. We were too far down the hall now, too far to shout. I had my phone, but I didn't know what he would do if I tried to make a call. I was afraid he'd take it, and then I'd really be out of options. I slipped my hand holding the phone behind my back, disguising the gesture in a glance around.

His movements were stilted, sluggish, as though he were under the influence of medication or had taken a hard knock to the head. His self-inflicted wounds didn't seem to cause him any pain. He pulled his hand from the wall, ending the streak of blood abruptly, and pointed a finger at me. "You took her from me."

I shook my head. Somehow I had to get him to believe me. "I didn't. Remember? I was with you when she died. It wasn't me, Tenchi. I swear."

"You *swear*?" His face grew ugly, twisting with grief and anger. "You killed her! She died because of you. You...you pushed her off that balcony!"

"I didn't." He'd backed me into a door. There was nowhere else to go. I pushed my fear down deep, reaching for the words I'd need to get him to believe me. "Trinity was beautiful, wasn't she?" It took everything I had to keep my voice from shaking, to keep it soothing, and him talking.

"Yes." His eyes filled with tears. The knife turned in his hand. "So beautiful."

"She was precious and special."

"Yes." He brought his hands up, the blade slicing his shirt through to the skin as it brushed his side and came to rest clutched over his heart. "She was everything."

I kept my gaze off the red stain blooming where the knife had made its mark. "She *was* everything. Everything good and wonderful." I felt for the buttons on my phone, tried to make a call.

"I loved her." He tilted his head up and to one side, as if searching for something. "Why'd she leave me? Why'd she have to leave?"

"I don't think she wanted to. If she'd had a choice, she would have stayed with you. I'm sure of it. She loved you, too." I didn't know any of this for certain, but what else was there to say?

He relaxed his stance a little, a small smile playing around his mouth. "She did. She loved me."

"She did love you, Tenchi. She loved you very much, and she wouldn't want to see you hurt. You're hurt. Let's get out of this hall. Let me help you." I reached a hand out, hoping he'd place the knife in it and not stab it straight through.

"I hurt so much." The knife wavered in his hands as he fingered the hilt, the point snagging a spot just above his navel. "So very, very much."

"I know you do. I want to help you. Let's go back down the hall where the people are. We'll get you that help."

"It hurts," he wailed, shaking now. He brought his hands up to his head, squeezing. "It hurts. Make it stop. Make it go away."

"Drop the knife and step away from her." Kennedy stood, feet braced apart, holding a gun on Tenchi. He'd angled himself so I was out of the line of fire. Alex and the wandering man from my hallway flanked him. "Drop the knife."

Tenchi whirled to face them. "Please kill me. Kill me like I killed him. It was me. My fault. I killed Dhane to stay with Trinity. Oh, God, did I kill her, too?" He curled in on himself, holding his head as though it would explode. "I want to die."

"Nobody's dying." Kennedy made a lowering motion with his hand. "Put the knife down now."

"I just wanted it to stop," Tenchi howled. "I wanted her to hurt like me. You should all hurt like me. It hurts so much."

Before any of us could move, Tenchi reared up, bringing the knife down hard into his stomach. He bent over and backed into me, then collapsed into a pile at my feet. I screamed—short, sharp bursts. The next thing I knew, Alex was holding me, ushering me away as Kennedy barked orders into a walkie-talkie.

He brought me out to the main hallway and held me at arm's length, examining me from head to toe, then yanked me back into arms. "Are you all right? God." He kissed the top of my head. "You don't know how frustrating it was to hear you through the phone and not be able to get to you."

I shook so hard it was painful. My mind couldn't wrap around what had just happened, what Tenchi had done. I clung to Alex, balling wads of his jacket in my fists. "Did you hear him? Did you hear what he said about Dhane?"

"Yes."

"Why'd he do that? I just wanted to help him. I just wanted to help."

"I know." He placed shaky hands on either side of my face and brought my head up. "God. Don't do that to me again." And then he kissed me and I felt everything and nothing. I threaded my fingers through his hair, bringing him closer. Drawing strength from our connection, I was swamped with the need for more. More of everything, him, this moment, and answers. I really needed answers.

I broke the kiss. "Tenchi said he didn't kill Trinity."

"No. Kennedy told me her death was ruled a suicide."

"Suicide." I could barely get the word out. "But how? How'd she get my flower?"

Alex wrapped me in his arms again as though he never wanted to let go. "Kennedy didn't give me specifics, just that he was certain she wasn't murdered. He thinks she might have found your flower or taken it from you."

I remembered what Jun had said about Trinity taking things from people she was obsessed with. Poor Trinity.

So it was over. All of it. Trinity had likely killed herself over the death of her brother, a death Tenchi was responsible for. No wonder he'd been so distraught. He loved Trinity and was inadvertently responsible for her death. I hoped Tenchi lived. I hoped he paid for what he did, what he took. My sadness boiled into anger. Tenchi had caused so much pain, so much suffering. I wanted him to live a long, terrible life, burning with the misery he'd caused so many others.

"Oh my God, Azalea!" Juan Carlos jumped me from behind, locking me in a double hug.

"Let her breathe," Richard said.

Juan Carlos pulled away suddenly and I turned in Alex's arms to see that Richard had plucked him off me and still had him by the back of his jacket. Instead of being upset with him, Juan Carlos transferred his hug to Richard.

"Hold me, big daddy." He pressed his face into Richard's chest. "I can't believe our Zee was nearly cut to shreds by a deranged killer." Richard patted him on the back, murmuring soothing words. "What is this world coming to?" Juan Carlos sniffed.

"I'm fine," I said to him. "Look."

Juan Carlos quit his histrionics and eyed me closely. "Not even a scratch? You're really okay?"

"I'm fine."

"What happened? Tell me everything and don't leave one bit of it out."

At that moment, we were all distracted by the arrival of uniformed police and paramedics. The wandering man from my hotel directed them down the hall, then came over to where we stood.

"We're going to need a statement from you," he told me.

"Who are you?"

"Detective Bolger. When Detective Kennedy is finished with the suspect, he's going to want a conversation with you. We're setting up a room now. Hang tight until I come and get you." At my nod, he went down the hall to where the paramedics worked on Tenchi.

Tenchi. I couldn't stop picturing over and over in my mind the look in his eyes, the way he'd moved. Why'd he do it? Why had he killed Dhane? And then I remembered what Jun had said about Dhane sending Tenchi away. Had he killed him to stay with Trinity, only to have her die, too? The pain and grief had hollowed him out, carved chunks as the blade of his knife had cut his flesh. He'd loved Trinity with a manic fierceness I couldn't imagine. What it must have been like to be loved like that.

Did Trinity know? Did she think of him when she died?

CHAPTER TWENTY-SEVEN

At the edge of the crowd, which had gathered to gape at all the excitement, stood a lone figure, fragile and pale. Jun. He looked confused until he saw me, and then his face lit up. What would I say to him? How would I tell him what his friend had done?

We moved toward each other, meeting in the middle.

"What's happening? Did somebody get hurt?" He looked at me with such open honesty and trust, it broke my heart.

"Yes, but the paramedics are working really hard to help them. Why don't you come with me?" I reached for his hand. He took it without question.

Alex didn't seem surprised to see me towing Jun.

"I don't want to stay here," I told Alex, trying to send him subliminal messages that I didn't want Jun to see Tenchi. "Can you tell Kennedy I'm going back to my hotel room?"

"Do you think that's such a good idea?"

"Hang on, Jun." I motioned for Alex to step away with me. "I'm safe. You heard Tenchi. He confessed. I don't want Jun to find out what his friend's done from someone else. He's lost so much."

Alex didn't look happy about it, but he agreed. "All right. I'll come with you." He looked around. "I'm not needed here anyway.

I'll tell Kennedy where we're going."

I went back to our little group while Alex went to talk with Kennedy. Juan Carlos was telling Jun what had happened to me. I walked up next to him and pretended to accidentally step on his foot.

"Ow! Watch it, Graceless. Look what you did," Juan Carlos said. "You put a dent in my shoe with your heel."

"Oh, I'm *so* sorry. Let me make it up to you." I pulled him away from the others and pretended to be interested in his shoe. "I'm trying to get Jun out of here." I hitched a thumb in the direction the paramedics had gone. "That's his friend back there."

"His friend is the one who—"

I clamped a hand on Juan Carlos's mouth, cutting him off. "Yes. So shut up and let's go."

Juan Carlos nodded, glaring at me. I eased my hand back.

"Your hand tastes nasty," he said. "If you're going to put it on my mouth, make sure it's washed next time. Scratch that. Don't ever put your hand on my mouth again. Disgusting." He faked spitting.

"I just washed it! Get over it."

"Not likely." He wiped his mouth with his sleeve to prove it.

I knew that to be true. Juan Carlos rarely got over anything.

We rejoined the group just as Alex returned. Together, we walked out of the hotel to catch a cab. I was never so glad to leave a place in all my life. Nothing good had happened here for me. For all its opulence and beauty, this hotel held nothing but bad vibes and negative memories. And ghosts.

The cab ride to our hotel was quiet and sullen. I was grateful for it. How in the world was I going to tell Jun his friend had killed Dhane and driven Trinity to take her own life? He'd been through so much in his young life. How many more hits could he take?

Alex slipped his hand in mine and gave me an uncertain smile. He'd gotten more than he bargained for when he'd agreed to fly to Vegas and help James get Vivian out of jail. I glanced up at him. He didn't seem to regret it. In fact, he seemed to enjoy—I guessed enjoy wasn't the right word. He thrived on all the intrigue and mayhem. Plus, he really seemed to want to build a relationship with me. Would it last once we were back home and our work and lives got in the way again? Once the forced proximity was gone?

I guessed only time and effort would tell. I decided to enjoy the moment and rested my head on his shoulder, snuggling up next to him while Jun chatted and chirped away about everything and nothing. By the time we got to our hotel, Alex was looking a little twitchy. Jun rode his nerves like the roller coaster atop the Stratosphere. I suggested Alex have a drink at the bar while Jun and I went upstairs.

As soon as I got to the room with Jun, I wished I hadn't let Alex off the hook. I could've used the moral support while I broke Jun's heart.

Sitting across from him in my hotel room, I almost lost my nerve. He watched me expectantly, as though he knew this was a moment he should pay attention to. I was afraid I'd let him down, as he'd been let down so many times in his young life. But as with anything, I supposed it was best to begin at the beginning.

"Jun—"

"Yes?" He reached for my hand, blinking his ridiculous Kewpie doll eyes at me.

"I need to tell you something. Something that might upset you."

"Okay." His trust in me was written all over his face. I only hoped I lived up to it.

"It's about what happened back at the Raine and…Tenchi."

His brows bunched together. "Tenchi?"

"Yes. He was there. He was the one who got hurt."

"Is he okay? Why didn't you tell me? I need to go see him." He made a move to stand, but I held onto his hand, pulling it for him to sit back down.

"I don't know if he's okay. We can find out after I tell you what happened. Please, just a moment."

He settled back down and squared his shoulders, as if preparing himself, like a good little soldier. I imagined him having to do this as a child, bracing for the blows that came too often for a young, abandoned boy.

I rubbed the back of his hand with my thumb. "Tenchi approached me in a hallway. He didn't look well. He was upset about Trinity."

Jun dropped his eyes and let out a shaky breath. "She died."

"Yes, she did. And Tenchi blamed himself for her death."

"Why? He didn't kill her. Tenchi wouldn't hurt anyone."

I wanted to press a hand to my heart to put pressure on the pain that had settled there. Instead, I wrapped Jun's hand in both of mine and inched closer, feeling he'd need someone to hold him when I told him the truth about his friend.

"He did, Jun. He confessed to me and the police that he was the one who killed Dhane."

Jun pushed my hands away, his mouth twisting down. "No." I tried to reach for him, but he shook his head. "You're wrong."

"I'm sorry."

Jun backed away from me, as though the distance would protect him. "You're wrong!"

I stood but didn't go to him. "I'm not wrong. That's what happened. I'm so sorry."

"No." His face crumpled and he dropped to his knees, his voice hoarse. "Tenchi, no."

"He came looking for me. He had a knife. He would have killed me if the police hadn't gotten there in time. Instead he hurt himself. He…he tried to kill himself."

"No," he whimpered, sagging under the weight of his emotions.

I dropped to my knees next to him and smoothed a hand over

his head. "It will be all right," I told him, not really believing my own words. "You'll be okay."

He reached up and gripped my wrist, holding too tight. Rising up over me, he pushed me back. Tears ran in black lines down his face. "You killed Tenchi."

I scrambled backward, trying to free my wrist. "I didn't. He hurt himself." I tried to twist free from his grip. "Let me go."

He yanked me toward him, holding me against his hard, tense body. His face molded and changed, as though he were shedding one mask for another. I didn't recognize this face. Or the voice that came from it. "You killed my brother."

Panic washed cold over me, crawling up my neck to choke me. "Your brother?"

He squeezed my wrist harder, putting pressure on bones as fragile as twigs. "I worked so hard." He grabbed a handful of my hair, holding my face close to his. "I kept us together. Tenchi didn't kill Dhane. I did. I killed him because he wouldn't let Tenchi be with Trinity. He made him go away." He jerked my head. "Do you hear me? I killed Dhane."

"No."

"What? You think I couldn't do it? I'd do anything for my brother." He shook me, his hand tightening in my hair, hurting me. "Anything."

I believed him. In that moment I believed he'd killed Dhane and he'd kill me, too. "I know you would. I believe you, Jun. I believe you."

He looked me over, as if seeing me for the first time. "I thought you were my friend."

"I am."

He shook his head slowly. "I don't think so. Dhane said he was my friend, and then he tried to make Tenchi go away."

"Dhane was wrong."

"You're not my friend." He released my wrist and put his

hand over my mouth, trapping my head in his hands. "You killed Tenchi."

My lips brushed against his fingers. "No, Jun. Don't do this." The horror of what he'd done, what he was willing to do, roared through me. I tried to kick out, but my legs were trapped beneath me. I gasped for breath. My screams trapped behind his hand. Blackness framed the edges of my vision.

I was going to die.

He applied more pressure with each word, cutting off my air. "You killed Tenchi. You're not my friend."

I clawed at his arms, his face. He shifted his body, pinning my arms down. A red haze filled my vision. This was how I'd meet my end. A strange stillness settled over me, blocking all sound. My vision narrowed, condensing down to nothing but the realization that the last thing I would ever see was the cold, empty eyes of my killer.

CHAPTER TWENTY-EIGHT

I'd been so terribly, terribly wrong about so many things. How I'd die was one of them. I closed my eyes on that thought.

There was a commotion behind Jun, startling him. His weight shifted. I bucked, wriggling free enough to bring up a knee, making just enough contact that his hand fell away from my mouth. I rolled to the side, sucking in air, most of my body still pinned under Jun's.

Suddenly the room filled with people and noise. So much noise.

"Azalea." Alex was at my side.

I tried to reach for him, but my arm wouldn't cooperate. He squeezed my hand. I hadn't known he held it. He pulled me up and into him, and I crawled the rest of the way into his lap, craving his safety. He held me hard, careful not to crush the air from my lungs.

Lips brushed mine and a hand smoothed my brow. I opened my eyes to find Alex's, very close and intent. "You're safe now."

Safe. It all came rushing at me at once. Tenchi. Jun. His hand over my mouth and nose. His eyes so close to mine, watching for my death. And the awful coldness inside him. I hadn't seen that. How could I have been so close, have liked him so much and been so wrong about him?

"What happened to Jun?" I tried to pull back, but Alex held me to him, turning us both.

Jun lay on his stomach a few feet away, hands cuffed behind his back. His eyes were eerily calm, his gaze watchful and empty. And when he spoke, his voice held a quiet petulance. "You're not my friend."

"No. I'm not your friend." My voice rasped rough, but I managed to put enough force in it to make him flinch.

"Get him out of here," Kennedy ordered.

Hands grabbed at him, but Jun didn't resist. He stared at me until he vanished from my sight.

"What's going to happen to him?" I asked.

"Why do you care?" Alex looked down at me, like he couldn't believe I was for real. "He nearly killed you." His voice broke at the end. He didn't try to cover it up.

"The paramedics are here," Kennedy said from behind Alex, his mouth set in that perpetual thin line of determination.

"I'm fine."

"You're going to let them check you over, or I'll cuff you and they'll take you to the hospital. Your choice." That Kennedy, always threatening.

"Jerk," I muttered.

"I think that's the sweetest thing you could say to me right now," Kennedy said, giving me a wink that didn't mask his relief.

The paramedics filled my line of vision, making me lay back down. They did their best to annoy me, poking and prodding, pinching and squeezing until they declared me ready to be transported.

"I'm not going anywhere." I sat up and was suddenly at the center of a merry-go-round. "Whoa."

"She should really go to the hospital," the paramedic informed everyone, as if I wasn't there.

Kennedy filled my vision, slipping his hand into mine. "I agree.

You don't looks so good, Ms. Smith."

"I'm fine. I just sat up too quickly. There, that's better." The room only spun half as fast now.

Alex crouched down next to me. "I think they're right. You should get checked out at the hospital."

"And miss Vivian's wedding? No. What time is it?"

Alex frowned, clearly on Kennedy's and the paramedic's side. "Ten thirty."

"I still have time to get there. Where's Juan Carlos? I need him to fix my hair." I reached up to touch my updo where Jun had pulled it and blew out a sigh of relief that I still had any left.

"They can go on without us or change their plans," Alex said. "Because you're not going anywhere."

Kennedy squeezed my hand in both of his, then released it, standing. "I'll leave you to deal with her. Good luck with that."

"Wait!" I struggled to stand with some help from Alex. The room tipped and me with it. I swerved, landing with a bounce on the bed. I put a hand to my head. "Oh."

"She really should go to the hospital," the paramedic insisted.

"Stop saying that. I'm fine." Mostly.

Kennedy looked impatient or worried, I wasn't real clear on anything at the moment. "What is it?" he asked.

"How's Tenchi? Did he…?" I couldn't bring myself to finish the sentence.

"He's alive," Kennedy affirmed. "In surgery, but he should pull through."

"Are Tenchi and Jun really brothers?" I asked.

"Is that what he told you?"

"Yes. Jun said that he killed Dhane because Dhane didn't want Tenchi around Trinity anymore. He was splitting them up. Jun killed Dhane so Tenchi could stay with Trinity, but Trinity killed herself over Dhane's death and Tenchi tried to kill himself over Trinity's death." I took a deep breath, realizing that I was a rambling moron and if I didn't hold it together, they would ship me off to the hospital without my consent.

"You got most of that right," Kennedy said. "All except the part about Trinity's death being a suicide."

I blinked up at him, trying to focus, but his face was all swimmy. "What are you talking about?"

But in the back of my mind I'd known it all along. Trinity would never have gone anywhere without Curio, not even to her death. And then I remembered something Jun had said early on about Trinity becoming obsessed with people and stealing from them. Was that how my flower had ended up in her hand when she was pushed over the railing? The same question that had been rattling around in my head since I'd found poor Trinity came up again.

"Who?" I asked. "Who would do such a thing?"

"Dhane's will left his half of Hjálmar to Trinity. But according to the will, if Trinity died, ownership would transfer directly to his business partner, Mackenzie Todd."

"Mac killed Trinity?" Although she'd been at the top of my list of suspects, I'd scratched her name off after Juan Carlos had told me about her applying for the product patent.

"The cameras in that hallway were repaired shortly after we discovered they'd been tampered with," Kennedy said. "We have Tenchi leaving, and then a couple of minutes later Mackenzie Todd goes in. When she comes out of the room a short time later, she looks like she's been in a fight. It didn't take long for her to break down under questioning. She wanted Dhane's half of the company. The only way to get it would be if Trinity died."

Wow. I nodded, struggling to process it all. What a totally screwed-up family they were. Poor Trinity. And poor Dhane. He'd tried to protect his sister, only in the end he wasn't able to. What a loss.

"I knew you'd be the lead I needed to completely solve this

case." Kennedy paused as if he were trying to decide something. "I'm glad I followed my hunch, and I'm glad you're okay."

So much made sense now. Kennedy letting me listen in while he questioned Jun, letting me take Jun with me, and that feeling in the hallway afterward of Kennedy setting a trap for me. I tried, but couldn't muster the anger I should've felt toward him. I was just so glad it was all over.

"You're good," I said to him.

"Yeah. I am."

"King Kennedy."

Kennedy angled himself to leave, his mouth twitching as though he held back a smart-aleck remark. "I've got to go, but I'm going to want you to come down to the station tomorrow. And *Ms. Smith*?"

"Yeah?"

"Try to stay out of trouble until then, will you?"

"I'll try."

Kennedy inclined his head with a smirk, as though he didn't believe me. He exchanged a handshake with Alex, then left.

The paramedics packed their things and tried one last unsuccessful bid to get me to go to the hospital. When they'd gone, Alex sat down next to me on the bed and drew me into his arms.

"What happened?" I asked. "What made you come into the room?"

Alex looked down and away. "It was Kennedy. Tenchi recanted his confession at the hospital when Kennedy questioned him before he went into surgery. Tenchi guessed it was Jun who had really killed Dhane. He tried to protect Jun by confessing. Kennedy figured he thought he'd take the confession to his grave and Jun would be safe."

"Kennedy rescued me?"

"Yeah." Alex didn't seem too happy about that.

"You wanted to be the big hero?"

He made a face.

I took his hand. "You're still my hero."

He looked at me with the goofiest grin on his face. I couldn't help but smile, like a big fool, back at him.

"Azalea?"

"Hmm?"

"I really want to kiss you."

"So why aren't you?"

He put his hands on my cheeks, gazing at me, like he was trying to impart some deep, important message. I grew impatient and threw my arms around his neck, dragging him toward me. Our lips met in a searing kiss that melted away all thoughts except for him and how he made me feel. We tumbled onto the bed, rolling around like two teenagers, all hands and hot mouths.

A fist banged on the door. "Azalea! Open up." The fist struck again louder. "Azalea!"

Alex dragged his mouth away from mine and looked down at me, like he couldn't believe his rotten luck…again. "I think he and I need to have a little talk." Alex rolled off me and opened the door to a frantic Juan Carlos and placid Richard. "Your timing sucks as usual." He made a sweeping gesture for them to come inside after they had already brushed past him without being invited. "Come on in."

"Oh, Azalea! Look at you." Juan Carlos turned to Richard with a smirk. "She's finally been properly smooshed." He returned his attention to me. "Good for you, girl. I knew Detective Drool-worthy would come through."

"I wish it was, but that's not my work," Alex said.

"What do you mean?" Juan Carlos looked from Alex to me. "What's he talking about?"

I told Juan Carlos and Richard about Jun with Alex filling in the spots where I was either not there or had nearly passed out from lack of oxygen. When we finished, Juan Carlos just stared at us, struck dumb for probably the first time in his life.

"I'm okay," I told him.

Juan Carlos shook his head. "Oh my God. Oh my ever-loving God. I knew it! I knew that Jun was no good. Rotten to the core. A bad seed. A wolf in sheep's clothing."

"Is that why you flirted with him?" Richard asked.

Juan Carlos sputtered, his mouth opening and closing like a landed fish. I laughed. I couldn't help it. I'd never seen Juan Carlos at such a loss for words.

"Will you help me put myself back together?" I asked Juan Carlos. "We have a wedding to attend."

"I will, but we haven't got much time. Considering what you went through, I won't complain about not having much to work with. Or remark on the travesty that is your hair. Or worry about where your other eyelashes went. Or…"

I held up a hand. "You're wasting valuable repair time, you know."

Richard escorted me to the chair he'd put up to the mirror and they both began their work on me. I tried not to look too closely at myself in the mirror. If I did, I might worry about the bruising that was just beginning to appear around my mouth, reminding me of what I'd just been through.

Instead I focused on the steady stream of Juan Carlos's commentary, ignoring the pain in my wrist and the bruises where Jun's fingers had left their mark. I hardly felt the tug on my tender scalp as Richard brushed my hair back into a twist or how each hairpin dug in, like a giant needle.

What had I called Jun? Innocuous? As dangerous as a basket of kittens under a rainbow? Something in him had called to something in me. I'd felt a kinship, a friendship with him from the start. How wrong I was. How terribly, horribly wrong. Alex had called it a gift, my wanting to see the best in everyone. I wasn't so sure of that. At the moment it weighed on me, feeling more like a defect.

No, I wasn't going to think about any of that. I turned my thoughts instead to Vivian.

"Promise me something, guys." I looked at all three of their faces in the mirror. "Nobody tells Vivian what happened today. Got it? This is her day. And I want her to have it."

They agreed, unable to hide the grimness of the secret. Tomorrow we'd tell her. If I couldn't give her Dhane back, I could at least give her a wedding day filled with joy and love.

CHAPTER TWENTY-NINE

I stood, waiting at the front of the Little White Wedding Chapel with Juan Carlos on my right as the man of honor and Alex on my left as the best man. James stood between Alex and me, his face split nearly in half by a gigantic grin. He looked impossibly happy, as though nothing that had happened or would happen could ever compare to this moment.

He was waiting for his bride.

The Elvis impersonator/officiant pressed a button on the podium and the wedding march began, a bluesy version of Billy Idol's "White Wedding." He sang the words, doing a pretty good imitation of The King. Vivian appeared at the end of the aisle, stunning in a red-and-black lace dress and black veil. My eyes filled with tears that I let spill over. She looked so beautiful. Her gaze fixed on James as she step-togethered her way up the aisle. Then she made an impatient face, picked up her skirt, and ran the last half of the distance.

James caught her and spun her around for a dip ending in a kiss that had Elvis mumbling, "Hunk-a hunk-a burnin' love."

I laughed, and it felt so good I didn't want to stop. Next thing I knew, Vivian was hugging me, exclaiming over my hair and dress.

We tittered like little girls over each other's outfits before Elvis cleared his throat and tapped his watch.

Vivian took her place next to James, slipping her hand in his.

"Dearly beloved," Elvis began, the reflection of Vivian and James in his sunglasses. "We are gathered here today to join this couple in the holy, holy bond of matrimony."

As Elvis did his thing, my attention wandered to Alex. He stood tall next to James, taking his role seriously, his gaze fixed on me. His mouth tipped up into that smile I had no defense against and the chaotic place inside me stilled. Maybe we'd make it, like Vivian and James, and maybe we wouldn't. I only knew in that moment, in that cheesy chapel with the fake flowers and faker Elvis, I had the strength to give it a try.

Nothing about this weekend in Las Vegas had turned out the way we'd planned, the way we'd wanted it to. But as I looked around at my friends I knew one thing for certain, none of our lives would ever be the same. Juan Carlos and Richard had found something they didn't know they could have. Vivian and James had pledged their lives to each other. And Alex and I were beginning an uncertain adventure, taking it very, very slow.

And maybe that's more than anyone could expect from a wild weekend in Las Vegas.

Acknowledgments

A very special thank-you to Debra Mullins for taking me under her wing when I had no idea how and when to use a comma and for gently suggesting that I forget there's a semicolon key on my keyboard because I clearly had no idea how to use it (still don't!). You will always be the honorary president of the Juan Carlos fan club...should ever such a thing exist.

Charity Hammond and Alison Diem contributed so much to this book and my journey as an author. I am forever grateful to you ladies for your friendship and advice.

This truly is the book of my heart and I'm so very thankful for whichever stars aligned just right to make my editor, Stacy Abrams, pluck these pages from her slush pile and decide they should be a published novel. Thank you for seeing the diamond in the rough and helping me polish it to a high shine.

And to my husband and sons who put up with a lot of frozen pizza and takeout so that I can write my stories. We're a little bit closer to that swimming pool, boys.

If you enjoyed this work, try these…

FIGHTING LOVE

by Abby Niles

Tommy "Lightning" Sparks is a former Middleweight champion and confirmed bachelor. His best friend Julie Rogers is a veterinarian who has secretly been in love with him since she was ten. A devastating fire brings them together, but will his playboy ways and her time spent with another fighter tear them apart? Can two childhood friends make a relationship work, or will they lose everything because they stopped FIGHTING LOVE.

SUNROPER

by Natalie J. Damschroder

Marley Canton nullifies power in those who aren't supposed to have it. Gage Samargo wants to cut off his younger brother's dangerous power source. Together they are tracking down a goddess insane with too much power from the sun. Gage falls for Marley's sharp wit and intense desire to right wrongs. But once he discovers that every time she nullifies someone she takes on some of the goddess's insanity, is it too late to back away?

TANGLED HEARTS

by Heather McCollum

Pandora Wyatt knows trying to rescue her surrogate father before he's executed will be difficult. She doesn't expect to have her life saved by the sexy Highland warrior Ewan Brody. After tricking him in to playing her husband at King Henry's court, Ewan quickly learns that Pandora is not only a witch, but also a pirate and possibly a traitor's daughter. When they discover dark secrets leading to the real traitor of the Tudor court, Ewan and Pandora must uncover the truth before they lose more than just their hearts.

TOUCH OF THE ANGEL

by Rosalie Lario

Interdimensional bounty hunter Ronin Meyers must locate an incubus who's using succubi as murder weapons or risk being deported to hellish Infernum. When he captures Amara, the beautiful succubus who stole his heart — and nearly his life — during the most mind-blowing hour of his existence, the happily-ever-after will have to wait. Before they can find salvation, they must bring down the madman hell-bent on destroying everything — and everyone — they love. And Ronin and Amara are at the top of his list.

BLACK WIDOW DEMON

by Paula Altenburg

Half-demon Raven is nearly executed on the orders of her fundamentalist stepfather. She escapes the burning stake using her otherworldly gifts with the help of a mortal stranger—retired assassin Blade. While she's set on revenge, Blade wants redemption. To get it, he must deliver her into the hands of loved ones. But as Blade's sense of duty becomes something more and threats, both mortal and immortal, stalk the woman he can't abandon, he could very well fall back into the life he's trying so hard to escape.